DIRK WAS FLES
AND BLOOD

Hot blood that caused his fingers to sear through the fabric of Andrea's dress as his hands trailed over her shoulders and inched their way to her waist.

Andrea shivered—from the heat, not the cold. Yielding to instinct, she pressed herself against him, and she knew immediately how fully he was aroused.

They were in perfect tune. They needed no words. It was natural to lift her face to his, to have their mouths fuse in a kiss that deepened in intensity.

Everything Andrea had told herself in the past became invalid as he held her. What did it matter if Dirk was her client?

A small voice warned that tomorrow she would regret her action. But this wasn't tomorrow, Andrea retorted silently as she curved her body into his. This was now.

My appreciation to Denis Sturtevant and Robert Petersen of the My Bread (Sunbeam) Bakery, New Bedford, Massachusetts, and to Terry Moran of the Kitchens of Sara Lee, Deerfield, Illinois, for taking time out of busy schedules to be so very helpful to me.

———————◆———————

MEG HUDSON
is also the author
of these titles in
SuperRomance

SWEET DAWN OF DESIRE
LOVE'S SOUND IN SILENCE
THOUGH HEARTS RESIST
A CHARM FOR ADONIS

and in
Love Affair

TO LOVE A STRANGER

NOW, IN SEPTEMBER

Meg Hudson

A SuperRomance from
HARLEQUIN
London · Toronto · New York · Sydney

First published in Great Britain in 1985 by Harlequin, 15–16 Brook's Mews, London W1A 1DR

© Koehler Associates, Ltd 1984

ISBN 0 373 70126 8

11/0185

Printed and bound in Great Britain by Cox & Wyman Ltd, Reading

For Luella and Jack, who gave us such wonderful memories of Michigan.

CHAPTER ONE

ANDREA CAMPBELL stood at the big window overlooking the Boston Common and watched the rain beading the streetlamp on the corner. Then, as if on cue, the light switched on, a wet pearl glistening in the growing dusk.

Behind her a masculine voice inquired with faint irritation, "Would it be too much to suggest that you might fix me a drink?"

Andrea turned and smiled at the man behind her. "Of course not," she assured him.

Mark Terrence grinned wryly. "But I suppose it would be asking entirely too much to suggest that you join me?"

She laughed. "No. Matter of fact, I don't think you'll even have to twist my arm!"

He shook his head. "You never cease to surprise me," he confessed. "You've always insisted that nothing stronger than coffee belongs in a business office." The grin returned, but this time it was without the wryness. "I think you're taking pity on my affliction. And if that's the case, I just may keep wearing a cast on my foot forever!"

Andrea had moved across the room to a corner cabinet and was withdrawing glasses and a bottle of Scotch, which she then placed next to an insulated bucket already stocked with ice. Mark watched her appreciatively as she began to make the drinks. In his opinion she was stunning. Tall, graceful, with an eye-arresting figure and hair of an unusual silvery-blond shade. She wore her hair quite long, curving just above her shoulders, and as she moved it swished in a way he found delightful. Although her profile was turned to him so he couldn't see her eyes, he knew they were a clear shade of green, as unusual a color as her hair. Andrea's mother was of Finnish descent and her father was Scottish, a combination that had produced their daughter's distinctive beauty.

Mark was sitting in a big comfortable armchair with his right leg propped up on a hassock. He looked strangely vulnerable to Andrea as she brought his drink over to him. Usually Mark sat behind the huge modern desk that dominated the large office. In fact he didn't usually sit at all. He presided.

Even now he was trying to preside, as he had been during the course of the hour-long conference they'd been having. But it was the end of the day for him, and she knew his ankle was hurting. It was also late in the day for her. True, she didn't have a broken bone to contend with, but she was bone weary in a different way. For the past few weeks she'd been realizing how much she needed a vacation. She'd begun to make plans to take one just before Mark's accident.

It had been a stupid accident, as Mark was the first to admit. He'd been spending Easter down in Connecticut with his sister and her family and had engaged in an egg hunt with the kids. Thinking about this, Andrea's lips curved in a smile. Mark tended to get into everything he did with considerable vigor, which was one reason why he was such a highly successful advertising executive. He'd given his all to the egg hunt and had stumbled over a rock in the course of it, twisting his foot in a freak motion that had pivoted him to the ground.

"I could hear the bone snap," he'd told Andrea morosely when she'd gone to visit him in the hospital.

He'd been away from the agency only a couple of weeks and returned with an impressive cast and a pair of crutches. The secretaries had loved this opportunity to fuss over him, for Mark was tall, lean, handsome and newly divorced in the bargain. Even Andrea had occasionally succumbed to his helplessness, as she was doing now. She didn't like to drink during working hours. Even a little bit of alcohol tended to make her sleepy, and advertising was a field in which every ounce of wit was needed. Now, though, she held up her glass and, smiling at Mark over its rim, said, "Cheers!"

"Cheers," Mark replied absently, and at once

Andrea was on the alert. It was one thing for Mark to be tired, but quite another thing for him to be staring across the room with a vague expression glazing his eyes. She'd seen that expression before, and almost always it had prefaced his asking her to do something she didn't want to do.

"I think," she announced, "it's time we called your evening cabbie and let him convey you home."

Since the accident Mark had used two cabs by arrangement, one driver picking him up each morning and bringing him to work, the other performing the return service in the afternoon. The morning hour of departure was always the same, but the evening one varied, depending both on Mark's physical endurance and the account with which he was dealing.

Andrea stood, about to move to the intercom and buzz Mark's secretary so that she could call the cab company, but he shook his head violently.

"No!" he blurted, with an explosiveness that startled her. "There's something we have to settle before I leave for the night. Anyway...."

"Yes?"

"When I do leave, I have a fantastic idea."

"Yes?"

"How about coming home with me and cooking our dinner?" he suggested.

"Not tonight, Mark," Andrea replied quickly. Maybe just a shade too quickly.

"If you don't want to cook," he continued, undaunted, "we could send out for Chinese food.

No. . . don't tell me you're not in the mood for Chinese food tonight. We could send out for Italian food, or maybe Greek food, or tempura shrimp, or—''

She cut him short, laughing as she shook her head. But she was very conscious at the same time of how easy it would be to say yes to Mark, and that was something she didn't want to do. She'd been with Saunders and Terrence for two years, and she wanted to stay with them. She loved her job, and until recently there had been no threatening personal problems. Carl Saunders, the senior partner in the agency, was a man in his fifties, happily married, the ultimate suburbanite, in Andrea's opinion. He commuted to Westwood nightly. Mark, until recently, had been involved in a crumbling marriage and then in a divorce, which had not been without considerable unpleasantness. It was only recently that he'd truly come up for air, and Andrea felt sure that his growing interest in her was primarily because she'd happened to be the first person he'd really seen at that point. But she didn't want to encourage him. She liked her job too much—she liked Mark too much—to let herself become involved with him on a romantic level.

He was watching her. "I'm predicting that, once again, I'm going to have to eat alone."

"Poor darling," Andrea murmured sympathetically. "Shall I get out your address book for you and we can see if we can't round up someone who. . . .''

"A pox on you, witch," he threatened, then held out his empty glass. "At the least," he told her, "you could do your bit toward assuaging a man's thirst."

She looked at him doubtfully. "Sure you can still navigate on those crutches after a second one?"

"Like an Olympic star," he assured her. "Anyway, I'm not going to be doing any navigating until I've gone over something with you."

"Oh?" It was impossible to keep suspicion out of her voice.

"I'm not about to suggest anything lecherous, Andi," Mark told her with feigned reproach. "Look, fix the drink and come over here and sit down, will you?"

"Yes, master," she said, executing a funny little bow. But as she filled his glass with ice cubes once again she felt uneasy. Whatever Mark was about to bring up with her was plainly important to him, and she wondered why he'd left it till this late in the afternoon to get into a serious subject.

He didn't satisfy her curiosity immediately. He twirled an ice cube around with his finger, frowned, then shifted position, wincing as he did so. Only at this point did he say, "I have a favor to ask of you, Andi."

"Something so serious?" Andrea asked, slightly taken aback by his gravity.

"No, not really serious. Something that wouldn't normally come your way, that's all. An account I intended to handle myself."

"Then why don't you?" she responded quickly.

"Because it involves traveling. Not just a single trip—I could maybe manage that in a couple of weeks. But I think this'll require some going back and forth between Boston and Michigan for the next several months, at least."

"Michigan?"

Mark smiled at her tone. "It's not the last frontier, Andi."

"I know that," she said swiftly. "I just wondered why a Michigan firm wouldn't use a Detroit agency. If not, maybe Madison Avenue. Why pick Boston? I mean...."

"It doesn't much matter what you mean," Mark said, the way he said it taking any potential sting out of the words themselves. "This particular firm wants us. Its president went to college with me."

"Not an old school tie!" Andrea moaned.

"You can leave out the 'old,'" Mark suggested.

Andrea was twenty-eight and Mark, she knew, was thirty-six. A very fit thirty-six under ordinary circumstances.

"All right," she said. "A school tie, then."

"You have something against school ties?"

"I've worked on a couple of accounts in the past where there was a friend involved, a friend of one of the agency executives, that is. In my experience, most 'friend' clients are bad news. They're much more demanding, they feel that friendship should breed favors. I'd rather deal with someone who walked in right off the street.''

"I can assure you that this particular client—if he becomes a client—won't ask any special favors,'' Mark told her. "Nor will he give any. These days, Dirk Van Der Maas is all business.''

"Dirk Van Der Maas?''

"He owns a bakery in Holland, Michigan,'' Mark said levelly.

She stared at him. "You've got to be kidding!''

"No. I'm serious.''

Andrea shook her head. "Old school tie or not, I can't see us becoming interested in a small midwestern bakery,'' she said flatly. "It's too...too remote from everything we do.''

"Small is a relative term,'' Mark replied obliquely. "By some standards I suppose the Van Der Maas bakery is small, yes. But Dirk has some very large ideas. That's why he wants us. Also, as I've said, small is relevant. Dirk's bakery isn't all that small, it's....''

"Please,'' Andrea said wearily. "It's been a long day, we're both tired, and you don't have to try to sell me, Mark. I'm not interested in the Van Der Maas bakery. I'm not interested in bakeries, per se. I don't even like to cook!''

"So you've indicated every time I've suggested you fix dinner for me,'' Mark reminded her. "Seriously, though, Andi...I can't let you turn this aside. It was my intention to go out to Holland myself and spend the necessary time with Dirk. I'll admit it was—initially, at least—to have been both business and pleasure. His mother keeps house for him, I was to stay with them, and Dirk and I planned to get in some sailing, among other things." Mark glared down at his foot. "This damned fracture put a stop to just about everything!"

"A very temporary stop," Andrea told him soothingly. "Surely your friend Dirk can wait to start his ad campaign until you're a bit more ambulatory."

"No, he can't," Mark contradicted flatly. "He wants to get into the preliminaries with us to be sure we're right for the account and the account's right for us. He's planning a large addition to his present plant which will enable the bakery to freeze its products. He wants to go for national distribution on a small scale, at first. Then he plans to expand, with some very carefully allocated franchises over which he'll keep tight control. I'll venture that within the next two to three years you and everyone you know will be buying frozen Van Der Maas baked products."

Andrea stared wonderingly at this man, who, technically, was her superior in the advertising agency. She said slowly, "You mean this, don't you? You're really optimistic about his prospects?"

"Very," Mark told her. "Dirk is an exceptionally...dedicated individual. When he makes up his mind to achieve something, he achieves it. In the past he's been up against a lot of odds, both personally and professionally. He's survived, where a lot of people wouldn't have, and become stronger because of what he's been through. In fact that's how I'd put him down. He's a survivor. Now he's made up his mind to expand, and I can assure you this was no overnight decision. Dirk is a clear thinker, a thorough thinker.... As a matter of fact, there was a time when I would have called him a visionary... and perhaps he still is one.''

Andrea couldn't repress a laugh, which only elicited a frown from Mark.

''Okay, think it's funny if you like,'' Mark said crossly. ''When Dirk makes a million with his grandmother's apple cake, you can laugh all the way to the bank if we're handling his advertising account.''

''His grandmother's apple cake?'' she echoed.

''That and a number of other tried-and-true Dutch recipes,'' Mark said staunchly.

''You expect me to muddle around in cakes and cookies and grandmother's apple whatever?'' Andrea asked incredulously. And then she remembered something.

''Mark,'' she said, leaning forward, ''since you called me in here this afternoon we've gone over every one of the accounts I handle.''

He nodded.

''I suspect,'' she said, a decided note of coolness edging her voice, ''that this was by design.''

"True. I wanted to get the up-to-the-minute status of everything you're doing," Mark admitted. "That was the only way I could know whether or not it would be possible to spare you from the Boston scene for a while."

"And?" she asked, her green eyes glinting dangerously.

"Don't look at me like that!" Mark pleaded. "I have enough troubles. I don't need a couple of emerald daggers stuck in me." He paused and sighed. "Andi, the fact is that your accounts are all doing fabulously...thanks to you. I'm not at all hesitant about letting a couple of the junior account executives handle them for a while. That," he explained, as he observed her reaction, "does not mean I'm taking them away from you. You'll be in Boston most of the time anyway, once you get things under way in Holland. You'll only have to fly out there occasionally. For that matter Dirk can fly here for consultation, as well. Okay?"

"No, it's not okay," Andrea said. She thought about commuting irregularly between Boston and Holland, Michigan over the course of the spring, summer and maybe into the fall, and the idea didn't appeal at all. Trying to work out an advertising campaign for a Dutch bakery appealed even less.

She forced Mark to meet her eyes. "Do I have a choice?"

Despite himself, he flushed. "I don't like to hear it put that way."

"Do I have a choice, Mark?" she persisted.

"I talked to Carl Saunders this morning. We went over this. We both think you're the best person for the job," Mark said unhappily. "So I guess that. . . well, that no, you don't have a choice, Andi."

IT WAS SURPRISING how quickly even important details could be attended to and everything wrapped up when it became expedient businesswise. Andrea found herself aboard an airplane headed for Michigan four days after her conference with Mark.

She changed planes in Detroit, then flew on to Grand Rapids. There she found a rental car awaiting her, one of the many arrangements that had been made for her by the agency.

A network of elevated highways encircled Grand Rapids, and Andrea's first impression was that the city had been built in a bowl. As she drove she glimpsed a river and a series of low waterfalls, but then became so involved in dealing with the heavy traffic heading south on Michigan's Interstate 96 that she didn't have time to take in much scenery.

Soon the suburbs yielded to open country, a gently rolling terrain studded with large farms sheltered by copses of trees, their leaves just now showing green.

The agency had booked accommodations for her at the Yellow Tulip Motor Inn, and once she'd left the Interstate at the Holland turnoff, she meticulously followed the directions that had been given to her and found the place without difficulty.

The Yellow Tulip was at the edge of town, and it lived up to its name. There were beds of tulips edging the grassy slope atop which the inn stood, and more of them around the low white buildings themselves. Hundreds of tulips, Andrea estimated, all of them in bloom now, and all of them yellow.

Her large pleasant room overlooked the slope and the tulips. It was charming, decorated in a delft-blue motif that was typically Dutch. Andrea was particularly captivated by a framed fabric print on the wall that showed a blue windmill with yellow tulips in the foreground.

It was midafternoon. Lunch had been served on her flight from Boston to Detroit, so she was not hungry. Nor was she tired. She was restless, though, possibly because she was eager to get on with the job and get it over with.

She unpacked quickly, thankful as she always was when she traveled for the wonderful fabrics that were wrinkle-proof and so easy to maintain. She liked clothes and she knew without conceit that she wore them well, an advantage of being both tall and slim. It was also nice, she thought ruefully as she zipped her suitcase closed and stashed it away in the closet, to have reached the point in life where she was able to think of being tall as an advantage at all.

Five-feet eight in her bare feet, Andrea was at the

eye level of many of the men she knew and taller than a number of them when she wore heels, but this no longer bothered her. Growing up, though, she'd also been on the skinny side, and she could remember early adolescence as a period when she'd felt gangly. Because of this she'd been something of a tomboy, and the nickname "Andi" had come naturally. She smiled. It had been "Andy" to begin with. She'd converted the ending to the more feminine *i* around the time of her sixteenth birthday.

Her unpacking finished, she stretched, wishing there was something else to do, something that would dissipate this mounting energy. She'd checked maps of the area before leaving Boston. Holland was right on Lake Michigan, so she supposed there must be a beach nearby. The water in mid-May would still be too cool for swimming, but she could at least get some fresh air by taking a long walk.

Or, she supposed, she could drive around town and locate the Van Der Maas bakery. But she easily dismissed that thought. Her appointment with Dirk Van Der Maas was for ten o'clock the following morning. She'd have more than enough time to find her way to his bakery then.

No...it was the thought of the beach that attracted her at the moment, and she sought directions from the receptionist at the desk in the motor inn, a plump middle-aged woman who looked delightfully Dutch with her flaxen hair and twinkling blue eyes.

As she drove north out of town, then cut to the west on Ottawa Beach Road, which would take her to a state beach on Lake Michigan, Andrea wondered if most of the people who lived in Holland were of Dutch descent. Which made her wonder in turn what Dirk Van Der Maas was going to look like.

It was foolish to paint mental pictures of someone you'd never met. Andrea knew this. But it was also difficult to resist doing so. She found that she was envisioning the baker as a middle-aged man, a short plump individual with fat ruddy cheeks, small blue eyes and thinning hair that probably would be turning gray.

She realized she was drawing a caricature of Dirk Van Der Maas rather than painting a portrait of him, and there were certain fallacies in her approach. For one thing, since Mark Terrence was eight years her senior, and he and Dirk Van Der Maas had been in college together, the baker must also be in his mid-thirties and thus hardly past his prime. If he did have thinning gray hair, it would be premature.

Because it was a weekday afternoon the state beach was virtually deserted. Andrea paid a small entrance fee to a uniformed officer at the entrance gate, then found that there were dozens of empty spaces in which she could park. Before long, she thought, as she strolled toward a long flat expanse of gold-toned sand, there'd be people at all the empty picnic tables, children playing, families enjoying time off together. Right now, though, she had the place pretty much to herself.

To the left was an inlet that led out into Lake Michigan, guarded by a bright red lighthouse. Across the inlet Andrea could glimpse high sand dunes, a vista repeated far to her right. She hadn't expected to see such high dunes along a lakefront, even a Great Lake front. The surf on the lake also surprised her. Wind whipped, the waves crested and broke in a crashing display of power. Andrea shivered. It would be a bad day to be out in a boat.

It was a perfect day for walking. She strolled for the better part of an hour, loving the feel of the cool wind on her skin but glad she'd thought to bring a bulky knit sweater along with her.

On her way back to town she glimpsed a large windmill silhouetted against a sky fused with the glorious colors of the approaching sunset. She'd noticed a display of literature about Holland and its environs in the lobby at the motor inn, and she was sure that a picture of this same windmill was on the cover of one of the brochures. She decided to pick up some of the various pamphlets on her return. Possibly she'd have some spare time on her hands, and she might as well see as much of the country as she could while she was there.

She had absolutely no idea how long that might be. Mark had stressed that she was to stay in Holland until the preliminary details involving the account were worked out. Of course he'd been presuming there was no doubt about their getting the account, a certainty she didn't share. There was always the chance that when they got down to the bottom line, Dirk Van Der Maas might decide not to give his business to his old friend. It wouldn't be the first time such a thing had happened.

Thinking about this, Andrea wished she'd talked more to Mark about his former college classmate, so that she'd have a better idea of what to expect the next day. She remembered Mark saying that his friend had at one time been "a visionary," and she'd thought this an odd choice of words to use in connection with a small-town baker. But then, Mark had spoken as if this was in the past, as if something, in the interim, might have happened to change Dirk Van Der Maas.

What else had Mark said? Andrea tried to remember, but Mark's exact words eluded her. Too much had happened too quickly over these past few days to remember everything. Still, she recalled Mark saying something about Dirk Van Der Maas being a survivor. Something about the man having encountered many odds "both personal and professional"—yes, she was sure that was the way Mark had put it—and having emerged a stronger character because of them.

Mark had also assured her that if they did get the account Dirk would not expect any favors because of friendship. At the same time he'd warned her that she couldn't expect to be on the receiving end of any favors, either. But then she'd never wanted "favors" from a client, as Mark very well knew.

She frowned. Despite his avowed friendship with the Dutch bakery owner, Mark had left her with the impression that Dirk Van Der Maas was going to be a difficult person to deal with.

As she brought her car to a stop in front of her motel unit, Andrea realized she was not looking forward at all to her first appointment with him.

CHAPTER TWO

THE VAN DER MAAS BAKERY was not far from the central business district, on the western edge of town. It was a three-story, pale-yellow brick building, and to Andrea it looked unexpectedly old and rather grimy. Nor did the two-story addition at the side of the building appear to be much newer or cleaner. It simply had more windows.

The neighborhood around the bakery was not very impressive, either. There was a large cannery in the vicinity, which she'd passed en route, and an assortment of other factories. She'd also crossed a number of railroad tracks, the rails so shiny it was evident they were still well used. But most of the buildings—even in the center of town—had seen better days, and their brick facades looked as if they could do with a good cleaning. Andrea found the effect of this kind of venerability depressing, and she wondered how a first glimpse of the Van Der Maas plant would have struck Mark.

She parked at the curb in front of the bakery, then found a door marked Office Entrance. Once inside she did have to revise her original estimate somewhat. The walls were painted in a soft shade of Wedgwood blue. The blond woman behind the reception desk wore a blouse and skirt of a slightly darker shade of blue, and there was an embroidered motif on the blouse collar that Andrea suspected must be the bakery's logo.

The receptionist smiled pleasantly when Andrea gave her name.

"Yes, Miss Campbell," she said. "Mr. Van Der Maas is expecting you. You'll find his office up one flight, to the left." She indicated a door at the side of the reception area. "The stairs are through there."

So the Van Der Maas bakery was not modern enough to boast elevators!

Andrea started up the long narrow flight of stairs, her reluctance mounting with every step. Her initial glimpse of the bakery was all she'd needed to cement her conviction that she was the wrong person to handle this account. She'd worked on a wide variety of accounts during the course of her career, but she'd had a basic enthusiasm for all of them. This was what had carried her through both the good times and the bad, and there was always a full quota of both in dealing with any account.

Her interest in promoting Van Der Maas bakery products was absolutely zero, especially now that she'd seen the site where they were produced. And she felt more strongly than ever that the account simply was not for the Saunders and Terrence agency, as she'd warned Mark in the first place.

Unfortunately it was too late to backtrack. She had to go through with her appointment with Dirk Van Der Maas, and because of his friendship with Mark she couldn't afford to deliberately antagonize him.

Mark, she thought resentfully as she neared the top of the stairs, had put her in a very awkward position. If she succeeded in getting the bakery's business, she'd be forced to work on something she really didn't want to do. If she failed, then the guilty feeling that she'd let Mark down would be unavoidable. As far as she could see, Andrea concluded gloomily, it was a no-win situation. And she was as professionally obligated to make a sincere pitch to Dirk Van Der Maas as she would be to any other prospective client.

She climbed the last step and found herself in a square foyer with several doors opening off it. Turning to the left, as the receptionist had instructed her to do, she saw a dark wood door with Office of the President stenciled in gold on it.

The door was partly open and Andrea stepped through it into a pleasantly furnished outer office, the comfortable chairs and sofas covered in a bright print, repeated in the fabric of the curtains at the windows.

The woman at the large center desk was plump and gray haired. Glancing toward her, Andrea decided that she might be Dutch, but then again she might not be. The same could have been said of the receptionist on the floor below.

"You must be Miss Campbell," the woman suggested, and when Andrea nodded assent she continued, "I'm Evelyn Bleeker, Mr. Van Der Maas's secretary. I'm sorry, but Mr. Van Der Maas had to go into the bakery. A problem with some yeast. He suggested you wait in his office. He shouldn't be long."

Andrea noted that Mrs. Bleeker's deep-blue eyes were very discerning, and she was glad she'd dressed carefully for her first meeting with Dirk Van Der Maas. She was aware that the secretary was taking in every detail of her appearance, from the collarless short jacket of her light wool, violet-colored suit to the ruffle down the front of her violet-and-beige plaid taffeta blouse.

Mrs. Bleeker, she suspected, was the type of secretary who'd be fiercely loyal to her employer, and in a working situation with anyone else she could be a powerful ally... or enemy, as the case might be.

At the moment she was smiling as she stood and led the way toward an inner office, holding the door open for Andrea. "Perhaps you'd like some coffee?" she suggested.

"Thank you, not just now," Andrea rejoined politely.

The secretary nodded. "Just make yourself comfortable, then. I don't think Mr. Van Der Maas will be very long."

Left alone, Andrea looked around curiously. Although the exterior of the bakery might appear an-

cient, the interior—what she'd seen of it so far—
was definitely modern, and the president's office
was starkly contemporary.

The decor was neutral in tone and the furniture,
Scandinavian in design, was totally functional. Like
most rooms furnished in an ultracontemporary
style, there was nothing at all intimate about this
one. Even the large desk of pale wood gave no clue
at all to the personality of the man who usually sat
behind it. There was an ivory telephone on one end
of it, and a matching intercom. An ivory leather appointment book and a slender gold pen had been
carefully placed alongside it. But there was nothing
else. No clutter, no photographs, not so much as an
old pipe or a crumpled pack of cigarettes.

There were two windows across the front of the
office, draped in an ivory fabric with a nubby
weave, and there were several framed pictures on
the walls. Moving toward them, Andrea saw that
they were architects' renderings of a number of
buildings, all of them extremely contemporary. She
frowned slightly as she examined them. She'd been
brought up in a small New England town and had a
strong streak of the traditional in her when it came
to architectural preferences. At best she preferred a
blend of the old and the new. But the sketches of
the high-rise buildings she was looking at left no
room for anything of the old. They had clearly been
designed to take full advantage of light and space
and were definitely bold in concept. Although not

to her personal taste, they were in their own way quite beautiful, a far cry from the stereotyped concrete monoliths so characteristic of most high rises.

She was still studying the drawings when she heard a door close behind her and knew that the moment of confrontation with Mark's friend was at hand.

She turned to face a tall man. He must have been a good three inches over six feet, and he carried his height well. It would have been impossible not to notice that he was exceptionally well built. The light-gray suit he was wearing was so perfectly tailored it drew instant attention to the slimness of his waist and to his broad, powerful shoulders and the length of his legs. They were muscular legs, which were fully revealed by the cut of his slacks.

It was also impossible to put the moment when she'd have to look him full in the face on indefinite hold. Slowly Andrea met his eyes to find that they were very light blue, not at all obscured by the amber-rimmed glasses he was wearing. In fact his eyes were so light a blue that they reminded her of winter frost at twilight, and there was precisely the same sort of chill about them.

She bit back a laugh when she remembered her imaginary picture of him. In actuality his hair was neither thinning nor blond, nor was it turning gray. It was a very light brown. The color of pecan wood, Andrea decided, the exact shade of the pecan table in her Boston apartment. He wore his hair styled, so that it was precisely the right length to frame his arrestingly handsome face and was perfectly contoured to mold the outline of his well-shaped head. But there was also a thickness to it, a softness. It was the kind of hair that made a woman want to touch it.

His hair, she decided, was the only inviting thing about him. For the rest, he was almost too perfect, too well groomed, too...too urbane. Again laughter threatened Andrea. "Urbane" was the last adjective she would have thought she would be using to describe a small-town Michigan baker.

Dirk Van Der Maas didn't look like a small-town baker, though. At least not according to her obviously erroneous concept. She could see him in the advertising business, perhaps a rising young executive on Madison Avenue. Yes, decidedly, he was the Madison Avenue type.

"Miss Campbell?" he asked.

Aware that she'd been staring at him, Andrea quickly recaptured the composure that came so easily to her after years of coping with all sorts of situations in the pressured advertising business.

"Yes, Mr. Van Der Maas?" she asked in turn.

He nodded, then crossed the room in a way that could have been called graceful, except that there was such an essential masculinity about his walk the word didn't suit. He moved like...well, like an athlete, Andrea decided, like a person in total control of his body and, she suspected, of his mind and emotions, as well.

He pulled out the chair behind his desk and waved her to a straight chair at the side of it, then he flicked the switch on the intercom and spoke into it. "Hold any calls, will you please, Evelyn?" he asked his secretary, and Andrea noted that his voice was low and well modulated, as sophisticated as everything else about him.

His profile was turned to her as he opened a desk drawer and glanced into it, then closed it without taking anything out. It was a rather severe profile, a rather severe face, for that matter, but this was in part because of his expression. His nose was straight, his cheekbones high, his forehead broad. His well-shaped eyebrows, a tone darker than his hair, arched above the rims of his glasses. The glasses were as fashionable as his clothes and were quite becoming, though they tended to add to an air of.... Andrea searched for the right word as if she was in the throes of writing ad copy until she finally came up with the perfect phrase. An air of aloofness, that was it.

Yet his mouth was not aloof. There was an intriguing curve to his full lips, giving his mouth a disturbingly sensual quality.

He surveyed her coolly, then said, with no change of expression, "I suspect this may be Mark's idea of a practical joke."

Andrea frowned. "I beg your pardon?"

"He'd told me he was sending Andy Campbell out here," Dirk explained. "I assumed he was sending a man. This poses an extremely cliché situation, I know, but. . . .''

"I don't think Mark intended you to be mistaken about anything like that," Andrea pounced.

"Do you know Mark very well?"

It was a question that could place the person responding to it in a damned-if-you-do, damned-if-you-don't position. "I've been working with Mark for two years," she evaded.

"Then you must know that at times he has a rather peculiar sense of humor," Dirk said flatly. "Did he really break his ankle, by the way?"

Annoyance flared, but with a slight inward struggle Andrea succeeded in suppressing it. Still, there was an edge to her voice as she said, "Yes, of course Mark broke his ankle."

"In an Easter-egg hunt?"

"He was playing with his nieces and nephews," she explained, her tone as cool as his.

"So I understand," he said dryly. "All right, I'll concede the broken ankle. But I do think Mark had some malicious mischief in mind when he chose you as a substitute."

"Malicious mischief?"

"He knows that I don't like to work with women."

It was anger rather than annoyance that surged this time, and Andrea pressed her hands together until her knuckles were white. "I notice you have a female secretary."

"I don't like to work with women on an executive level," he explained. "If I were to give Saunders and Terrence my business and you were placed in charge of my account, then obviously that would put you on an executive level."

"Yes, it certainly would," she agreed evenly. Then added, almost curiously, "You really don't mind confessing to such chauvinism, do you?"

"No, not particularly."

"Very well then." Andrea forced a tight smile, determined not to let him know that he was ruffling her. "If you feel that way about working with women, Mr. Van Der Maas," she said sweetly, "I see no point in our wasting each other's time any further. In a few weeks Mark should be able to come out here himself. Perhaps in the interim you could meet with him in New York and discuss your preliminary planning. If that won't do, I imagine he can find you another account executive. A male account executive," she amended. "The agency has a reasonably large staff."

Was she imagining it, or had that surprisingly attractive mouth of Dirk Van Der Maas's just twitched slightly, a sign that in anyone else she would have read as suppressed amusement.

It had been such a fleeting expression she couldn't be sure of it. Nor could she be sure there was a somewhat warmer tone to his voice as he asked mildly, "Do you always make your decisions so swiftly, Miss Campbell?"

She wanted to demand rudely, "What's that supposed to mean?" She managed to mellow it to, "I don't think I understand you. I wasn't aware that I'd made a hasty decision, Mr. Van Der Maas."

It occurred to her suddenly that she liked the sound of his name. Dirk Van Der Maas. There was a cadence to it and. . . it suited him.

"I was under the impression that you just tossed my account back to me before I'd even had the chance to hit the ball into your court, if I may paraphrase Madison Avenue," he told her, and he was smiling. A slight smile, but a decided improvement.

"I was under the impression you wouldn't consider working with a woman," Andrea said bluntly.

"Then perhaps the misunderstanding is mutual," he conceded. "Actually I said that I don't like working with women. I didn't say that I'd refuse to work with a woman."

Was he backtracking? Andrea considered this possibility, then decided against it. It wouldn't be his style, she suspected, to give up ground so easily.

"Mark's idea of humor and mine sometimes don't jibe," he continued.

"This wasn't a joke on Mark's part," she said stiffly.

"Yes, I'm beginning to believe that." He picked up the slim gold pen that lay by the ivory leather appointment book and twirled it between fingers that were long and slender. Andrea noticed that his hands were well formed, graceful, like the hands of an artist. Capable hands, she found herself thinking. Strong though they might be, she sensed they could also be very gentle.

Dirk Van Der Maas pushed back his desk chair then, unexpectedly, ran one of those gentle, capable hands across his hair as if to smooth it—except that his hair didn't need smoothing. It was a gesture that Andrea would have put down to nervousness in anyone else.

"Would you like some coffee?" he asked her abruptly. "And perhaps a *banket*?"

He pronounced the word with a broad *a*, and she repeated it. "What's a *banket*?" she asked him.

"A Dutch pastry, filled with almond paste." Without waiting for her answer he pressed the intercom again, and when his secretary answered said, "Bring us some coffee, will you, Evelyn? And a *banket*?"

Flipping the switch off, he turned back to Andrea. "There are a number of very good Dutch pastries," he told her. "From some preliminary experimenting we've done, I'm convinced they'd freeze well, and I think we could introduce a very successful new bakery line with them. My thought is to first plot out a strategic selection of varying locations across the country where we could do some trial runs. At the same time I'd like to see enough national publicity—and advertising—generated so that people in areas where Van Der Maas products are now unknown would be demanding them from their local food outlets. It's a big enterprise, I admit. But a couple of decades ago who would have believed in the tremendous future popularity of Chinese frozen foods, Italian frozen foods, gourmet-quality frozen dinners, layer cakes, cookies, you name it. Even if we just limit ourselves to thinking about croissants," he added, "the scope becomes mind boggling. Croissants have taken the country by storm. You can now buy almost any kind of frozen croissants from chocolate to raspberry in the smallest towns in the United States."

"But the original, plain French croissants remain the best," Andrea put in.

"That's true," he agreed. "Ah, here's Evelyn."

To Andrea's surprise, he didn't wait for his secretary to bring the tray she was carrying over to his desk but went and took it from her, thanking her as he did so.

It was a large pewter tray, an old one, Andrea observed. There was a flower-sprigged china pot for the coffee, and the cups and saucers were English bone china. The spoons were silver, engraved with a heavy monogram. Andrea could not repress a smile. It was beginning to appear that perhaps everything in Dirk Van Der Maas's life was not so strictly contemporary after all.

The *banket* was a fairly large, rolled pastry. Dirk cut a wide slice, put it on a plate and handed the plate to Andrea with a fork. "I always ask that it be served warm," he explained, "so that makes it rather difficult to eat with your fingers. Try it."

She did so and found that it really was delicious. "Very good," she told him. "But then I've always liked almond flavoring."

"So do most people," he said. "And for those who don't, we plan to offer some excellent alternatives."

She couldn't resist it. "Like your grandmother's apple cake?"

He had just cut himself a piece of the *banket* and was transferring it to a plate. He looked up at her blankly. "What?"

"Mark mentioned that your grandmother's apple cake features prominently in your plans," she explained.

"My great-great-great grandmother's *appel koek*," Dirk corrected, with no change of expression. "At least I think it was my great-great-great grandmother, rather than my great-great. My mother could verify that, I suppose, and perhaps you might want it verified when we launch a campaign for the apple cake."

We. Andrea clutched at the word and didn't want to let it go. It was the most encouraging thing he'd said to her. She felt further heartened when he added, "I imagine you'll want to know more about Holland's Dutch heritage?"

"Yes, I will," Andrea agreed.

Did this mean that he'd cast his vote for her to

handle his account, despite his prejudice against women executives? Or were they still dealing with preliminaries? Andrea was not about to risk asking him, so she continued, "I'll want as much background as possible. At this point I'd say that there will be a time when local references might be used advantageously in our copy. Anyway, I always feel it's essential to know as much as possible about a subject I'm to be dealing with, and since we're featuring the 'Dutch' aspects of your products, that takes in the Dutch heritage of Holland, of course."

He nodded. "The Netherlands Museum here in town would be a good place for you to do some research," he suggested. "Holland has quite a long history. It was settled in late 1847 by Albertus Christiaan Van Raalte."

"Was he a relative of yours?" Andrea asked.

"Distant, perhaps. Not a close one." Dirk helped himself to another piece of *banket*, having first determined that Andrea had not yet finished her first one, then slanted an ice-blue glance in her direction. "As you've suggested, Miss Campbell," he told her, "playing up the Dutch background will be essential to the success of our campaign, and you'll find no dearth of material in that regard. Mrs. Bleeker can help you with any specifics, but I would advise you to explore around on your own, to get the feeling of this locale and its heritage. I don't suppose you've ever been here before?"

"No," Andrea said, put off slightly by his tone.

She couldn't avoid the feeling that he was talking down to her.

"That's to the good," he said. "First impressions are inevitably the most vivid ones. Later we tend to see things as we wish they were, rather than as they are."

It was a provocative statement, but Andrea didn't want to explore it with him. Her own first impressions—not of Holland, but of his bakery and its surroundings—had been much too negative.

Abruptly he asked, "Do you like to cook?"

To Andrea the question smacked of sexism. She felt as if he was about to cast her into a hausfrau role, and resentment simmered. "No!" she blurted, more emphatically than she'd intended.

Unexpectedly he smiled, and Andrea glimpsed a charm that surprised her. "Did I touch a sore point?" he asked.

"No," she said hastily. "No, of course not. And. . . I *can* cook. It isn't my forte, that's all."

She wanted to add that there was no particular reason why it should be. She'd come here to handle his advertising account, not to work in his test kitchens. But her professional caution came to the forefront before she blurted out anything she might regret. Until she felt much more sure of her ground with Dirk Van Der Maas than she did right now, she was going to live up to the old Latin proverb and "make haste slowly."

Although not a great believer in so-called female

intuition, Andrea knew from past experience that her own instincts where clients were concerned were valid more often than not. A part of her success in her field could be attributed to her ability to determine early on the best way to handle a new client, and thus to establish as soon as possible the most effective business rapport.

She was already sure that Dirk Van Der Maas was a man who was going to set and maintain his own pace in his relationship with his advertising agency, and it didn't take much talent to recognize that he was not about to be rushed into a decision about Andrea Campbell, or anything else.

She was even more certain that because she was a woman she was going to have to prove herself, and her professionalism to him, and she had the strong feeling that it was going to be quite a challenge.

He would be testing her every step of the way. Andrea, with no visible change of expression, girded herself for battle, knowing she'd have to be ready for him.

CHAPTER THREE

LESS THAN HALF AN HOUR AFTER she'd finished having coffee with Dirk Van Der Maas, Andrea was seated behind the wheel of her rental car wondering what to do next.

Her interview with the bakery president had been brought to a close when his secretary had knocked on the door, circumventing the intercom, to tell him that there was an important phone call for him.

To Andrea it had seemed that a significant glance passed between Dirk and Mrs. Bleeker. But he'd said only, "I'll call back in five minutes, Evelyn," and with that he'd made it clear that his time with Saunders and Terrence's representative was up.

He had politely ushered Andrea to the door. "Where can you be reached?" he'd asked at the threshold.

"I'm staying at the Yellow Tulip," she'd answered, wishing she could stall long enough to have the opportunity to pose a few questions of her own. She knew Mark would be expecting a phone call from her. What was she going to tell him? Did they have the account or didn't they? On the one hand, she was sure they did. On the other hand. . . .

Dirk had brought her conjectures to a temporary end by saying, "We'll be in touch." The editorial "we." Did this mean he'd be calling her personally? Or in future dealings—if there were to be any future dealings—was he going to turn her over to someone else? It was not the usual rule of thumb to have the president of a company act as liaison between his organization and the advertising agency chosen to represent it. On the other hand, she suspected that Dirk Van Der Maas was not inclined to operate by the usual rules.

Mrs. Bleeker had been on the phone in the outer office, so she'd merely nodded goodbye, and Andrea had returned the nod. By the time she'd reached her car she felt limp. Her initial interview with Dirk Van Der Maas had been surprisingly fatiguing. The problem, of course, was that he'd disconcerted her with that initial statement about his dislike of working with women. It was the first time she'd ever encountered that sort of attitude, and it had been hard to accept, especially coming from someone as coolly sophisticated as Dirk Van Der Maas.

Blast Mark! A surge of irritation came with the unspoken exclamation. He should have warned her that his old college tie was a woman hater, or a chauvinist at the very least, Andrea thought grimly.

As she drove away from the bakery she was tempted to go back to the state beach and take another walk along the shores of Lake Michigan. But though she knew this might be calming, it would do little toward solving any of her present problems.

She supposed that she should start in on her homework about Holland, Michigan and its inhabitants, as Dirk Van Der Maas had suggested. But she wasn't in the mood for a visit to the Netherlands Museum at the moment, so she decided to shop around for some basic research material first.

Browsing along the main street, Andrea window-shopped until she came to a bookstore. There she found what she was looking for. A variety of books and pamphlets about Holland and its history.

She bought a number of them, as well as a copy of the daily *Holland Sentinel*, then, as she walked on up the street, a gift-shop display caught her eye. Although she hadn't intended to do any souvenir shopping at this point, she couldn't resist going in and buying a piece of delft china, made in the shape of a Dutch shoe, for herself, and a pewter pendant, fashioned like a windmill, to send her mother.

Since her father's retirement from business, her parents had been fulfilling their lifelong dream of moving wherever their fancy took them. At the moment they were living on a houseboat berthed along Florida's section of the Intracoastal Waterway. Every now and then Andrea caught up with them, and their reunions were always wonderful. Her parents seemed to have an eternal blitheness of spirit that she envied and often wished she could emulate. But then, she reminded herself, they were still as much in love with each other as they'd been when they'd married thirty years ago. Even more so, for their love had deepened both with trial and with time.

She could not say the same for her own experience with love, Andrea thought broodingly as she left the gift shop and continued on down the street. So far she hadn't been fortunate in the matter of love. Twice she'd come close to marriage. The first time had been while she was still in college. The romance had come to a crashing end over the summer vacation when her prospective husband had taken a job down on Cape Cod and had fallen in love with someone else before Labor Day.

The second near-marriage had been more recent, and considerably more traumatic. A few months after joining the staff of Saunders and Terrence, Andrea had met a young Boston attorney at a house party given by mutual friends in Newton. George Cabot came from a branch of a famous old Boston family; he could definitely be classified a Boston Brahmin. Andrea, with her Scottish-Finnish background, was not in the same class genealogically, a fact that hadn't bothered her at all. She was just as proud of her own antecedents as George was of his.

In due course George had taken her to the family's home in Marblehead, and Andrea had been instantly aware that his mother didn't like her. But it was not Mrs. Cabot who'd caused the final dissolution between George and herself.

The shock of what ultimately happened was still profound. Ironically it had been at a house party quite similar to the one at which they'd met several months earlier. Different people, different locale, but the same atmosphere. Midway through the evening, Andrea had become increasingly aware that George had deserted her, and that there were some knowing glances being passed around, some of them, when they chanced to rest on her, laced with pity. Then George had returned...not with a woman on his arm but with a man.

Andrea still shrank from the memory. George had given her a ring, and they'd come perilously close to setting their wedding date, something that was still very difficult for her to think about. In fact, the entire episode had taken a toll from which she hadn't yet recovered. She'd been warned that only time would help her deal fully with these memories.

The warning had come from the psychologist she'd consulted, a wonderful woman whose chief function was to listen, and Andrea had come to realize that being able to truly listen to someone else was one of the rarest of qualities. The sessions with the psychologist had strengthened her, given her a deeper understanding and—most important of all—the volition to go on with her own life. But there were times when she was still...very tired. When she still felt the need to get away from Boston and the job that usually suited her so well. She'd been on the verge of putting in for a vacation at precisely the moment Mark had met with his ludicrous accident. And now....

And now, she thought wryly, she had Dirk Van Der Maas to cope with. Or did she?

It was a question that could not be resolved until she heard from either Dirk or some representative of his firm. She forced a mental shrug, then determined to forget her own problems for the moment and concentrate on the things around her.

She'd noted that there seemed to be a tremendous spirit of expectation in the air, and when she stopped in a small café for a lunch of Dutch pea soup and thick home-baked bread she found out the reason why.

The waitress who served her confided that she hoped to be able to go home early that day so she could get her costume ready.

"Costume?" Andrea asked.

The waitress nodded, then added, "You did come for the festival, didn't you? And to see the street scrubbing?"

Andrea's perplexed expression was answer enough, and the woman laughed. "By tonight the town will be mobbed," she said. "Tulip Time starts tomorrow. I can't believe you came here at this season of the year without knowing that! How did you manage to find a place to stay? Usually everything's reserved way ahead."

Andrea hesitated, then said, "Friends made my reservations for me." Strictly speaking, this was the truth. She considered just about everyone in the agency a friend, and she didn't want to get into the business reasons for her trip to Holland. She paused. "I take it that Tulip Time is quite a big event?"

"The event of the year in Holland," the waitress confirmed. "Have you been out to the island?"

"What island?"

"Windmill Island, where De Zwaan is," the waitress said. "The big windmill."

"No. I've seen the mill from a distance."

"You must go," she urged. "Despite the crowds. There are thousands of tulips in bloom there now. I'm sure there's nothing like it to be seen, except in the Netherlands, perhaps."

"There must be more tulips just around the town here than there are anyplace else in the world, except perhaps the Netherlands," Andrea said with a laugh.

"The tulip is our symbol. A symbol of Dutch heritage," the waitress explained. "Although there are not many first-generation Hollanders among us any longer, Holland's background is mostly Dutch." Then she added, "Tomorrow everything starts with the street scrubbing."

"Are you saying people actually get out and scrub streets?" Andrea asked incredulously.

"Yes. The main street of town, in fact. And no—everyone doesn't get out and scrub," the waitress added, her blue eyes twinkling. "Just women and children."

The waitress's statement immediately made Andrea think of Dirk Van Der Maas. Perhaps he had come by his attitude to women honestly. Maybe his environment had influenced him. Mark had said he still lived with his mother, Andrea remembered, and she pictured an overworked elderly woman trying through endless toil to satisfy her demanding son. The concept made her feel sorry for Mrs. Van Der Maas. Dirk, she suspected, would be a hard man to please.

Her lunch finished, Andrea decided to go back to the motel and look over the literature she'd bought. But this project was to be delayed. As she entered her room the message light on the telephone was blinking furiously. The sight of the flashing red button stopped her cold. Had Dirk Van Der Maas come to a decision? Had he called?

Andrea faced up to the knowledge that the moment of truth regarding the Van Der Maas account and herself might be at hand, and she was daunted to realize that she wasn't ready for it.

It was unusual for her to let emotion sway her when it came to an account. But that was exactly what was happening. She felt so mixed about this. Common sense told her it was folly to try to work with someone who was prejudiced about you, even though it was not a personal prejudice. Evidently it was directed against her entire sex.

On the other hand, she hated the thought of giving in to Dirk Van Der Maas and his archaic ideas about women and their capabilities. There in his office she'd told herself that she'd meet any challenge he might fling at her, but in just these few hours since she'd left him she'd weakened.

Was this because she wondered if the struggle would be worth it? She didn't like the thought that she might be shying away from a challenge because she couldn't face up to it. True, one shouldn't have to face up to this sort of personality clash in a business situation, but then who'd ever said that business—especially the advertising business—was a bed of roses?

If she got the account it would not be the first time she'd had to teach a male client a lesson, Andrea reminded herself. Because she was a young and attractive woman she'd had to set the ground rules more than once in the past with the men she worked with. And she'd succeeded. Always, before she was long into a relationship with a client, her skill and her professionalism had won the respect and resulting rapport necessary to do a good job.

Maybe this would also prove true with Dirk Van Der Maas. Admittedly, her previous problems with male clients had revolved around initial efforts to be amorous, something she didn't have to worry about where the bakery president was concerned. He hadn't appeared to be the least bit interested in her on a personal level.

No, handling Dirk Van Der Maas would be far, far more difficult than dealing with men, generally old enough to be her father, who initially responded to her as a woman. In fact she doubted if she'd ever be able to "handle" Dirk Van Der Maas at all, nor did she see why she'd have to.

They were adults. Intelligent adults, she added. They should be able to respect each other as professionals in their respective fields and to take their relationship from there.

I want to try! She nearly spoke the words aloud. *I want his account, damn it! I want to* show *him that he's wrong about women executives!*

She glanced dubiously at the phone's blinking light, knowing that her moment of truth couldn't be put off any longer. She picked up the receiver to be told that there were four messages for her, all with the same number to call back. But it was a Boston rather than a Holland number. It was Mark who'd been on the phone consistently over the course of the day.

There was nothing to do but return his calls. No use stalling. She knew Mark well enough to know that he'd keep on phoning until he got her.

She was unprepared, though, for his greeting when his secretary switched her through to him.

"Congratulations!" he said immediately.

Perplexed, Andrea asked, "About what?"

"For cinching the account, beautiful," Mark told her. "Dirk called late this morning and I've been trying to reach you ever since. I knew you could do the job for us! I'm proud of you. As I'd warned you, even our friendship wouldn't be enough for Dirk to give us the account unless he was sure we were the right agency to do the job. You must have given him a super sell!''

"He called you?'' The single fact leaped out of the context of everything else Mark had said.

"Yes, he called me,'' Mark said, sounding faintly puzzled. "Didn't you expect he would?''

"It. . .it isn't that,'' she hedged. "It's just that I. . . .''

"It did seem to me, as time slipped by, that you might have put a call in for me yourself,'' Mark told her, trying to be stern and reproachful at the same time.

"I'd intended to phone you this evening, Mark,'' she told him. She *had* been intending to call him, though she hadn't been in the least sure what she would have said to him.

Mark laughed. "Okay. I'll forgive you. You're our shining star right now, anyway. I've the feeling that you're going to do terrific things with this account.''

Andrea didn't know how to answer this, but since Mark was continuing to talk about a variety of things she was spared the necessity of doing so. Meantime, chaotic thoughts were racing through her head. A super sell? She hadn't attempted to sell Dirk Van Der Maas on anything at all. In fact, it had been very much to the contrary. . . .

A direct question from Mark came to interrupt. "Have you any idea how long it'll take you to get things going out there, so you can come back to Boston?"

"No," she said, "No, I don't. I've no idea at all. I...."

"Relax," Mark advised. "It's okay. I want you to consider the Van Der Maas account your top priority. If that means staying in Holland a few days longer, I'll just have to console myself with some of the other beauties around the office. Saunders's secretary is on vacation incidentally, and you should see the replacement. Gorgeous red hair and eyes that are almost as green as yours!"

She had to chuckle. "You're incorrigible!" she accused.

"And you're not even jealous, are you?" he countered sadly. "No, don't answer that question. My ego might not be able to take the blow. By the way, what do you think of Dirk?"

The question had its own curve, as it was thrown at her. Mark and Dirk Van Der Maas, she reminded herself, were old friends. She tried to think of a reply that would be diplomatic and noncommittal, and then decided to settle for honesty. "I'm not quite sure," she admitted.

"He's handsome enough," Mark observed morosely.

"He's attractive, yes."

"Do I detect an edge of understatement in your voice? Come on, Andi, you don't have to hedge with me. I know the two of you must really have hit it off. Dirk isn't usually one to make important decisions swiftly. I thought he'd have to brood over your presentation for a time."

Andrea had dutifully written a presentation to help obtain the account before leaving New York. She'd taken it along in her briefcase that morning, the case she carried with her as routinely as she did a purse. Now she remembered that she'd never even removed the neat folder with its twenty-page treatise from the case, and her cheeks flamed.

"Whatever you did, remember the formula," Mark was saying. "I think you've stumbled on the secret to instant success. Anyway, while I have you on the phone...."

Mark went on to speak briefly about a couple of matters dealing with one of her other accounts, then they touched on the weather, the progress of his broken ankle, and after that concluded the call.

Glancing at her watch, Andrea saw that it was not quite four o'clock, and again she was restless. She could start studying the literature she'd bought in town, but she wasn't ready to settle down with it, not yet.

Remembering what the waitress in the café had said about the tulip display on Windmill Island, she decided this would be a good time to go see the flowers for herself. The next day with the opening of Tulip Time, the island would surely be mobbed.

It was less than a ten-minute drive from the motor inn to the island, which was literally a stone's throw from the downtown business district. Yet Andrea had the sense of entering into a completely different time slot as she found and secured what was probably the last parking space in the Windmill Island lot. The Tulip Time crowds were definitely descending.

She'd picked up a brochure about Windmill Island in the motor inn's front office, so she knew that it was located in the middle of the Black River, which emptied into Lake Macatawa in the very heart of Holland, the lake finding its outlet into Lake Michigan via the narrow channel she'd seen at the state beach the day before. The brochure had also explained that the people of Holland, following the tradition of their forebears, had reclaimed part of the floodplain along the river. They'd converted it into a beautiful park, and in the center stood the giant De Zwaan, a historic two-hundred-year-old windmill that had been brought from the Netherlands and reassembled at this perfect site.

There were thousands of tulips in bloom on the island, planted in masses of varying colors, and with the windmill in the background and everyone who worked on the island dressed in traditional Dutch costume it would have been easy to imagine this was really the Netherlands.

The windmill was on an arm of land separated from the other attractions in the village by an impressive double drawbridge over a canal. The small guidebook she'd been given when she purchased her admission ticket told Andrea that the bridge was a reproduction of one that generations of Dutch had used in crossing over the Amstel River at Ouderkerk, Noord Holland.

Everything about the village was authentic. The administrative center was housed in a charming building that was a faithful reproduction of a Netherlands fourteenth-century inn. Then there was a "Little Netherlands" display in a colorful, three-gabled building surrounded with blooming tulips, a panoramic exhibit depicting the way life had been lived on Marken Island in the Zuider Zee in another era. There were hundreds of tiny figures, buildings, boats and windmills in the display, all of them beautifully executed, and Andrea was fascinated.

After she'd toured the various buildings on the island and paused to admire the *draaimolen*, an authentic Dutch carousel imported from the Netherlands, she crossed the drawbridge to De Zwaan itself.

The old mill had been moved to Michigan by special permission of the Netherlands government and could boast the claim of being the only authentic Dutch windmill in the United States. It was still a working mill, Andrea learned, and the grain produced by it could be bought on the island. In this lovely setting, with the colorful tulips blooming everywhere, it was an unusual sight, and Andrea wished she'd brought a camera with her. She hadn't brought one to Michigan at all, and decided maybe she'd go into town later and buy an inexpensive one so she could record these memories in her own way. Postcards were fine, but not personal.

She was still caught up in a sense of the past as she made her way back toward the drawbridge over the canal. She'd nearly reached it when she saw the little girl standing along the bank at the canal's edge, leaning forward, her attention evidently attracted by a black goose with a red face that looked like a carnival mask. Andrea had noticed when she'd first crossed the drawbridge that there were several geese of varying species in the canal, and the black ones had attracted her attention, too.

Now, though, her eyes became riveted on the child, who seemed too close to the edge of the bank for safety, given the high waters from the spring flooding. And then, as if predestined, it happened. The child's foot slipped, and in another instant she'd plunged headfirst into the canal.

CHAPTER FOUR

ANDREA WAS NOT AN EXPERT SWIMMER, although she was able to take care of herself in the water under ordinary circumstances. She knew later, though, that even if she hadn't been able to swim a stroke she'd have done the same thing. She streaked toward the canal edge and dived in. Water that was cold and black and murky closed around her.

She surfaced and was aware of people shouting. She could hear feet pounding in her direction. But there was no time to be wasted. She dived again, searching frantically, and was rewarded by the glimpse of something pale. The little girl's dress! At least she prayed it was the child's dress. She clutched at fabric and then felt the solidity of the sturdy body. Lifting the child's head above the water, she started with her toward shore.

Fortunately the distance was a short one. Yet the effort of supporting the child, who was evidently unconscious, and trying to swim at the same time took a surprising amount of strength. It was with what she felt might well be her last gasp that Andrea surrendered her burden to a pair of the many outstretched arms.

Other arms reached toward her, and she shook her head at first, but then she let herself be lifted out of the water. She was glad she hadn't tried to do it on her own, because suddenly she'd gone weak all over. There was no protest left in her as she was gently placed on the grass at the top of the canal bank.

A quick call for help must have been sent out, because as she leaned forward, fearing she was going to be sick, Andrea saw men dressed in white arriving on the scene. She heard mumbled voices, then became so giddy she nearly blacked out. This bout passed, and she looked up just in time to see two of the rescue-squad men carrying a stretcher with a very small form lying prone upon it.

She became aware that a rotund middle-aged man wearing a Dutch costume was holding her hand and gazing down at her anxiously, his broad ruddy face creased in a worried frown. Simultaneously one of the rescue-squad attendants dropped to his knees at her side, questioning her gently as he began to examine her.

It was a routine check, superficial really, and when he had finished he sat back, apparently satisfied. "I think you'll be fine," he told her. "But to be on the safe side, how about letting us take you over to the hospital emergency room so we can be sure?"

Andrea shook her head. "There's no need, really," she managed to say. Then added, "The little girl...."

"She's going to be fine, too," he assured her, but Andrea suspected this might merely be reassurance, aimed to keep her calm.

She didn't have the strength to go into it, though, or to ask any more questions. It took all the energy she could muster to get to her feet, and then she was swaying, thankful for the steady grip on her arm from the older man at her side.

Noting his costume again, she realized he must be an employee of the village, which was confirmed when he guided her across to the administrative center, a journey she'd never have been able to make under her own power. There she was fussed over by other costumed employees who insisted upon plying her with hot coffee.

Her clothes were soaked, the water had been icy cold, and she was shivering. One of the ladies summed up the situation and disappeared briefly, returning with a woolen skirt and sweater and a pair of loafers, which she insisted Andrea put on.

"They will be sizes too large for you," the woman told her, with a wry smile, "but you must have something dry. Otherwise you could become ill."

Andrea didn't protest. She was given a place in which to change, and towels to dry herself off. When she emerged dressed in the borrowed garb, which was much too big for her, there were protests about her leaving until she'd had more coffee and something to eat. This was mandatory, her benefactors said, since she was insisting on driving herself back to her motel.

Andrea managed another cup of coffee, which she was beginning to think must be Holland's favorite beverage, but it was impossible to force down a single bite of food. Finally she was allowed to go, but only after she'd heard all sorts of instructions as to how she should care for herself for the next twenty-four hours or so.

"It was a shock to you," the avuncular man who had first approached her said solemnly as he guided her across the parking lot to her rented car. "You are a strong young woman, I'm sure, but don't dismiss the effects too lightly. If you have any doubts, go over to the hospital and let them look you over. Will you promise me that?"

Andrea managed a faint smile as she made him the promise he'd asked of her. He was as solicitous as her father might have been, and she felt warmed by this attention. In fact the people she'd met in Holland so far—with one exception—were the friendliest people she'd ever met anywhere. And Dirk Van Der Maas, for that matter, had not been unfriendly, though he certainly hadn't displayed any of the same kind of warmth she'd just been shown.

The drive back to the Tulip Motor Inn took more out of Andrea than she would have thought possible. She was glad the parking space in front of her own door was vacant, and once inside her room she collapsed on the bed, staring wide-eyed toward the ceiling.

The afternoon's incident had a nightmare quality to it. She imagined she could still feel the fabric of the child's dress, and there'd been an instant when she'd feared it was going to slip through her fingers and she wouldn't be able to grasp it again.

She shivered. It was frightening to think how quickly things could happen, how quickly a pleasant moment in a sunny spring afternoon could swing toward tragedy. She knew she'd have to find out how the little girl was or she'd never be able to sleep that night. After a time, she promised herself, she'd call the Holland hospital. It shouldn't be too difficult to locate the child. There couldn't have been that many children pulled out of the canal on Windmill Island in one day.

But at the moment she lacked energy to so much as reach for the telephone, and it wasn't that far a reach. Andrea chided herself for being so weak. Then the memory of that black, cold water engulfing her swept over her, and she shuddered. Suppose the child had eluded her grip? There would have been others diving to the rescue, she knew that, but she felt sure their efforts would have been too late. Her own effort might have been too late, for that matter. The child's body had been dead weight, yet curiously limp.

She tried to estimate the girl's age, but she'd had such a fleeting glimpse of her it was difficult to do so. She'd looked to be around six or so, and evidently she hadn't been able to swim a stroke. She must have swallowed water as she went under, and. . . .

There was no point in speculation, Andrea told herself wearily. She should phone and find out. But she still made no move to do so.

The last of the daylight had faded and it was dark in the room. Dark, and surprisingly quiet. A major highway ran not far from the motor inn, yet even the traffic noises were subdued just now. Everything seemed to be in limbo. . . .

Andrea's eyes closed and she drifted into sleep. Fortunately it was a dreamless sleep. Time passed, and she had no idea whether she'd been asleep for five seconds, five minutes or five hours, when she was awakened by a thunderous banging on her door.

She sat bolt upright on the bed, her pulse racing. Fear turned her cold. Dazed, half-asleep, she could only think that it must be the police at her door, and if so, they'd come about the child. They'd come to ask her questions about the incident. And that could only mean. . . .

The banging persisted with a fierceness that made her wonder the wooden door didn't splinter. She cried out, "I'm coming," and hoped she would be heard. She managed to switch on the bedside light with trembling fingers, and she weaved, crossing the room, as if she'd had too much to drink.

She flung the door open, prepared to face the police. Then she had to clutch at the doorknob in order to keep her balance at all, because her legs were turning to rubber and in another instant they wouldn't be able to support her.

She swayed and felt strong arms encircle her, drawing her close, holding her up.

Dirk Van Der Maas's arms!

She shook her head dizzily, wanting to speak to him, wanting to ask him what he was doing there, wanting to try to make sense out of what was happening to her...but she couldn't find either the voice or the words to say anything. And it didn't matter anyway, because he was drawing her across to the bed, half carrying her, then depositing her on it.

She leaned her head back against the pillow and closed her eyes, ready to imagine that she was dreaming all of this, and when she woke up, everything would somehow right itself. Then she felt a blanket being drawn over her gently, and an added weight on the bed. She opened her eyes to find that he'd sat down beside her.

His glasses reflected light from the bedside lamp so that she couldn't see his eyes clearly, but his face looked as if it had been wiped clear of any expression. Only the tautness of his mouth betrayed his tenseness, and even in her present foggy state Andrea found herself wondering why he should be so tense?

He asked abruptly, "How are you?"

It was not an idle question, she knew that from his tone, and she glanced at him, surprised. "I'm all right," she said mildly.

"I'd like to be sure about that," he answered, to her further surprise. "Have you seen a doctor?"

"What?"

"Have you seen a doctor?" he repeated, and she saw a muscle twitch at the side of his jaw. Then, in a moment she'd never forget, the mask slipped, and as he bent toward her she could see his eyes, and they were anything but icy. "My God," he said, "that water must have been freezing!"

So he knew about the episode at the canal. Evidently news traveled fast in Holland, but she was puzzled nevertheless. How could he have found out that she had been the one out on Windmill Island that afternoon? She'd given her name to the rescue-squad attendant, but even so. . . .

"It was cold," she found herself answering him. "Quite cold, but certainly not freezing."

He ran an agitated hand through his hair, and she followed the course of his fingers with her eyes. His hair, she saw, was as thick as she'd thought it would be, and she was sure it would also be as soft. She had an almost irrepressible urge to reach out and touch it.

He'd rumpled it slightly, and it was astonishing what a difference even such a simple alteration as this could make in someone's appearance. As he stared down at her now he looked younger and considerably more vulnerable than she would have imagined possible.

"Look," he said, "if you haven't seen a doctor I think you should. You should have been taken over to the hospital in the first place. I can't imagine what the rescue squad was thinking of, just...just leaving you there like that."

"They didn't just leave me," she corrected him. "I was examined. One of the emergency medical technicians suggested that I should go to the hospital, but I felt sure I didn't need to, and I'm even more sure of it now. And I knew they'd be busy with the little girl." She paused. Since he seemed to know so much about the matter, there was the chance he might know one thing more.

"Do you know how she is?" she ventured.

"She's home," he said with an abruptness that surprised her. "Somewhat frightened, still, but physically she's fine."

"You speak as if you know her," Andrea found herself saying.

His glance held surprise. "Of course I know her."

"I didn't realize that," Andrea put in. "I...I don't even know her name."

"Johanna," he said, with that same surprising abruptness. "Johanna Van Der Maas."

He wasn't looking at her as he spoke, and Andrea was thankful. She could imagine that the range of feelings this revelation had brought about in her would be echoed on a face friends had always told her was extremely transparent.

Her gaze strayed to his hands, but she knew even before she looked that she hadn't seen a wedding band on his finger. If there'd been one, she would have noticed it when he poured coffee for them that morning.

She reminded herself that this didn't necessarily mean he wasn't married. And why should it matter to her?

He said slowly, "We want to thank you. They told us at the hospital that your quick action probably saved Johanna's life."

"You...you're sure she's all right?" Andrea stammered. This was something she had to be sure of herself, for her own peace of mind.

He looked faintly surprised. "Yes."

"How...how old is Johanna?" she managed to ask.

"She'll be seven in just a couple of weeks," he said. "She's a first grader. Ordinarily she'd be in school, but she'd been kept home for a few days. This afternoon Anna Poest, who used to work for our family and sometimes still comes to care for Johanna, thought it would be a treat to take her to Windmill Island to see the tulips. Anna is not as young as she used to be, and some forty pounds too heavy. She was talking to some friends she'd met, and when she looked around Johanna was gone.

Then she saw all the people running toward the canal. . . ."

Dirk sighed. "Anna is still in a state of shock," he said. "I was afraid her heart was going to give out on her at one point. I was sufficiently concerned, in fact, that I've arranged for her to have an electrocardiogram tomorrow."

"I'm sorry," Andrea said feebly.

"You?" he asked. "You have no reason to be sorry about anything. As I said, we're very grateful to you. . . ."

"There's no need for gratitude," she told him. "I'm glad I was able to reach Johanna in time, that's all."

Johanna. Knowing the child's name added dimensions to her personality. Or, Andrea asked herself perceptively, was this the result of knowing that she was Dirk Van Der Maas's daughter?

For a moment he was silent. When he spoke again he was almost as imperturbable as he'd been when she'd met him that morning. That morning? It seemed a long, long time since she'd heard a door close behind her in his office and had turned to confront him.

He said rather stiffly, "My mother would like it very much if you'd have dinner with us Thursday night. She's involved in various activities concerning the opening of Tulip Time tomorrow or she would have suggested we make it then. Anyway, she'd like to have the opportunity to thank you herself."

His mother. His mother, not his wife.

It occurred to Andrea that he might be divorced. Or he might be a widower.

She said, almost as stiffly as he had, "I appreciate the invitation, but there's really no need for your mother to feel obligated. . . ."

"I didn't say she felt obligated," he cut in. "Johanna would also like to meet you, though I thought that was something that could be accomplished sooner. First, though, will Thursday night be convenient for you?"

"Yes, of course," she said.

"As to meeting Johanna—originally we were going to let her take part in the street scrubbing with Anna, but Anna is not up to it and I think that for this year it would be better if Johanna were simply a spectator. So I wonder if you would come with us to the street scrubbing? It opens our annual Tulip Time celebration," he began to explain.

"Yes, I know," she cut in.

Interrogative eyebrows arched above the rims of his glasses, and there was something very attractive, even provocative, in the action. "Are you learning about our Dutch customs so quickly?" he asked her.

"It was impossible not to realize there was celebration in the air when I went downtown after I left you this morning," she told him. "Then, a waitress in the café where I stopped for lunch said she wanted to get home early so she could fix her costume. One thing led to another."

He had stood up. Now he wandered across to the dresser where she'd spread out the various publications about Holland she'd bought that day, and he glanced down at them, picking up one book to finger it.

"I see you've been busy," he commented. "Do you always do your homework so thoroughly?"

He looked across the room at her, book in hand, and Andrea felt as if her breath was slowly being drawn out of her. She hadn't noticed until now that he was wearing casual clothes, a total contrast to the way he'd been dressed when she'd met him in his office that morning.

His snug faded jeans had seen plenty of wear, and there was a comfortable look about his thickly knit light-gray sweater. Though Andrea couldn't understand why, these clothes gave an added impact to his appearance, a very sensual impact. Maybe it was because they underscored a highly potent masculinity, because they made her all the more aware of his body, all the more conscious of him as a man.

She also became conscious of the odd intimacy implicit in their present situation. He was here in her motel room with her, she lay stretched upon the bed, and she couldn't understand why it all seemed so...so natural.

Awareness made her sit up, and at once she felt dizzy again. She swung her legs over the side of the bed, then propped her elbows on her knees and rested her head in her hands, waiting for the feeling to pass. But it didn't pass swiftly enough and she heard his voice close by, underlaid with anxiety as he asked, "Are you about to faint on me?"

She managed to shake her head, and then to raise it. This time as she looked at him their glances meshed, and Andrea felt a tremor run through her that had nothing to do with her recent ordeal. It was electric in its impact, a vibrating current that passed between this man and herself. A purely physical— very physical—reaction, she told herself, and she wondered if he was aware of it too.

If so, he wasn't about to let her know it. "You wouldn't happen to have some whisky or brandy with you, would you?" he asked her.

"No," she told him.

He frowned. "You could do with a stiff drink. I don't imagine you've had anything to eat, either, have you?"

"No," she admitted.

"I should take you home with me right now," he said, making the statement sound close to a threat.

She managed a weak smile. "I'm really not up to visiting tonight," she pointed out.

"No, you're not, are you?" he conceded. "Look, there's a reasonably good restaurant just down the road from here. I know the owner, and I'm going to stop by and see that they send you over something hot to eat. They don't serve alcoholic drinks, nor do I imagine the laws would permit them to deliver them if they did, so we'll have to forgo that. But I want you to promise me you'll eat, and then you'll take a hot bath and go to bed.''

His tone was severe, but the expression on his face belied it. There was concern, a lot of concern, in the way he was looking at her. Concern and... and some intangibles she couldn't put together, not in her present fuzzy state.

"The major festivities don't start until two tomorrow afternoon," he went on, and she knew he was referring to the Tulip Time celebration. "That's when the streets are scrubbed, and there's also a parade and *klompen* dancing. I have reserved seats at a good spot along the route, so we don't have to worry about getting there early. Just be sure, will you, that you've had both breakfast and lunch and plenty of rest before I pick you up?"

She nodded, aware that he hadn't given her the chance to either accept or refuse his invitation.

"The Tulip Time festivities will be a good introduction to Holland for you," he went on. "Did you call Mark, incidentally?"

"I returned his call, yes. His several calls. He'd been phoning here most of the day before I reached him."

Dirk's lips twitched, and then he smiled. Again it was a heart-stopping smile. Andrea found it impossible not to stare at him.

"He seemed pleased that you'd convinced me I

could work with a woman," he said, a surprisingly teasing note in his voice.

"Did I convince you of that?" It took a bit of daring to pose the question.

"We shall see," he responded enigmatically. "In any event, tomorrow's a holiday here in Holland. There won't be too much business accomplished anywhere. Perhaps on Thursday afternoon you and I can have a preliminary conference about the account and then go directly out to my house for dinner."

He was at the door, his hand on the knob. Gazing across at him, Andrea wished that he wasn't about to leave her. She hated being alone just now. She still felt wobbly, and the thought of having his strength to lean on was strangely desirable. Regardless of the ambivalent feelings she'd had about him ever since they'd met the previous day, she welcomed the idea of his nearness. It would be comforting to have him hold her in his arms as if she were a child, like Johanna, until she drifted off to sleep.

What am I thinking about? Andrea demanded of herself, angry at her own lack of control.

It was dim in the room with only one light on, and she hoped that Dirk was not able to see her clearly enough to be able to read her. She already suspected that he was much too astute about a lot of things.

But he said only, "Good night. And be sure to eat your dinner."

"I will," she said, nodding, and then had to ask him one thing more. "Are *you* sure your daughter will be up to so much activity tomorrow?"

"Johanna?" he answered. "Oh, yes. Kids recover fast from bad experiences, though Johanna may not do as well in that department as some children."

He didn't amplify his last remark but, standing in the open doorway, he paused.

"Andrea?" he asked. It was the first time he'd used her first name and she liked the way he said it.

"Yes?"

"Johanna is not my daughter." Then, with a brief wave, he closed the door behind him.

CHAPTER FIVE

THE MOTEL MANAGERESS brought coffee and hot rolls to Andrea the next morning and lingered on the threshold long enough to congratulate her. "Everyone in town's talking about your saving the little Van Der Maas girl's life," she said tremulously.

Andrea tried to be deprecating about the rescue, but the manageress would have none of it. "You were very brave," she insisted.

As she ate the rolls and drank the coffee, Andrea reflected that it was rather pleasant to be a heroine, if only briefly.

After a time she showered, then she found that the events of the previous day had taken more out of her than she realized, and she succumbed to the idea of a late-morning nap. It was afternoon when she woke up again, and she watched television for a time before starting to get ready for her "date" with Dirk and Johanna.

At exactly quarter to two there was a knock on the door. Opening it, Andrea had to concede that Mark had been right when he'd said his friend was handsome. Dirk Van Der Maas was disturbingly handsome.

One of the mental-caution flags that Andrea always kept in good supply fluttered briefly. *Remember that you're here for business, not pleasure,* she reminded herself sharply. *Any encounter with a client comes under the heading of business, and you'd better not forget it!*

But it would be easy to be forgetful with a man who looked as attractive as Dirk Van Der Maas did on this day, she acknowledged with a slight inner smile. He was wearing beige slacks, a Harris-tweed jacket and a deep-brown turtleneck, giving him an appearance that fell somewhere between the Madison Avenue man and the far more rugged individual of the night before.

Andrea had wondered just how to dress for the occasion and had settled on cream-colored slacks with a matching lace-collared cotton knit sweater. She'd applied her makeup carefully, using a bit more blush than she might have normally and a touch of green eyeshadow, Even so, she knew she still looked rather wan, and she felt like wriggling under Dirk's intent scrutiny.

Surprisingly he said, "You remind me of a piece of fine porcelain."

"What's that supposed to mean?"

"Beautiful, but fragile. I have the feeling you could break very easily just now. Did you sleep well?"

"Yes, I did." This was true. She'd obediently eaten the dinner the restaurant had delivered to her, then taken the prescribed hot bath and after that there'd been no problem in getting to sleep at all. Nor had the bad dreams she'd feared come to haunt her.

Despite her answer, Dirk frowned. "Are you sure you're up to going out?" he asked bluntly.

"Absolutely," she said, then added, "Where's Johanna?"

"In the car. I'm parked just outside. So hurry, will you please? I don't like to leave her alone, after what she went through yesterday."

"I hope her experience hasn't left any bad effects," Andrea ventured. "Is she all right?"

"Yes...surprisingly," he answered, a taut note in his voice that caused her to look up at him swiftly.

Just who was Johanna? This was a question Andrea had asked herself several times since Dirk had left her the night before, and she did so again as they left the motel unit and she saw, just outside, a silver-gray Mercedes with a child sitting in the rear seat.

At that instant Dirk, speaking in a voice so low she could barely hear him, said, "I should have told you more about Johanna. I will, later. For the moment, though, just go along with things, will you? Don't ask any questions."

Mystified, Andrea nodded.

There was no smile on Dirk's face as he went over to the car and opened the back door, but his tone was kindly enough as he said, "Come on out, Johanna, and meet Miss Campbell."

The little girl needed no second invitation. She clambered out of the car with alacrity, and Andrea stared down at her, transfixed.

Johanna looked like a little Dutch doll. She was dressed in an enchanting Netherlands costume, and Andrea was sure it was authentic, from the tip of the winged, white lace cap to the curve of the hand-carved wooden shoes. Her long full skirt, striped in pink, blue and lavender, came to her ankles, and the navy smock she wore was edged with lace and a band of the same striped material.

She was a beautiful child. Dark chestnut curls tumbled to her shoulders, and her wide eyes, inspecting Andrea now, were not blue but a deep velvety brown.

Andrea's breath caught at the edge of an emotional wave that threatened to bring on a tidal wave of tears, and she had to force a careful control as she said, "Hello, Johanna."

There was something enormously appealing about the child, and it was the kind of appeal that tugged at the heartstrings. Andrea wished that Dirk had told her more about the girl. She felt herself on thin ice. He'd warned her not to ask questions, which automatically gave rise to the thought that there must be forbidden subjects with Johanna. But what subjects, and why?

She felt an impatience toward Dirk because he'd introduced her to the child without first filling her in about any of these things, and this showed in the glance she leveled at him as he held the front door of the car open for her.

"You can get in back again, Johanna," he told the little girl, and she nodded. But she paused before climbing into the back seat to survey Andrea with the kind of direct gaze only a child can give. Then, to Andrea's astonishment, she said, "My uncle says you saved my life, Miss Campbell."

Andrea gulped. So, Dirk Van Der Maas was Johanna's uncle. This opened up an entirely new line of thought, but she dismissed it to concentrate on Johanna's statement, and she felt a surge of resentment toward the diffident, handsome man still holding the car door for her. She would have preferred that he hadn't told the child anything so dramatic.

"I only happened to be near when you needed a little help," she said, trying to make it sound as if this was something that could happen to anyone, anywhere, anytime.

Johanna nodded, but before she turned to climb into the car Andrea caught a glimpse of her face, and the child's expression shocked her. Her small face mirrored stark terror. Johanna was frightened to death about something. Impulsively Andrea moved toward her, instinctively wanting to reach out to her. But she was stopped by a firm hand gripping her arm, and Dirk Van Der Maas said, his voice tight, "Get in, will you please?"

It was a tense beginning to what was supposed to be a festive occasion. As they drove out of the motor-inn parking lot toward a street that would lead to the center of town, all three were silent. Andrea's thoughts swung, pendulum fashion, first to the man at her side and then to the little girl huddled in the rear seat, and then back again to Dirk, whose mouth was set in a taut line as he drove.

Something was wrong, very wrong, and Andrea had no inkling as to what it might be, no idea of how to begin to cope with this situation. Her frustration was intense.

Finally she asked, "What is *klompen* dancing?" and her relief was vast when she heard a chuckle from the seat behind her.

It seemed to her that Dirk, too, relaxed visibly, and he said, with a much lighter note to his voice, "Tell Miss Campbell what *klompen* are, Johanna."

"I have them on," Johanna announced proudly. "*Klompen* are wooden shoes. Dutch wooden shoes. The *klompen* dancing is fun, and it's very pretty."

"You'll see plenty of it," Dirk added. "There are groups of girls in Dutch costumes *klompen* dancing somewhere in downtown Holland every half hour during Tulip Time. They're mostly high-school students, not only from Holland but from the surrounding area. Over a period of fifty-odd years the dances have been elaborated on, so they've become more and more intricate. There will be several hundred dancers performing along Main Street during the opening festivities this afternoon. I think you'll enjoy watching them.''

"I wish I could help scrub the streets," Johanna said wistfully.

"Next year," her uncle promised. "Anyway, I'm sure you'll want to point out everything that's going on to Miss Campbell this time around.''

Dirk had arranged front-row seats for them along the main street, thronged today with thousands of spectators who had come to see the street scrubbing and the parade that opened Tulip Time. The festivities traditionally started with the mayor and members of the city council inspecting the city streets, then finding them dirty and ordering that they be scrubbed.

The street scrubbing itself was hilarious, women and children entering into it with a contagious enthusiasm. Everyone participating had to wear a Dutch costume, regardless of age, so even the babies being pushed along in strollers by mothers wielding brooms or scrub brushes were wearing white-peaked caps and miniature wooden shoes.

Men dressed in Dutch costume, some of them with wooden shoulder yokes from which large metal pails of water were suspended, set the scene for the scrubbing by tossing water out of the pails in high arced streams, the cascading spumes glinting rainbow colors in the bright afternoon sunlight. The women in the first row started to scrub, and then the others joined in, going at the job with high-spirited exuberance.

When the last of the scrubbers had disappeared from view, Johanna, sitting at Andrea's side, sighed and said, "I think that's the best part. Except, I guess, for the *klompen* dancers."

By the time she'd seen the parade and the *klompen* dancers, Andrea had to admit that she was hard put to decide which she liked best herself, the street scrubbing or the *klompen* dancing. Both had been unique in her experience, she told Johanna and added, "You must be very proud of your Dutch heritage."

To her surprise, Johanna said solemnly, "I'm not all Dutch. My mother was part French."

That accounted for those beautiful brown eyes—and brought to mind so many questions. But, remembering Dirk's admonition, Andrea said quickly, "My mother is Finnish. At least her parents came from Finland. It's interesting, isn't it, how we Americans have roots in different countries all over the world?"

At that instant she glimpsed a balloon seller moving toward them along the street edge, and impulsively, she asked Johanna, "Would you like a balloon?"

"Oh, yes, please," the little girl answered quickly.

"What color?"

"Yellow," Johanna said promptly.

Andrea had fished in her handbag and taken out a dollar bill as she spoke. She handed it to the balloon vendor even as Dirk Van Der Maas said crisply, "Here. Let me get that."

"No, please," she told him. "I want to give Johanna a present."

She took the balloon from the vendor and handed it to the girl, and was disconcerted when she touched Johanna's small hand. It was cold, almost clammy.

She started to say something to Dirk, because it occurred to her that the coldness of Johanna's skin could be a delayed reaction to the previous day's episode, but then she thought better of it. The opening festivities were nearly over. People were beginning to leave the scene, and Dirk said, "Why don't we let the crowds thin out a bit, and then we'll go?"

"All right," Andrea nodded.

She looked down at Johanna to see that the little girl was gazing up at the yellow balloon, clutching the stick from which it was suspended with chubby fingers.

"Hold it tightly," Andrea advised. "They're filled with helium, and they can escape and fly away very easily."

Johanna nodded without looking at her, and Andrea had the uneasy feeling that the child had gone far away from her. She seemed so . . . so remote.

Inadvertently she glanced at Dirk. As she'd suspected, he was watching his niece. But there was an intentness about his expression, and something more. She saw raw pain in his eyes, pain so primitive she was taken aback by it and left with the feeling that she'd stumbled into a prohibited area, a corner of his life into which he was not about to let anyone venture.

He was quick at putting his mask back on again, though. "I think we could start out now," he said. "It would be easiest to go right down the middle of the street."

Johanna walked between them as they made their way back to the car, the yellow balloon bobbing with every step she took.

Dirk opened the back door first, for Johanna. "Take care with the balloon," he suggested. But she only gave him an odd look.

Then, so quickly it was over before either of the adults knew what she was doing, Johanna opened her hand wide and seemed to be urging the balloon upward as it took off in a quick, graceful flight.

For just a second Andrea thought this had happened accidentally, and she was afraid the child was going to be upset. Then she realized that Johanna had let the balloon go on purpose.

She couldn't keep from voicing the question, regardless of Dirk Van Der Maas's prior instructions. "Why did you do that?" she asked Johanna gently.

"Because I wanted my balloon to be free," she said, her voice low. "If something is free, then it never needs to be afraid."

She looked up at Andrea as she spoke, and Andrea saw that the velvety brown eyes were shimmering with tears.

Johanna had freed her balloon. . . and yet Andrea was terribly aware of how much the little girl had really wanted to keep it.

"THERE'S A PLEASANT EATING PLACE a few miles out of town along the lake," Dirk said, as he started the car engine purring. "Are you in the mood for either a very late lunch or a very early supper?"

"I am!" a small voice from the back seat rejoined promptly.

Andrea's answering laugh was tinged with relief. She tried to tell herself that she was probably imagining things about Johanna that had no basis in reality. Because of that strange comment of Dirk's, she was creating a mystery about the child.

Children, she reminded herself, sometimes lived in worlds all their own. It was quite possible that Johanna's statement about the balloon stemmed from something in a bedtime story someone had read her. It could be as simple as that.

But somehow Andrea doubted it. She hadn't misread the expression of pure terror she'd seen earlier on the child's face when they were starting out.

What could Johanna be so afraid of?

"Are you agreeable, Andrea?" Dirk asked, and she realized she'd made no response to his invitation.

"Yes," she said quickly. "Yes, of course."

He nodded but said nothing more, and she realized there were times when he spoke less than anyone she'd ever known. Just as she wondered what caused Johanna's fear, so she wondered what had happened to Dirk Van Der Maas to have made him build up such a tremendous reserve around himself. That's what it was. He'd all but buried himself behind a wall of inviolable privacy.

Yet the night before she'd glimpsed a different sort of person. He'd been concerned about her when he'd come to the motel. Concerned and caring. And just now she hadn't imagined the tortured emotion in his eyes, more revealing than anything else. A person did not show such pain—even in an off-guard moment—without very good reason.

As they drove she became aware that the silence was beginning to get to her. Because she had to say something, because she had to break this tension-provoking stillness, Andrea casually asked, "How long does the tulip festival last?"

At first she thought Dirk hadn't heard her. He was staring straight ahead, but she suspected his concentration was not entirely on his driving. No, he'd gone miles away from her.

"I beg your pardon?" he asked, then evidently remembered the content of her question after all. "The tulip festival?" he echoed. "It lasts four days. Traditionally it opens on the Wednesday nearest May 15 and concludes the following Sunday. During the course of the four days there are all sorts of special events...."

"Yes," she interrupted dryly, "I'm sure there are."

The glance he shot toward her blazed with blue flames. Though a second before she'd felt as if she was traveling with a statue, now she knew, deeply and instinctively, that this man at her side was anything but a statue. Perhaps he'd tried to cast himself into a marble mold, Andrea conceded, for reasons she couldn't even begin to imagine. But there were moments when the marble cracked in places and the man showed through, and there was something very provocative about even a glimpse of that man.

"I've been thinking," he said now, abruptly.

"Yes?"

"About tomorrow. My mother's delighted that you'll be coming to dinner, and she sent her apologies again for not being able to meet you today. She's on the Tulip Time board of directors, so this is a tremendously busy period for her."

"Then won't tomorrow be a busy time for her, too?"

"She's determined to be free tomorrow evening," Dirk answered. "Meanwhile it occurred to me that it might be a good idea for you to tour the bakery before we get down to any details about my future plans."

Business. She'd almost forgotten she was here to conduct business with him. The personal had intruded, and she'd become so wrapped up in it she'd actually forgotten she was about to start handling his account for Saunders and Terrence.

She said rather stiffly, "Of course, if you think so."

"You should be familiar with our history, and with the products we're producing now," he told her. "We've been trying out some of the purely Dutch products, like the *bankets*, throughout this region, but though the *bankets* and some of the other things keep remarkably well, I'm not fond of old baked goods. So I've limited the distribution."

"Which, of course, can be greatly expanded once you start freezing your products," she stated, rather than asked.

"Exactly. You'll be concentrating primarily on our frozen-foods division," he said, then added with a slight smile, "It's still in an embryonic stage."

"But you're definitely going ahead with it?"

"Yes," he nodded. "I'm definitely going ahead with it. It's time for Van Der Maas to expand. Past time, probably, but I haven't been able to get to it sooner. Anyway...."

"Yes?"

"I'd suggest you plan to tour the bakery tomorrow morning," he said. "Then you and I can meet Friday and begin to get some of the details down."

"Very well," she agreed.

He nodded as if something had been accomplished between them.

Andrea noted that they'd passed the turnoff she'd taken on Monday on the way to the state beach. "We're going out toward Sandy Point," Dirk informed her, and she told herself she'd have to remember to get out her map again once she got back to the motor inn.

The place Dirk had suggested for their lunch was not the beach shack Andrea had expected it might be. It was a spacious restaurant on the Lakeshore Drive with an added cocktail lounge, which sometimes had some pretty good entertainment at night, Dirk told her.

To her surprise he suggested they preface their repast with Bloody Marys. Reminding herself that they were not yet involved in business conferences, Andrea agreed.

As he lifted his glass and said, "Cheers," Dirk smiled somewhat wryly. "You thought I was a teetotaler, didn't you?" he teased.

She had, and her expressive face gave her away.

He laughed. "That shows you," he said, "that you should watch out for first impressions. They're not always valid."

"No, they're not," she agreed, and all at once they were staring at each other. A quivering sensation began deep inside Andrea, and it grew as she and Dirk continued to look at each other. A wonderful warmth invaded her body, and she felt an awareness and a sense of being such as she'd never experienced before.

A small voice murmured, "You should have said *Welkom Vrienden*, Uncle Dirk."

Dirk looked down at his small niece uncompre-hendingly. "What?" he managed.

"You should have said *Welkom Vrienden*," Johanna repeated. "Because I think Miss Campbell is very welcome, don't you, and she's going to be our friend, isn't she?"

Only Johanna failed to appreciate the intensity of the brief moment of silence that followed her ques-tion. Then Dirk asked, casually enough, "Are you going to be our friend, Miss Andrea Campbell?"

It was a simple enough question, a harmless enough question, and one posed by Johanna in the first place. But when voiced by Dirk it had a devastating undercurrent of meaning and it wedged between them, overwhelmingly important.

It took effort, but Andrea managed to keep her voice steady, to sound almost as casual as he had. "Yes," she answered. "Yes, I certainly hope to be."

THEY WERE AT THE EDGE of Lake Michigan, and after lunch Andrea expected that Dirk would suggest they might go for a walk along the sandy shoreline and explore. She was an inveterate beachcomber and had been collecting shells and rocks ever since she was a child.

Cape Cod, where she'd spent most of her sum-mers, was a mecca for both. The rocks, most of which could more accurately be called pebbles, were wonderfully varied, because the Cape was glacial moraine territory. Andrea didn't know what the Lake Michigan shore had to offer but she was eager to learn. She'd seen few shorelines where there wasn't something interesting and purely regional to discover.

When they left the restaurant, though, Dirk led them directly back to his car. Andrea was tempted to suggest they take a beach walk, but there was something about his attitude—a renewed stiffness—that kept her from doing so. And Johanna seemed content to clamber into the back seat again without so much as a glance toward the water.

During lunch Johanna had behaved like any other high-spirited seven-year-old child. She'd had a hamburger and a chocolate milk shake, and she'd shared orders of both French fries and onion rings, proof there was nothing wrong with her appetite. Once in the car, though, she lapsed into silence again, her bright chattering stilled.

At the motor inn, Andrea hoped Dirk would escort her to her room so that she'd be able to have a word with him about Johanna. But as they pulled up alongside her own car, Johanna piped, "Can I see what your room looks like, Miss Campbell?"

"Of course," Andrea said, hoping that she was concealing her disappointment, especially from Dirk.

There was little to see, so the tour was a brief one. But Johanna was intrigued by the idea of having a color TV in one's own room, and also by the red message light that once again was blinking on the phone.

"Probably Mark," she said, in answer to Dirk's inquiring glance. "I'll get back to him later."

"He does keep tabs on you, doesn't he," Dirk remarked mildly. Or was it mildly? When he used that cool tone of voice, she'd already discovered, it was difficult to know what lay behind it.

"It's not a question of keeping tabs," she answered, a bit abruptly. "He's interested in the account. And I forgot to tell him today would be a holiday here in Holland."

"You underestimate yourself," Dirk said, surprisingly, and then turned to his niece. "Okay, Johanna, we'd better get along."

The child paused on the threshold and turned toward Andrea, her arms upstretched. Andrea knelt instinctively, and felt herself being hugged while Johanna's soft little mouth brushed her cheek.

"Thank you for coming today," Johanna said, then added, "And thank you for saving me!"

Andrea didn't dare look at Dirk as she listened to Johanna's words, and once the door had closed behind him and his niece, she was unable to suppress an inexplicable rush of tears.

CHAPTER SIX

THE PHONE RANG at eight o'clock Thursday morning, just as Andrea was emerging from the shower. She wrapped a towel around herself as she raced for it, sure it would be Dirk Van Der Maas calling. He probably wanted to set a time for showing her around the bakery.

She was surprised at the sharp sense of disappointment that pricked her when it was a woman who responded to her own, carefully modulated, "Hello?"

"This is Evelyn Bleeker, Miss Campbell," Dirk's secretary said crisply. "Mr. Van Der Maas asked me to telephone you. He's arranged a bakery tour. Could you be here by ten o'clock?"

"Of course," Andrea said, noting that Mrs. Bleeker had made no apologies for calling her at such an early hour. In Boston it would have been unusual, to say the least, to make a business call at eight o'clock in the morning. The working day must start at dawn in Holland.

"Come directly to Mr. Van Der Maas's office, will you please?" Mrs. Bleeker instructed, and Andrea assented.

After she'd hung up, she tried to assess the secretary's tone of voice. She'd concluded after meeting her that Mrs. Bleeker could be a powerful friend or a powerful foe. She appeared to be well entrenched in her job, and Andrea suspected she'd held it for a long time. She also suspected that the secretary knew as much about the Van Der Maas family as anyone else in town, and her own curiosity about Johanna, about Dirk himself, for that matter, had been heightened by the time she'd spent with them the previous day. But she suspected that getting information out of Mrs. Bleeker might be a shade more difficult than getting gold out of Fort Knox.

As she toweled her hair dry, Andrea thought about what she should wear for her tour of the bakery. She wanted to look both attractive and efficient. This was the day when she was going to convince Dirk Van Der Maas that a woman could be as effective professionally as a man. She was going to show him that Mark's confidence in her was not misplaced. But after carefully scanning her wardrobe she discarded her more discreetly tailored clothes in favor of a red knit dress that did just the right things for her figure. It was unadorned except for a shoulder flounce, and she wore the dress with a wide, black patent-leather belt and matching low-heeled shoes. By the time she'd brushed out her shimmering hair and added some subtle makeup touches her mirror told her that she looked very, very feminine—and she found herself retorting to the mirror that there was no reason why a woman had to dress like a man in order to prove herself capable in her chosen career.

There was a restaurant that served breakfast within a short distance of the motor inn. Andrea decided to walk over to it. She felt as if she needed the exercise. Although not particularly athletic, she did do a lot of walking when she was in the city. Out of the city she loved to take long hikes in the woods, especially during the fall when New England's foliage was so glorious. And many times, on a winter weekend, she'd drive down to Cape Cod and stroll for miles along the beautiful, deserted beaches. Andrea reacted sharply to visual impressions. The glory of the fall foliage, the power of the winter sea, golden sunlight, for that matter, or a gray veil of mysterious fog were all balm to her soul.

There wasn't much to be said, though, about walking from the motor inn to the restaurant. She had to go along the grassy strip at the edge of a well-graveled highway in order to bridge the distance, and though it was safe enough, there was nothing in the least relaxing about such a safari.

As she made her way back to the Yellow Tulip after breakfast she decided that in future she'd drive to the restaurant and put her walking time in elsewhere, in more tranquil surroundings.

She arrived at the bakery a few minutes before ten to find that the door to the president's outer office was wide open. She hoped this was a good sign.

Mrs. Bleeker, presiding at the desk, looked up with a polite smile impossible to interpret. "Mr. Van Der Maas will be with you directly, Miss Campbell," she said after greeting Andrea.

"Thank you," Andrea murmured politely. She sat down on one of the comfortable chintz-covered chairs, remembering what a contrast there was between this cozy room and the austerity of Dirk's office.

A minute later she heard Mrs. Bleeker say, "Ah, here you are." Andrea looked up, expecting to see Dirk, but the man standing at Mrs. Bleeker's desk was considerably younger than Dirk, and very blond.

"Miss Campbell," Mrs. Bleeker said at exactly that second, "this is Klaus Van Der Maas."

It had not occurred to Andrea that Dirk might have other relatives involved with him in the bakery business, her mistake, she saw now. She stood and the young man—as tall as Dirk but slighter in build—came across to her, his hand extended. "I'm Dirk's younger brother, Miss Campbell. I understand I'm to have the pleasure of taking you on a tour of the bakery."

Again Andrea felt that sharp stab of disappointment, but this time it was edged with resentment. Dirk *was* the president of Van Der Maas, Inc. True, he was in the throes of an expansion campaign, and she didn't doubt that he had plenty of other things to do. Nevertheless, the fact that he was not taking the time to show her through the bakery himself for this initial overview left her with the feeling that she was being put in her place in a rather subtle way.

Andrea hoped her face wasn't as transparent as usual. The last thing in the world she wanted to do was to telegraph any messages involving her ruffled feelings to Dirk's brother.

She managed a convincing smile as she shook Klaus Van Der Maas's hand. Looking up at him, she said, "I appreciate your taking the time to show me around."

He was good-looking, more classically handsome than Dirk, she decided. His eyes were a deeper blue than Dirk's, and there was none of his older brother's aloofness about him.

Whatever had happened to affect Dirk so tangibly evidently hadn't touched his younger brother. At least not seriously.

And Klaus was considerably younger. Andrea had already concluded that if Dirk and Mark had been in college together, Dirk must be thirty-six or so...eight years older than she was. On the other hand, Klaus Van Der Maas could not be much beyond his early twenties.

"Shall we go along?" he suggested, and Andrea nodded absently. She had noticed that the door to the president's private office was closed, and she wondered if Dirk was in there, sitting alone at his barren desk.

Klaus led her toward the staircase as he asked politely, "Did you enjoy the street scrubbing and all the rest of the festivities yesterday?"

"Yes," Andrea nodded, rallying. There was no point in taking her hostilities out on an attractive young man who was merely doing something he'd been asked to do, and being very pleasant about it.

"Johanna had a great time," Klaus said. "You made a big hit with her. You should be pleased. Johanna doesn't take to strangers easily."

Something glimmered at the back of Andrea's mind. Klaus, too, was a Van Der Maas. He was Dirk's brother, so he must also be Johanna's uncle. He was hardly old enough to be her father.

Being with Klaus, Andrea thought now, could be quite a plus. Klaus was friendly, and he must know all about Dirk. He must know, for instance, why Dirk was so repressed. Repressed? No, that wasn't the right word for it, she mused, as she walked down the long flight of stairs. Encased in a shell of his own making. That was more like it.

For the first time in her life Andrea contemplated getting to know someone primarily so she could pry all the information possible out of them to satisfy her curiosity about someone else. She was vaguely ashamed of herself as she admitted silently that she was going to do this with Klaus Van Der Maas. She only hoped he wouldn't become aware of her strategy.

She decided to start with a direct question.

"Has Johanna been ill?" she asked Klaus.

They'd come to the foot of the stairs, and Klaus stopped in the small square foyer.

"Johanna?" he asked. "No, she's a healthy kid. Otherwise I guess she could have caught a cold from falling in the canal like she did. We're all very grateful to you about that, Miss Campbell."

That wasn't what she wanted at all. "I didn't do that much," she said. "Chances are Johanna would have managed to get back to the canal bank by herself if I hadn't reached her so quickly."

Klaus shook his head. "I doubt that," he said. "Johanna panicked. They said at the hospital she'd already swallowed a fair bit of water. Johanna's so terrified of the water I don't think there's much doubt she would have drowned if you hadn't gotten to her when you did. Anna," he added, "feels terrible about it."

Andrea remembered that Dirk had mentioned an elderly woman who had been with Johanna. She also recalled that he'd said he'd insisted Anna Poest get an electrocardiogram as a result of the incident.

"How is Anna?" she asked now.

"Her heart's okay," Klaus said. "Dirk was worried about that. But he feels it would be a good idea for her to take a real holiday anyway. He's sending her to visit a sister who lives in California. Frankly, I doubt Dirk would trust Anna to care for Johanna again."

"Can't Johanna swim at all?" Andrea asked. "I

mean. . .you live so near Lake Michigan. I would think. . . ."

"Johanna can swim like a fish," Klaus said surprisingly. "She started to swim almost before she could walk. It isn't that." Klaus hesitated. Then he asked slowly, "Didn't Dirk tell you about Gerrit?"

"Gerrit?"

"Johanna's father. Our brother. Dirk's twin. They weren't identical. They didn't look alike at all, so it's easy to forget they were twins. Dirk," Klaus added, with a strange sort of smile, "was five minutes older."

He said this as if it was important, and Andrea was puzzled.

Then she realized that Klaus was speaking in the past tense in his reference to Gerrit.

"Gerrit was drowned not quite two years ago," Klaus continued tersely, his face almost as expressionless as Dirk's usually was. "He and his wife. Marietta. They were out on the lake in Dirk's sloop. Gerrit had borrowed it. A sudden squall came up. Johanna was with them. She had a life preserver on—that's what saved her. But she saw the whole thing. . .she remembers the whole thing. She still wakes up in the night screaming. Screams that make your blood curdle. . . ."

Klaus was speaking softly, almost as if he was speaking to himself, and now he shook himself and forced a smile. "I'm sorry," he said gently. "I shouldn't have told you that. It's disturbing, I know, to think of a child being so...upset, for such a long time."

"No," Andrea said quickly, but her pulse was pounding and her throat felt dry. "No, that's all right. I'm glad you did tell me. I knew there was something that bothered Johanna deeply, but your brother didn't have the chance to talk to me about it. When we went to the street scrubbing yesterday, he only had time to warn me not to ask Johanna any questions. And there were a couple of times when I realized that...that there must be things that terrify her."

Suddenly she felt ashamed of herself. Abjectly ashamed. "I'm sorry, Klaus," she said sincerely, using his first name unconsciously. "I didn't mean to pry."

"That's all right," he said. Then he asked, "What's your first name?"

"Andrea. My friends call me Andi."

"That's all right, Andi," Klaus told her. "It's something you should know if you're going to be around Johanna—and I understand you're having dinner with us tonight. Otherwise it would be easy for you to say something about swimming, or boating...."

"Doesn't anyone ever mention swimming or boating in front of Johanna?"

"We try not to," Klaus admitted. "My mother's been taking Johanna to a psychiatrist in Grand Rapids who specializes in children. This was at the suggestion of her regular pediatrician. They go to Grand Rapids about once a month. Matter of fact, the appointment was for this past Monday, which was rough on mother with the Tulip Time activities coming up.''

So that was why Johanna had not been in school for a couple of days.

''Johanna lives with mother,'' Klaus went on, and then stopped, his smile sheepish. ''I'm boring you with all this family history,'' he said, ''and, anyway, they're waiting for us in the bakery.''

He could not have been more wrong about boring her, but Andrea was in no position to enlighten him. She followed him through a door on the far side of the foyer, and at once they were in a different world.

Regardless of the exterior appearance of the building, the bakery was strictly modern. To her surprise, Andrea discovered that it was also virtually odorless, and this was a disappointment. There was none of the delicious aroma of fresh-baking bread, and when she asked Klaus about this he told her it was because of modern air-venting technology.

They were greeted by a man dressed in a pale-blue coverall emblazoned with the same insignia Andrea had first noted on the receptionist's blouse. The man wore a white hard hat, and she wondered about this. She'd never thought of working in a bakery as a particularly hazardous operation.

Klaus introduced the man as Jan van der Houten, and Andrea gathered that he'd been with the Van Der Maas bakery for a long time and was in charge of its overall production.

"Jan can tell you how many loaves of old-fashioned white bread we baked yesterday, for example," Klaus said.

"One hundred and twenty-five thousand," van der Houten retorted promptly.

Andrea was staggered. "One-hundred-and-twenty-five-thousand loaves of bread in a single day?"

"One-hundred-and-twenty-five-thousand loaves of white bread," the baker corrected her. "We also baked thirty-five-thousand loaves of whole wheat, fifteen-thousand loaves of dark rye and another thirty-thousand loaves of various specialty breads. These are baked on different days of the week. We bake the white, the whole wheat and the dark rye every day. Then there are the English muffins and the rolls, and of course the doughnuts...."

He was smiling at the astonished expression on her face.

"That much, in just one bakery?" Andrea asked, incredulous. At the last instant she had deleted the word "small" from her question, for the Van Der Maas bakery was beginning to sound anything but small to her.

Jan van der Houten nodded. "We have the franchise for several brands of national breads and bakery products too," he confided. "I keep those tabulations separate. We bake them and distribute them via Van Der Maas through this region of Michigan. And, as Mr. Dirk Van Der Maas has probably already told you, Miss Campbell, we are also baking Dutch specialties from time to time."

"Our trial balloons," Klaus interposed.

Jan van der Houten produced two white hard hats similar to his own, and Klaus immediately put his on. After a moment Andrea followed suit, asking as she did so, "Why are these necessary?"

"We have a lot of machinery in action," the baker told her. "Large machinery. Overhead conveyor belts, for one thing. In any plant where there is machinery on this scale, there is always the danger of accident. We do everything we can to prevent mishaps, and to instill in our workers that they must always be thinking of safety. Their own safety and the safety of their fellow workers. But even so...."

He was leading Klaus and Andrea along a wide corridor as he spoke, and then, as they turned a corner, she quickly saw what he was talking about. She'd never seen so much machinery in one place before, all of it in operation.

"Let's go upstairs first," van der Houten suggested. He led them along an inner wall to another door, which opened onto a narrow stairway. At the top they stepped into a vast open space compartmentalized only by the differing activities taking place in each area.

"Here we first mix the yeast and liquids," van der Houten explained, pointing to a series of electric mixers that were like giant versions of the household appliance. "Flour is added automatically," he continued, "measured by computer. When the flour and the liquids have been blended to a prescribed consistency, the dough is turned out into these vats to rise."

He indicated enormous rectangular metal vats, all of which looked well used, and he added, with a grin, "Don't touch. If you do, you'll get grease on your fingers. That goes for most of the things around here. Everything has been buttered."

"How many loaves of bread do you get from the contents of one of those vats?" Andrea asked.

"Two thousand of the white bread," van der Houten said laconically. "Somewhat less for the whole wheat and rye, because the batters are more dense. The dough is left to rise for three hours. After that, it is pounded down—again by machinery—and then it will be left to rise once again. Now...you see this chute," he said, pointing to another large machine, set into the floor on one side of the room.

"Yes."

"The dough is poured down the chute, where it is automatically cut into lumps. Each lump goes into a buttered bread tin and then is conveyed to a temperature-controlled unit we call a 'proofer,' where it will be allowed to rise again. As you'll see when we go back downstairs, the tins are next conveyed along a belt to a point where a machine makes an automatic slit down the center of each loaf, into which a narrow stream of melted butter is poured. After that, the loaves are baked, then they go to a cooling oven. Then they are sliced and wrapped... all of these completely automatic processes."

As they progressed through the bakery, Jan van der Houten elaborating on each step of the baking process along the way, Andrea was struck with the strangeness of seeing so many familiar objects in giant size, from rolling pins to the enormous ovens in which the bread was baked.

Everything appeared to have been arranged in units of five, five bread pans linked together, five rolls or muffins or doughnuts to a unit.

"That's for easier counting," the baker told her. "We are accustomed to counting everything in fives. But then when it comes to packaging," he added with a smile, "our machines have been taught to count in units of six, so that we come out with a dozen muffins or rolls."

The huge units were all carefully marked: proofers, coders, mixers, depanners. Conveyor belts, as intricate in their layout as a network of superhighways, transmitted loaves of bread or pans of rolls or doughnuts along to the next step in their preparation. All the while additional conveyor belts whirred overhead, carrying freshly baked bread to the cooling oven, or on a circuitous ride down to the level where machines waited to slice the cooled loaves. After being sliced the loaves were slid into waxed-paper covers, a machine sealing over the fold of each loaf as it emerged and then pushing it along to the terminal collection point where the loaves would be stored on tall metal racks, which were taken out to the waiting delivery trucks.

The bakery employees all wore the same light-blue coveralls, and they all wore white hard hats. Each person had a specific task, some assigned to posts from which they seldom took more than a couple of steps in the course of their working hours. Many of the jobs involved supervising the workings of the machinery, making certain that each step in the processing was completed without error.

"I never realized that there have been machines invented for quite so many things," Andrea admitted as she watched. "Precision to the nth degree."

"Automation," Klaus put in. "That's what it's all about. Modern technology."

Van der Houten shrugged. "To produce a quarter of a million loaves of bread a day you have to have modern technology," he said simply.

"True," Klaus conceded. He smiled. "Are you going to give Andi the guest package?"

"Of course." The production manager smiled back. He walked into a small side office and came back with a plastic bag printed with the bakery's insignia. "A souvenir for you," he told Andrea.

She accepted the bag and couldn't refrain from peeping into it. She saw a loaf of fresh bread and a box of doughnuts and some other things she couldn't at once identify.

"Balloons and coloring books and a paper hard hat, among other items." Klaus grinned.

"We have a lot of school children tour the bakery from time to time," Jan van der Houten explained. "We like to give them something to take away."

"Good public relations," Andrea approved.

The mention of balloons had immediately reminded Andrea of that strangely poignant moment when Johanna had set the balloon she'd bought her free. She forced herself to thrust the memory to the back of her mind as she thanked the baker and was invited to come back any time or to call him with any questions she might have. Then she and Klaus stepped through the door that led into the little foyer.

When the door had closed behind them, Andrea realized the building was remarkably soundproof. Here she heard none of the bakery noises, and it was also at least twenty degrees cooler. It had been quite warm in most of the bakery, despite the air controlling Klaus had mentioned, and extremely hot in the immediate vicinity of the giant ovens.

Klaus glanced at his watch. "Just short of noon," he told her. "Could I suggest a bite of lunch?"

Andrea suspected he was merely being courteous

and, although she would have liked to have lunched with him, declined. "Thanks, but I'd better be getting along."

"Then I'll see you tonight," Klaus said.

Tonight. The very thought of the evening ahead was beginning to give her qualms. She felt uncomfortable about dining in Dirk's home with his family. Maybe because she'd been so wrong in her imaginary picture of Dirk himself, she'd been trying to rid herself of her preconceived ideas about his mother. The image she'd projected originally of an overworked elderly woman trying with all her might to please a difficult son no longer seemed to fit. The previous day when Dirk had spoken about his mother's activities as a member of the Tulip Time board of directors a momentary vision of a big-bosomed club woman had flitted across Andrea's consciousness, and now the image recurred.

Mrs. Van Der Maas must be prominent in local society, that stood to reason. The last middle-aged woman Andrea had known who was important socially and civically in her community—and a colossal snob to boot—had been George Cabot's mother, and the analogy was an unfortunate one.

Klaus was looking down at her and he asked, "What's the matter, Andi?"

"Nothing," she said hastily.

"You have a very expressive face," Klaus observed, and Andrea was tempted to reply, "And it's often been my undoing!"

"Dinner's to be around six-thirty," Klaus continued. "Mother likes to have it on the early side when Johanna's going to join us, and we'd be hard put to keep Johanna away with you coming. Suppose I pick you up at six?"

"What?" Andrea asked dumbly.

"Shall I pick you up at six?"

Was this Klaus's idea, or had Dirk told his younger brother that he was to take care of their guest's transportation that evening? Even as she posed the question, Andrea was sure she knew the answer. At this point Dirk had relegated her to those in lesser authority. But then it had been foolish to expect that he'd give her his undivided attention. There was no need for it.

She said to Klaus, "Thanks, I'll be ready at six."

"Fine."

"I'm at the Yellow Tulip," she added.

"Yes, I know."

He was such a friendly person, Andrea decided, clutching the goodies bag Jan van der Houten had given her. She wondered exactly how old he was, and if there were any other "surprise" Van Der Maases between him and Dirk. She also wondered how many times he'd had to drag visitors through the bakery. At best it must be a bore to be the company president's baby brother.

"Thank you for taking me through the bakery, Klaus," she said, then added, with a rather wry smile, "There must have been a lot of other things you'd rather have been doing."

"Not at all," Klaus Van Der Maas told her quickly. "It was a pleasure!" And he said it so fervently Andrea almost believed he meant it!

ANDREA HAD TIME ON HER HANDS after she left the bakery. There were several hours to pass before Klaus would be coming to pick her up at her motel, so she decided to visit the Netherlands Museum, as Dirk had previously suggested.

The area was thronged with visitors, and Andrea edged her car into one of the last spaces in the parking lot. Inside the small museum, a smiling white-haired lady wearing a traditional Dutch costume was detailing some of Holland's early history to a group of visitors, and Andrea paused to listen.

The people of the Netherlands had been enduring religious persecution for many years, she learned, when, toward the middle of the nineteenth century, Dr. Albertus Van Raalte, like a number of other Dutchmen, was forced to the reluctant conclusion that the only hope for the future was to leave the homeland and immigrate to another section of the world where the inherent Dutch love of liberty could be pursued.

Van Raalte had headed a band of one hundred men, women and children who had set sail from Rotterdam in the fall of 1846. He'd left most of his band in Detroit while he continued west in search of a place to settle, and they'd followed him when he'd decided on Holland as the preferred site.

It had been an especially cold winter, the snow more than two feet deep most of the time. But the first settlers had cleared the land, building log houses with the trees they chopped down, and by the following spring other immigrants from the Netherlands had begun to arrive by the hundreds.

Some of those immigrants would have been Dirk Van Der Maas's ancestors, Andrea mused, as she moved away from the group of tourists toward a diorama that depicted Dr. Van Raalte kneeling in prayer on ground thickly covered by snow as he asked for divine guidance in selecting the site where the new settlement was to be founded. They had been strong people, determined people.

Dirk had received a valuable inheritance from them. Although she still didn't know him very well—would anyone ever be permitted to know Dirk Van Der Maas really well? she wondered—she had no doubts about either his physical or his mental and emotional strength.

From the diorama, Andrea moved on to explore the charmingly furnished rooms in the museum, and it was obvious to her that everything within this small building had been put together with a great deal of loving care. There were beautiful displays of heirloom blue-and-white delft pottery, old Dutch pewter and exquisite, handmade furniture brought from the Netherlands long ago.

Andrea lingered in the museum longer than she'd intended to, welcoming this chance to view the many things so reflective of Holland's Dutch heritage. She was especially entranced by a one-hundred-fifty-year-old dollhouse that was remarkable in its craftsmanship, a miracle of miniature detail.

Inevitably the dollhouse made her think of Johanna, and she felt a pang of pity for the girl. Johanna had already had more than her share of tragedy in her life. And so, Andrea suspected, had Johanna's uncle.

CHAPTER SEVEN

KLAUS VAN DER MAAS was prompt that evening, and Andrea wondered if it was a family characteristic.

To her surprise he did not call for her in a car nearly so opulent as his brother's Mercedes. Klaus's car was an aging hardtop that had seen much better days. It looked like a college kid's car, but then, Klaus looked like a college kid. It surprised her that he wasn't still in school. Or did the Van Der Maases believe that the men in the family should start working in the bakery offices early in life?

It was a beautiful spring evening. The sunset was going to be gorgeous, and Andrea wished that instead of going to dinner she could drive out to a beach on Lake Michigan and just walk and walk and watch the sun go down back of the water. She could imagine wading in shallows turned to turquoise and rose and apricot by the last rays of the sun. Then she glanced down at her slim, open-toed, cream-colored shoes and wrinkled her nose. So much for imagination. There'd be no beach walking on this particular evening in May!

She was tempted to take the mirror out of her handbag and look at herself again, an act she'd performed a dozen times in the past ten minutes before Klaus had called for her. She'd done everything she could do with both her hair and her makeup, and after careful consideration she'd picked what she hoped was the right attire for the occasion. It was a two-piece outfit of cream-colored raw silk, belted by a matching stretch belt with a cloisonné buckle. The turquoise in the cloisonné was picked up in the silk scarf she wore tied in a loose bow and was further echoed in her earrings and bracelet. The whole effect was understated yet with a decided elegance about it, and knowing that she looked right should have been giving her confidence, she told herself. But it wasn't.

Klaus had driven past the bakery and then taken a turn onto a curving road that veered toward the west. In a very short time they entered a different world, an obviously exclusive section. The road was bordered with huge pines, elms and maples. Mansions fronted the spacious lawns that stretched back on either side of the street, and to her right Andrea could see the sparkling blue waters of Lake Macatawa.

The houses were imposing, all of them obviously very expensive. On the lake side, the grounds of many of them led down to private docks, where yachts of varying types bobbed at anchor.

The driveway into which Klaus turned belonged

to one of the most impressive homes of all. It was a three-story red brick with large French windows across the front, which were interrupted only by the formal, white-pillared entrance.

Klaus pulled up in front of the entrance with a flourish and turned to grin at her. "Here we are!"

Andrea had realized that the Van Der Maases were probably well-to-do, but she hadn't expected such opulence. As the car had rounded the curve in the driveway she'd seen that the property ran clear to the lake and—yes—there was a private dock. But there was no yacht tied up alongside it.

The house in itself almost made her gasp. It was a showplace. She noted on closer inspection that the French windows were fashioned of leaded glass and were bowed at the top. They overlooked grounds that were beautiful and perfectly manicured. There were beds of the ever-present tulips, but also other flowers and shrubs blooming in a glorious range of spring colors. And the air, was redolent with the fragrance of the towering pines that edged the property on either side.

"What a wonderful place!" she exclaimed appreciatively, and caught an odd expression on Klaus's face.

"Yes, isn't it," he agreed indifferently.

"You grew up here, Klaus?" she persisted.

He nodded. "Yes." Then he grinned, but it was a lopsided grin. "There weren't many kids around to play with," he confessed wryly. "So I guess I can't say as much for it as I would if I'd had some brothers or sisters closer to my own age."

"I'm an only child," she told him. "But I think I would have loved growing up here."

"Oh," Klaus admitted, "it had its good moments. I used to pretend I was a pirate...."

She laughed. "A pirate?"

"Our property extends down to Lake Macatawa, and we have quite a stretch of lake frontage," he told her. "There used to be an old stone hut down near the lake, and I'd pretend it was my pirate fort. Once I got hold of an old rowboat and painted it black, and I ran up a Jolly Roger flag. Gerrit had a small outboard engine and I swiped it and started out on the lake, and, believe it or not, the boat sank right offshore. Gerrit was mad as hell because his engine was ruined. We brought it up, but it was no good after that."

"And Dirk?" she couldn't resist asking.

"Dirk thought it was pretty funny. He said he admired my adventurous spirit and he got Gerrit to lay off me."

Klaus opened the car door. "Come on," he urged.

As Andrea got out of the car she wished she could postpone the moment of confrontation with Dirk and his mother. She lagged as she followed Klaus up the shallow steps to the front door.

She wondered if Klaus would produce a key to the impressive paneled door, or if he would ring the brightly shining brass bell so that they could be admitted—probably by a butler in perfect livery.

Klaus did neither. He pushed the door open, and Andrea gaped.

"Do you mean to say you leave it unlocked?" she demanded, a practice unthinkable to her after a few years of city living.

"We lock up at night," Klaus told her, and then motioned for her to precede him.

She stepped into a spacious entrance hall with a curving staircase at the far end, which lead to a landing where there was a huge duplicate of the French windows across the front. The ceiling in this hallway was the full height of the house—three stories—and Andrea saw that it was dominated by a massive crystal chandelier. The furnishings were exquisite, each chair, each table, perfect in its own right, probably all of them heirlooms, she surmised. Gilt-framed oil paintings hung on the walls, and there were bowls of fresh flowers everywhere.

"I think mom'll be in the family room," Klaus said, interrupting her reverie. "It's at the back."

He led the way and Andrea followed, a thousand impressions of Dirk Van Der Maas's home crowding in on her along the way. They passed a door that led into a drawing room, and she glimpsed a concert grand piano in one corner. A second door opened into a library with floor-to-ceiling bookcases, then beyond that Klaus turned into a big airy room where the furniture was comfortable and well used, the colors a bright mélange of blues, reds and yellows. Windows stretched across the far end of the room and overlooked a large swimming pool surrounded by lawn and gardens. Beyond this was the vista of Lake Macatawa, its waters deepening to sapphire in the early-evening light.

"Hmm," Klaus mused, and Andrea, transfixed by the glorious colors in the western sky, tore her gaze away from the windows to find that he was frowning. Abruptly he said, "Mom must still be upstairs. I'll go get her." And with that he left the room.

Andrea turned back to the windows, frowning herself because there was so much that perplexed her. She was intensely conscious of the beauty of Dirk's house and the many things it implied. Considerable wealth, for one thing. His wealth.

Also, the place where Dirk lived was at such variance with the place where he worked. Remembering the starkness of his office, Andrea decided that the man was a true enigma, and she wondered if she would ever figure him out.

To do so was important. Very important. It was her premise that in order to understand what a client wanted, in order to relate fully to his business needs, it was imperative to understand the client himself. Doing this sometimes did pose a problem because there was a line that had to be drawn between the personal and the professional. Andrea had always been careful to tread carefully on that line, giving herself the opportunity to only look into the personal, where her clients were concerned, never to stray into it. Never in her life had she made a social engagement with a client, for very good reasons. Never until the day before, she reminded herself. Going to the Tulip Time festivities with Dirk and Johanna and then out to lunch with them could hardly be classified as a business conference, even though Dirk had delved into business briefly during the course of the lunch. But then, the excursion had been for Johanna's sake, which put it into quite a different category.

There had been moments when she'd felt a surprising closeness to both Dirk and his niece, though, and she warned herself that this was something she was going to have to watch, at least as far as Dirk was concerned. True, she didn't appear to have too much to worry about in that department. He'd shuffled her off to his younger brother, a gesture that spoke for itself. Nevertheless, she'd be seeing him there this evening, and there were bound to be business conferences in the future that would bring them together.

Her reaction that morning when she'd thought it would be Dirk who was calling her and instead it was his secretary had been disproportionate, Andrea told herself sternly. The same could be said about her feelings when Klaus had appeared to show her through the bakery and then had told her he'd be picking her up that night. But the fact of the matter was that she'd *wanted* to hear Dirk's voice on the phone that morning, just as she'd wanted him to guide her through the bakery and escort her to his home. She'd wanted to see him again, to talk to him again, and she found his absence very dismaying.

Andrea was so deeply involved in a private struggle between her professional principles and some very disturbing personal feelings that for a moment she imagined someone was speaking her name. But then it was repeated.

"Andrea!" A small frisson of pleasure left a tingling sensation up and down her spine as she recognized Dirk's voice and turned to see him standing in the doorway.

It was a surprisingly intense moment. Their eyes met across the intervening space, met and clung, and all of Andrea's carefully erected defenses suddenly seemed as fragile as a house of cards.

It took a lot of effort, but with a remarkable outward show of serenity she said, "Hello, Dirk."

A brief smile touched his lips as he started across the room toward her. She saw that he'd loosened his tie and taken off his suit coat, which was draped negligently over his shoulder. The pencil-striped shirt he was wearing looked slightly rumpled, and Dirk himself looked tired. Shadows of fatigue were smudged under those arresting light-blue eyes.

Andrea sensed that for a moment, as their glances had meshed, his composure had faltered even as hers had. But she marveled at how quickly he was able to regain control, his tone casual as he asked, "What are you doing here all by yourself?"

"Your brother went to get your mother," she managed, not as sure of her own emotional steadiness as Dirk evidently was about his, and hoping he wasn't astute enough to sense this.

"Klaus?" he asked, clearly a question that didn't require an answer. He tossed his coat down on the nearest chair. "Hasn't anyone even offered you a drink?"

She shook her head. "No. But we just got here. Klaus and I, that is."

She hadn't noticed the small bar at the far corner of the room. Now Dirk headed for it, calling back, "What's your pleasure?"

"I . . . it doesn't matter," she said lamely.

"Vodka and tonic?" he suggested.

"That would be fine."

"Did you enjoy the bakery tour?" he asked as he clinked ice cubes into two glasses.

Without pausing to consider her words, Andrea answered him. "No," she said, and then was appalled at her own bluntness.

Dirk came over to her carrying two glasses, one of which he held out to her. "What was the matter?" he demanded. "Didn't Klaus show you the things you wanted to see?"

"It had nothing to do with Klaus," she said quickly.

"Then what did it have to do with, Andrea?" Dirk persisted.

"I don't like automation."

"You don't like automation?"

She nodded. "That's right. Oh, I appreciate the need for modern machinery, and I fully realize how remarkable it is that something mechanical can accomplish so much more than a man can in the same given time, with a far smaller margin of error. But there is something oppressive to me about the thought of someone standing in the same place watching a machine do the same thing hour after hour, day after day, through all the years of a working life.

"The doughnuts, for instance," she plunged on.

"What about them?" he asked, and she caught the steel edge to his voice.

"Well, there's a machine that operates on a—a kind of slant, and its function is to seal the flap at the end of each box," Andrea explained.

"Yes?"

"There's a man who stands in back of it and watches, and all he has to do is to be sure the seal meshes every time. I...I guess that isn't the right word for it," she added, aware at this point that she'd gotten the evening off to a very bad start.

" 'Mesh' will do," he assured her abruptly.

She took a long sip of the drink he'd given her, the cold liquid trickling down her parched throat.

"Dirk..." she began.

The sharpness of his tone surprised her. "Don't try to backtrack!"

"I'm not trying to backtrack," she protested. "I should learn to hold my tongue, that's all. Or at least to say things in...in better context."

She turned away from him as she was speaking and stared out the window toward the lake, angry at herself for being so indiscreet. It was his business she was attacking, it was an account she was going to be dealing with. If it bothered her to see people standing around like robots, that was something she should have kept to herself—or held in until a more appropriate moment. After all, she was a dinner guest in his home, about to meet his mother, and....

She felt a firm finger tilt her chin, the action making her turn toward him as surely as if he'd swung her around himself. She was almost afraid to look at him. She got as far as his mouth...to find it curved into a smile that was rueful, to say the least.

"It's refreshing to discover a woman who's so blatantly truthful." And before she knew what was happening, the mouth that she was staring at had descended to claim her lips in a kiss that was swift, incisive, yet so penetrating.

In a highly charged moment, Andrea felt herself reeling toward him, blindly following impulse. She felt his hands close on her shoulders, the warmth of his grip sending a giddy, intense wave of desire plummeting through her, and there was no telling what she might have done, what she might have said, had Johanna not interrupted them.

The child virtually exploded into the room, crying, "Miss Campbell, Miss Campbell!"

Andrea turned, fighting for composure as she did so. She felt as if she'd been set afire. She was trembling from the warmth of rocketing emotions she couldn't possibly have anticipated, and she tried, very hard, not to look at the man who'd caused them.

Johanna was an enchanting vision in a full-skirted yellow dress, a matching bow clipped to her brown curls, and it was good to be able to vent some feeling openly. Andrea bent and clasped the little girl, hugging her as enthusiastically as she was being hugged in return.

"Gran will be down right away, with Uncle Klaus," Johanna reported.

"About time," Andrea heard Dirk mutter, and saw that he was heading back to the bar to fix himself a second drink.

"I was in the children's parade this afternoon," Johanna was reporting excitedly. "You should have come!"

Andrea had not been aware there was a children's parade, but she said only, "I couldn't, Johanna. I was busy."

"When you went through the bakery, did you eat some of the doughnuts?"

"No," Andrea said, not daring to glance toward Dirk. "No, I didn't."

"I like the cinnamon-and-sugar ones best," Johanna confided, and then trilled, "Here's Gran."

Andrea turned to confront a woman who was neither elderly nor—at least not visibly—overworked. Monica Van Der Maas was tall, slender and stately, and beautifully garbed in a lilac silk dress with a lace bodice and a high neck. She'd probably been blond when she was younger. Now her hair was a soft gray, fashionably styled in a French knot.

Her face was very youthful, and Andrea would have found it impossible to guess her age. To have a son as old as Dirk, though, she would have to be in her mid-fifties at the least.

Mrs. Van Der Maas's eyes were the same bright blue as Klaus's, and they were as friendly as her smile. She clasped Andrea's hand warmly as introductions were made. Surprisingly Klaus performed this function rather than Dirk.

Dirk seemed intensely preoccupied, and his mother looked up at him inquiringly as he came across to hand her the drink he'd made for her. Andrea sensed she was on the verge of asking him a question but evidently thought better of it.

For the next fifteen minutes they talked casually about a variety of things, centering the conversation around Holland and the local festivities. Then they were summoned to dinner by a rosy-cheeked woman whom Mrs. Van Der Maas introduced as Mabel.

"Mabel and her husband, Henry, run this

place," she said with a pleasant laugh. "We say that Henry's in charge of the outdoors and Mabel is in command of the indoors!"

Candles had been lit in the dining room. A white lace cloth covered the long table, which was beautifully set with choice china, crystal and silver. The massive centerpiece was filled with an array of spring flowers, and Andrea felt sure Mrs. Van Der Maas had done the arrangement herself.

The meal was relatively simple but delicious. Creamed asparagus soup was the first course, then succulent roast lamb served with a mint sauce and tiny roast potatoes, and dessert was an ambrosial fresh strawberry tart. Andrea, though she relished the meal, was surprised there was nothing typically Dutch about the menu choice. She'd expected that Dutch cuisine would be featured in the Van Der Maas household, especially when an out-of-town guest was being entertained.

The conversation at the table was general, Johanna being allowed—in fact encouraged—to express herself. Mrs. Van Der Maas was clearly an accomplished hostess, making Andrea feel perfectly at ease, and Klaus contributed his share by adding an occasional note of humor. Only Dirk was silent. Andrea had never met a man who could keep so entirely to himself. If he so desired, she mused, Dirk Van Der Maas could feel alone in the middle of New York's Time Square on New Year's Eve.

Andrea had thought they might adjourn to the

drawing room for coffee, but instead Mrs. Van Der Maas led them back to the family room. The evening had turned chilly, and when she suggested a fire be made in the big stone fireplace, it was Dirk who took on the task. He built a fire with the same proficiency with which he probably did most things, Andrea reflected, watching him. In no time at all golden flames were crackling on the hearth.

Andrea accepted Mrs. Van Der Maas's offer of a second cup of coffee and slowly spooned some sugar into it as she stared at the blazing fire and the man standing in front of it. He was in silhouette from her vantage point, his strong, beautifully built body highlighted by the orange glow of the spiraling flames. Watching him, Andrea felt as if everything within her was tightening, her emotions clutching at her throat, and it was all she could do to swallow down the coffee she'd just sipped.

She hadn't expected Dirk's kiss, she hadn't been ready for anything like that, but honesty told her it would have been impossible to have avoided her reaction to him if they'd rehearsed the scene a hundred times. Honesty told her, too, that there'd been a current between them ever since that first moment when he'd walked into his office to find her studying the architect's renderings on the wall. She'd ignored the current, true. So, she suspected, had he. But that hadn't stopped its flow, and she knew that it would be a lie to deny the strong physical attraction that existed between them.

The intensity of Dirk's kiss, brief though it was, had been an affirmation of that attraction. But now she sensed that he was just as prepared to fight his feelings as she was.

Why? Maybe it was only that, like herself, he didn't believe in mixing business and personal relationships. But she didn't think that was the entire answer. It was likely, she decided, that there was no place for a woman in Dirk Van Der Maas's life, and that automatically posed yet another "why?" Had he once been so badly burned by a woman that he'd built a flameproof shield around himself?

Andrea became aware that Mrs. Van Der Maas had asked her something, and to her chagrin she had to respond, "I beg your pardon?"

A different kind of awareness came when she realzed that she'd been caught staring at Dirk, and that Dirk's mother was a very astute lady. Something flickered in Monica Van Der Maas's eyes, but she said only, "I asked if Dirk had told you I'd suggested that you stay here with us, while you're in Holland."

Dirk had poured himself out a second cup of coffee and had claimed an armchair directly across from the one Andrea was sitting in.

Before Andrea could rally enough to say anything, he answered, "No, I didn't tell her. As I mentioned to you, mother, there didn't seem much point in Andrea making the move for just a couple of days."

Just a couple of days? Andrea voiced the question with her eyes as she looked across at him.

"I think it's too bad you have to fly back to Boston on Saturday," Mrs. Van Der Maas commented. "You'll be back here again, though, I'm sure, and I insist that you be our houseguest then."

Fly back to Boston on Saturday! These were the words Andrea plucked from her hostess's statement, and she bristled as she met Dirk's cool blue eyes. How could he possibly sit there looking so innocuous?

Had he decided against having her handle his account, after calling Mark in Boston and stating the exact opposite? If so, what had happened to change his mind?

Andrea heard Klaus's voice and forced herself to listen to what he was saying. He was addressing his older brother, and there was a note not only of surprise but of indignation in his tone as he asked, "What's this about Andi going back to Boston Saturday?"

Klaus had not accompanied the others to the family room directly after dinner, and Andrea was appalled to think that until now she hadn't even been aware that he'd rejoined them. She was concentrating too much on Klaus's older brother.

Dirk said wearily, "Hey, look! It's not my idea." At his words, Andrea looked up in surprise.

"Mark Terrence called this morning and said he wants Andrea back in Boston on Monday. He suggested she fly back on Saturday so she'd have Sunday to recoup, as he put it. He's her boss." Dirk shrugged in conclusion.

Andrea had always disliked the word "boss." She'd never thought of anyone as her boss, much less Mark Terrence. Mark was a colleague and a friend, and a partner in the advertising agency she worked for. But she was damned if she considered him her "boss," she decided, annoyed.

The annoyance was echoed in her voice as she addressed Dirk. "Why didn't Mark call me himself and tell me this?" she demanded.

"He tried to," Dirk said simply. "Several times. You were out."

"He could have left a message," she said, bristling.

"He tried that," Dirk replied evenly. "If you'll remember, the message light was lit on your phone when Johanna and I took you back to your motel yesterday. You said you imagined it was Mark."

So she had... and she hadn't returned his call. She'd dialed the desk to learn that it had been Mark who'd phoned, and she'd let it go at that. She hadn't wanted to speak to Mark, not then. She was sure he would have wanted to talk about Dirk, and she hadn't been ready to discuss him.

"So?" Dirk asked now.

"I'll call Mark in the morning," she temporized.

"Telephone him now, if you like," Mrs. Van Der Maas suggested. "If you have his home number, that is. You can use the phone in the library."

"I'd just as soon speak to him in the office," Andrea said. "Thank you for the offer, though."

Monica Van Der Maas tactfully switched the conversation to other subjects, including Johanna, who then insisted that Andrea come up to her room so she could show her her doll collection.

Andrea was glad to escape, glad to follow the little girl up the wide curving stairway into a room that would have been any child's delight. There was a four-poster maple bed with a dotted swiss canopy, and plenty of shelves on which to display Johanna's extensive doll collection.

There was only one bad moment, when Johanna picked up a dark-haired doll and said, "This one looks like my mummy." But Andrea managed to steer her toward a boy doll that looked very much like Dirk, and the tears that had threatened momentarily were averted.

When they went back downstairs Klaus had disappeared, and Dirk and his mother were quietly talking in the family room. Dirk had drawn his chair up close to his mother's, and Andrea saw that he'd taken off his glasses. As he glanced up at her, she got the full impact of those unusual light eyes, and she learned that it was almost harder to read him with the glasses off than it was when he was wearing them.

He looked different without the glasses. Not younger, exactly, but more...vulnerable. As if he sensed this, he reached out to the side table where he'd placed them and whipped them on again.

Out in the entrance hall, a clock chimed. Automatically, Andrea counted. It was nine o'clock, which must be close to Johanna's bedtime, if not past it.

"I really should go," she said, and looked around for Klaus, expecting that he might be within hearing distance and reappear. But it was Dirk who got to his feet slowly.

"I'll drive you back," he stated, and there was no way of telling whether it was a task he looked forward to, or a chore he'd been forced into assuming.

CHAPTER EIGHT

DIRK WAS TIGHT-LIPPED and silent as they went out to the car, and Andrea admitted to herself resentfully that he tended to make her feel guilty, as if she'd done something she shouldn't have done, which was ridiculous. The fact of the matter was that she'd done nothing at all that should bother her conscience in the least, where Dirk was concerned.

The Mercedes was parked just beyond the entrance. Andrea slipped into the front seat without waiting for Dirk to hold the door for her. With a shrug, he walked around the car and took his place behind the wheel.

When he reached the end of the driveway, he made a turn to the left, rather than to the right, and this registered with Andrea at once. They were heading away from town, rather than back toward it.

It was a beautiful night, a romantic night, the moon obligingly occupying its right place in the sky, the stars as brilliant as if they'd been rubbed with jewelers' polish. Sitting next to Dirk, it was impossible not to be aware of the night and the potential it would hold with the right man. Instead, Andrea thought wryly, she was with a statue who gave no indication of toppling from his pedestal.

After a time she asked, "Where are we going?" In reply she was favored with a sideways glance that scorched her. The blazing intensity of Dirk's eyes seemed to light up the car's darkened interior.

"I want to talk to you," he said testily.

"Then pull over and park."

"I'd rather have a little more breathing space," he retorted.

She subsided into silence, aware that they were passing the residential area, the houses becoming farther apart. The road edged the lake and she saw a marina well filled with boats, their white hulls brushed with a ghostlike silver by the moonlight. They came to a turnaround that marked the end of the pavement, and Andrea spotted a sign that read, Private Property—No Trespassing. But Dirk disregarded the sign, driving on along a sandy lane that came to an apparent end just short of a cluster of pines.

He stopped the car there and got out, coming around to open the door for Andrea and to stretch out a hand. An inviting hand? She wasn't sure, but she took it anyway, looking up at him uncertainly. His tenseness was communicable and put her on edge.

"Come along," he urged, and he led her toward

a path that ran up through the pines toward high, sloping sand dunes.

"Won't we be trespassing?"

"No," he said shortly.

"The sign said something about property owners only," she persisted.

"Oh, come on, will you?" he exclaimed, exasperated.

She'd let go of his guiding hand as she questioned him and now he went ahead of her. Tree shadows obscured the path and Andrea was sufficiently agitated that it wasn't any great feat to trip and fall flat on her face. . . which she promptly did.

She struggled to sit up, feeling sand in her mouth, her eyes, her nose and her hair, and knowing, too, that a storm of tears lurked just over her personal horizon. This man had the damndest effect on her and he could be so. . . exasperating!

She heard a muffled oath, and Dirk said, "Andrea, where the hell are you?" Then, disbelievingly he called out, "Andrea!"

He came to stand over her as she slowly got to her feet, brushing away the clinging sand as she did so, and she felt an almost irrepressible urge to hit him. It would have been only common courtesy for him to have helped her to her feet. And anyone else would have asked solicitously whether or not she'd been hurt.

As it was, Dirk demanded, "What did you do? Fall over a twig?"

"No!" she snapped, then added, thoroughly irritated, "Funny, aren't you! But then I suppose you've never done anything awkward in your whole well-ordered life, have you?"

There was a moment of silence, and Dirk seemed stunned by her comment. A shaft of moonlight crossed his face, and she saw that he'd taken off his glasses. Those light eyes of his were silvered by the moon, twin mirrors, and looking into them Andrea felt herself plunging into depths that reason warned her were going to be dangerous.

Dirk reached for her and she went into his arms. Shaken, they didn't need words, they didn't need explanations, they didn't need anything except each other.

His lips singed hers, but the fever in her rose to match his, so the burning didn't hurt. Rather, it only intensified her yearning for this tall intriguing stranger—he was still a stranger—who seemed bent on proving to her that he was anything but unfeeling.

Dirk Van Der Maas was flesh and blood, hot blood that caused his fingers to sear through the fabric of her dress as they trailed over her shoulders and inched their way to her waist. She shivered— from the heat, not the cold—as those fingers found their way beneath the top of her dress, and then slowly started upward again, trailing a path over her skin, making her quiver.

Yielding to instinct, she pressed herself against

him. And she knew, immediately, how fully he was aroused, his desire translated so tangibly there was no doubting her effect on him. Over the years Andrea had built up a whole series of warning flags when it came to men. Now her cautions escaped her, one by one, wisps dissolving in the darkness as she trembled with a kind of wanting that was new to her.

Dirk's kiss deepened, his tongue seeking, probing, then, abruptly, moving away from her mouth to follow a course across her cheek until, finally, he began to encircle the delicate inner curves of her ear and she thought she'd go mad from the spasms of delight that darted through her.

She was moaning softly when, incredibly, he pulled away, and after a taut second she heard him chuckle.

"You've got sand in your ear!"

The moonlight etched his face as he spoke. In its silver light Andrea saw him grin, and all at once things swung back into perspective. The humor of the situation struck her as forcibly as it had him, and she dissolved into laughter.

Then she felt his arms around her again and he pulled her close, but this was a different kind of an embrace. Passion had been put on hold, Andrea acknowledged reluctantly, but now there was a genuine affection between them, something she had never before experienced with any man. She felt warmed all over, a good kind of warmth. She glowed from it.

Dirk was staring down at her intently, and she knew he was about to speak, but for once she didn't want him to say anything. She didn't want this unexpectedly lovely mood between them to be broken.

He must have sensed this, because after a moment he smiled at her and, tugging her hand, said, "Come on. Are you up to a climb to the top of the dunes?"

"Is that a challenge?"

"Sure," he said with a grin. "You're a city girl, after all!"

"I'll show you!" she vowed, and scrambled ahead of him.

He had no difficulty catching up with her. It was hard climbing in the shifting sand, and the dunes were steep. After a time she paused for breath, and Dirk said, "Not much farther. It'll be worth it when you see the moonlight on the lake."

He was right. Lake Michigan stretched before them, an immense silvered sea, and Andrea shivered slightly as she looked at it.

"So much beauty," she said softly.

The man at her side didn't answer, but he didn't have to. They were in perfect tune. It was natural to turn to him, it was natural to have their mouths fuse into a kiss that catapulted Andrea into an entirely new dimension. Tenderness and passion merged to become distilled into an elixir so potent she could only cling to Dirk, knowing herself to be far more helpless than he realized. Everything she'd told herself in the past, everything she'd taught herself, became invalid as he held her. What did it matter if Dirk was her client!

A small voice warned that tomorrow she would regret her actions. But this wasn't tomorrow, Andrea retorted silently, as she curved her body against his. This was now!

It was Dirk who put a stop to what promised to be a very natural procession of events. Andrea could actually feel the emotion draining out of him and the tension coming in to take its place. He grasped her arms with firm hands, and for long moments they both stood very still. Without even looking at him, Andrea knew their time was over. The spell had been broken.

What had broken it? She hadn't been the one who'd turned off that ecstatically wonderful current that had been flowing between them. No, once again it had been Dirk who'd taken control, and once again the all-important question concerning him became "why?"

Had the touch of her lips, the taste of her mouth, reminded him of someone else?

Almost blindly Andrea followed his lead, and they slowly climbed back down the dunes and followed the path to the place where he'd parked his car.

It was only when they were on the road again, this time heading in the direction of town, that Dirk said, "I'm sorry my mother brought up the subject of your leaving Saturday before I'd had the chance to speak to you about it.''

Andrea's response came without warning. . . even to herself. "I'm not going back to Boston Saturday," she said firmly. "It would be ridiculous, Dirk. Even if you and I were to spend all of tomorrow getting down some of the preliminaries for your advertising campaign, we couldn't possibly lay enough groundwork. You know that.''

"It isn't necessary to lay much groundwork just now," Dirk responded, to her surprise.

Suspicion stirred again. Had he decided he didn't want her handling the account—maybe because he *was* attracted to her?

There was only one way to find out. "Have you changed your mind?" she asked him bluntly.

He'd put his glasses back on and the lenses glinted as he glanced at her. "About what?" he asked.

"About having me work with you?"

He shook his head. "No." Then added, "I would have told you, if that were the case. I don't play games when it comes to business, Andrea. What I'm saying is that it's unlikely I would have agreed to have you handle the account in the first place if I'd thought there was any danger of my changing my mind. But if such a thing had come to pass, I certainly would have told you about it before I told anyone else. . .including Mark. You'd come highly recommended, you know that. But I had to meet you myself, I had to judge you for myself. . . .''

"Yes?"

He smiled and said unexpectedly, "I think our only problem will be trying to work together without our blood pressures constantly elevating to dangerously high levels!"

Then, before she could answer, he continued, "Right now I'd say that to work out anything in detail would be premature. We're not breaking ground for the new plant until next week. Fortunately we've got several months of good weather ahead of us, so the building itself should go up quickly."

"Where will it be located?"

"We're expanding to the rear of the present buildings," he told her. "Ultimately the entire plant will be much more attractive than it is now. I envision entirely new facades, plus a joining together of the old and the modern in a way that will be pleasing, visually...and highly efficient when it comes to our operations. The new plant will be used entirely for the production of the specialty items. They'll be frozen on the site and then shipped all over the country...in due course," Dirk finished with a slight smile. "I know it isn't all going to happen overnight, but I have confidence that I'm heading in the right direction on this. There's always room for something new in the market, when the product is an excellent one. All of our Dutch baked goods will be top quality, and—"

He broke off. "Sorry," he said, and his tone was

disturbingly cool. "I had no intention of getting into a business dissertation tonight. To get back to the question of your returning to Boston on Saturday...."

"Yes?" she asked, determined that her coolness was going to match his.

"I think it makes sense," he said. "I told Mark that. If you and I meet for a couple of hours tomorrow morning I can fill you in on my thoughts for the future sufficiently so that you can map out a few very general ideas we can go over later. I have to be in New York in a few weeks, and I can fly up to Boston and meet with both you and Mark then."

"Are you saying you want Mark in on consultation all the way along the line?" Andrea asked.

"Is there anything so wrong about that?" he countered.

"No. Except that I can't help but suspect it may denote a lack of confidence."

"You think I don't have confidence in you?"

"Maybe not enough," she answered reluctantly.

"That's not it at all, Andrea," he said, and that note of impatience she'd heard before crept into his voice. "I'm of the opinion that if two heads are better than one, then perhaps three heads are better than two, provided the right 'heads' are involved."

"I hate old sayings," Andrea found herself spouting angrily.

There'd been a mounting tension between them, but strangely this broke it. Dirk laughed. "Do you, now," he teased. "Okay, I plead guilty. Like most of us, I tend to take refuge in the old clichés while I'm trying to find the right thing to say."

"Just what is the right thing, Dirk?"

"I want you to know that I do want you to handle the account, and there's no doubt in my mind that it's you who are going to be in charge of it. I also want you to know that I do want you to come back to Holland and—"

He broke off, and Andrea couldn't resist asking, "And?"

"That's enough for now," Dirk told her enigmatically, and a moment later he was pulling up in front of her motel.

She soon realized that he didn't intend getting out of the car to open the door for her. Was he afraid they might fall into each other's arms if he walked her to her door? As it was, his hand brushed her breasts as he reached across to unlatch the door for her and she shivered involuntarily, but he didn't seem to notice.

Damn the man! she thought resentfully. *I'm going to have to put some steel in my spine if I'm going to work with him!*

Shoving the car door open slightly, he said, "How about coming to my office around ten tomorrow?"

Andrea nodded and slipped out with a quick good-night. He waited till she'd opened the door to her unit, and knowing that he was there at the wheel

of the car, watching her, made her fumble and she
nearly dropped her key. But then finally she was inside the room. She heard the roar of his car engine
as he drove off, and she discovered she was glad
that he'd gone. The evening had held its full quota
of emotions, and she felt drained by them. She'd
had enough.

ANDREA SLEPT RESTLESSLY that night. Upon awakening, she knew her dreams had been filled with
Dirk, and they'd been disturbing.

She chose her most severely tailored outfit for her
appointment with Dirk, a lightweight suit in a soft
shade of mauve. She even twisted her hair into a
French knot as if to reemphasize the fact that she'd
recast herself into a career role where Dirk Van Der
Maas was concerned. As she walked into his office,
she was determined that this was the image she was
going to live with.

Dirk stood to greet her. He was wearing a three-
piece, light-gray suit, and once again he looked as if
he could pose for an ad in a men's fashion magazine. But there was an added tautness to his mouth.
She suspected that his sleep had been as troubled as
hers.

Without preamble she said, "I phoned Mark
after I got back to the motel last night."

"Yes?" he asked politely.

"You were right, of course. It does seem logical
to go back to Boston tomorrow."

"Yes, I think it does," Dirk said, and she glanced at him sharply. Was she imagining it, or was he giving this simple sentence a double-edged meaning? "Incidentally," he added, "just for the record I want you to know that it was Mark's idea for you to go back just now. I gather the agency's somewhat short staffed at the moment. But I agree that it was a good idea.

"I'm going to arrange for you to take back a variety of samples of the different bakery products we plan to freeze," he continued. "If you don't mind carrying an extra parcel aboard the plane, that is."

"No, of course not," Andrea assured him quickly.

"I'm having a box packed that will include *krakelingen, Jan Hagels, St. Nikolaas koekjes*—although normally we make those only at Christmas—and a few other things. We'll get into cakes and pastries later."

Andrea stared at him blankly, the Dutch names totally strange to her.

"Recipes will be included," Dirk went on, "so that you can see exactly what we'll be handling. Meanwhile...."

He opened a desk drawer and extracted a long roll of stiff paper. Andrea watched as he spread it open over the top of his desk.

"This is a rendering of the new plant," he explained. "If you'd like to come take a look at it...."

She moved around to his side of the desk and at once was much too aware of him. His masculine scent filled her nostrils and she drew a deep, unsteady breath. He used a shaving lotion that had a faintly spicy aroma—not the sort of thing she would have thought he'd have favored, yet it suited him perfectly.

Andrea forced herself to glance down at the architect's rendering spread out before her, the edges of the paper held firm by Dirk's slim tanned fingers, and briefly her attention was wrested away from the man. The plan for his new bakery was arresting in concept, the old and the new blending, just as he'd said, into a harmonious whole that was aesthetically pleasing. The frozen-foods division stretched across the rear of the present bakery buildings, the lines clean and simple.

"The finish will be a white material that gives the effect of stucco," Dirk explained. "No windows in the frozen-food division, but there will be strict interior climate control, of course. What you're looking at, I should explain, is really a three-phase program. Construction of the frozen-food plant will take up the first phase. After that, this building will be constructed in front of the present bakery buildings." One long finger pointed to an impressive, two-story structure that was starkly modern and almost all glass.

"Our offices will be housed here. I've allowed ample space for office expansion, which will be essential if we grow as I hope we'll grow," he added, with a faint grin.

"In phase three," he went on, "the new type of facade will overlay the exterior of the old buildings. Once we've moved out of these present offices, this entire section will be completely renovated to be used as an addition to the present bakery facilities. The expansion of our regular bakery sales has been limited only by lack of space, and this'll solve that problem."

He smiled, but it was a very perfunctory smile. "Any questions?"

"Yes," she managed. "This is a terrific rendering. Who's your architect?"

His answer completely floored her.

"I am," he said simply.

"You?"

She saw Dirk's mouth tighten, and he rolled up the rendering and returned it to his desk drawer. "I was an architect before I was a baker, Andrea."

"Then...then you did those sketches on the walls?" she asked, staggered by the revelation. With that kind of talent....

"Yes, I did. Now...I see you brought a notebook with you. Suppose we get down to some of the specifics."

Quickly and effectively, he'd shut off the hundred questions she was yearning to ask him. There was nothing she could do but go back to her chair and sit down, get out her slim silver pen and open her notebook. One look at Dirk's closed face was enough to convince her she had no chance of getting him to enlighten her any further. Not now, at least.

For the next hour he did let her into his life... but on an entirely different level.

"I'm certainly not a pioneer in the field of frozen baked goods," he began. "Most of the credit in that area should go to Charles Lubin. Right after World War II, working on the concept that people would be willing to pay a good price for a really high-quality bakery product, he introduced a cheesecake that he named after his daughter... Sara Lee. It was such a success that he soon founded Kitchens of Sara Lee and started to add other items to his bakery line.

"He operated in the Chicago area," Dirk continued, "and it was one of his experiments in food packaging—the invention of an aluminum-foil pan in which a product could be baked and sold in the same container—that paved the way for today's frozen-baked-goods industry. The story goes that when a Texas grocery supplier happened to taste some of the Sara Lee cheesecake while on a visit to Chicago, he asked Lubin to ship his cheesecake to Texas. At this point Lubin tried freezing the cheesecake so that it could be shipped and also retain its freshness, and it worked. By the early 1960s, frozen Sara Lee products were available on a nationwide scale.

"Now... my thought is to specialize in a variety

of frozen Dutch baked goods, and my hope is that they'll also prove successful on a nationwide scale, in due course. As I've said, I don't expect miracles to happen overnight.

"The addition will house an automated freezer-warehouse, and we hope eventually to have our own fleet of refrigerated trucks for maximum distribution. I think—I hope—that we've pretty much worked out the technical bugs, but that's not your concern anyway. What is your concern," Dirk said, pushing back his desk chair as he spoke and crossing his legs, "is to put across this particular, specialized concept."

"We'll need a slogan," Andrea said. "Something very catchy. And a logo that will be eye provoking and...unforgettable. And...."

"All of that and more," Dirk agreed.

Briefly they discussed a few possible approaches as Andrea tried to get a firm idea of what Dirk had in mind. Then, to her chagrin, he glanced at his wristwatch. "I think you have enough to keep you going until we meet in Boston in a few weeks," he announced. Then added, "I'd like to ask you to lunch with me, but unfortunately I have a prior engagement."

There was no reason at all to feel so rebuffed, Andrea told herself, but her tone was icy as she said stiffly, "Of course."

"If you'd prefer to turn in your rental car here in Holland, I'm sure Klaus would be glad to drive you to the airport tomorrow,'' Dirk offered politely.

Inwardly she winced, feeling as if he'd slapped her.

"Thanks just the same," she said, "but I'd rather turn the car in where I got it."

"As you like." He stood, looking very tall and dignified and handsome...and amazingly unapproachable.

"Have a good trip back, Andrea."

CHAPTER NINE

ANDREA FELT AS IF SHE'D BEEN AWAY from the agency so long that it was a shock to see Mark still hobbling around on crutches.

He stood in her office doorway and said, "How about coming into my sanctum, sweet child? The hassock's already pulled up to the armchair, ready for me to prop my foot on it."

Andrea had been at work only an hour, but she knew that even if Mark had given her a five-day reprieve she still would not have been ready to confront him. She shied away from the thought of being questioned about her trip to Holland. . . especially about Dirk.

Leaving Holland had been somewhat frantic. At the last minute she'd remembered that she still had the clothes the woman on Windmill Island had lent her the day she'd dived into the canal after Johanna. In fact they were still at the cleaner's where she'd left them, and she felt the least she could do was pick them up and return them to their rightful owner.

Doing so had left her with little time to spare to

get to the airport and turn in her rental car. So it wasn't until she'd been airborne that there'd been a chance to think of Dirk and the letdown that had come in the wake of their meeting.

When she'd left his office, it had been almost impossible to accept the fact that he was the same man in whose arms she'd virtually swooned on top of those wonderful dunes overlooking Lake Michigan. Dirk, cool, impassive, had said goodbye to her without even a flicker of an eye.

Well, she'd thought resolutely as her plane was winging its way toward Boston, two could play at that game. And really, what Dirk had done was to put things between them back in proper perspective. Grudgingly she conceded that she owed him a vote of thanks for that.

Andrea vowed that she would never again forget that Dirk Van Der Maas was a client. Nor would she ever again permit herself to forget her self-imposed commandments about clients, the first of which was, "Never let yourself become involved personally with someone whose account you are handling."

Her homecoming had done nothing toward uplifting her spirits. The apartment had been hot and dusty, and there had been an accumulation of bills and other mail, none of it very interesting. Andrea had spent a dull weekend by herself sorting things out, and it had been therapeutic to walk into the agency, to greet friends, to take her place behind her own desk and to start going through the papers stacked in her "in" basket. The bad part had been knowing that sooner or later she'd have to face up to Mark. And the summons, unfortunately, had come "sooner."

She followed Mark into his office, where he sank into his armchair, propped up his foot and then looked at her speculatively. "Coffee, before we get started?" he suggested.

"Thanks, not for me," she said. "I just had my third cup." She didn't add that her nerves were already jangling so badly the last thing in the world she needed was an added jolt of caffeine.

"You looked tired," Mark observed.

"Jet lag," Andrea told him.

"From a flight from Michigan to Boston?" he asked, raising his eyebrows. "Come on, now, Andi."

"I'm not crazy about flying," she said, which was true. She wasn't afraid of flying, it simply wasn't her favorite form of transportation. She preferred ships. Cruise ships, she decided. Right now she'd like to take a cruise to nowhere on a ship that would keep sailing on and on and on.

"How was it?" Mark asked her.

She was thinking about sailing over water that was the same clear, pale blue of Dirk Van Der Maas's eyes, and she asked vacantly, "What?"

"Your trip, Andi," Mark said patiently. "Holland, Dirk. The whole package. How was it?"

"It was. . . fine," she said cautiously.

"I can imagine," Mark retorted dryly. "Dirk called me at home last night. He wanted to be sure you'd gotten back to Boston all right. What's the matter? Did the two of you have a fight?"

"No," she answered promptly. There had been nothing nearly so emotional as a fight about her parting scene with Dirk.

Mark gave her a long questioning look but he said only, "Okay. So tell me what went on out in Holland. Where do you want to begin?"

"Mr. Van Der Maas plans to come to Boston in a few weeks," Andrea stated primly, only to be interrupted by Mark's snort of laughter.

"Mr. Van Der Maas? What is this, Andi?"

She flushed. "All right then, Dirk. He has to go to New York on business, and he's going to fly up here before he goes back to Holland. By then I hope to have something comprehensive mapped out that I can turn over to you—"

"Turn over to me?" Mark interposed. "Why do you put it that way?"

"You'll want to check anything I do on the account, won't you?"

"Not necessarily," he informed her. "Dirk made it fairly clear that you're to have free rein on this project."

"Oh?"

"Wasn't that the way you understood it?" Mark asked, eyeing her narrowly.

"He wasn't that specific, really," Andrea said, then amended her reply. "Yes, I guess, basically, that's the way I understood it." She drew a deep breath. "We had a conference Friday, and I think I have his overall plan fairly well in mind. The frozen baked goods will be marketed under the Van Der Maas label, but we'll want a new emphasis for them, an identification that, in time, should be recognizable from coast to coast. A prime need will be to come up with a really good slogan, and a visually effective logo." Andrea paused, hoping that she was coming across to Mark the way a rising young advertising executive should, because her heart wasn't in this.

"That reminds me," she added, "I have a whole box of bakery samples that we can test out with coffee later in the morning. Some of the things Dirk hopes to market on the national level."

"Yummy!" Mark said flippantly, and then asked, "Aren't you afraid they'll give us indigestion?"

"Of course not," she snapped. "They're not 'bakery fresh,' I suppose. Dirk would be the first to point that out. But...."

"I was being facetious, Andrea," Mark said, emphasizing the statement by the use of her full name rather than the nickname he usually favored.

"Oh," she replied weakly.

"Why not level with me? Come clean with your old Uncle Mark. What happened out there?"

The truth—at least the whole truth—about what had happened to her in Holland was the last thing Andrea intended to reveal to anyone, especially Mark. She settled for just an edge of the truth. "Dirk Van Der Maas is a rather difficult person to understand, that's all," she said, thinking this must surely be the understatement of the century.

"I was afraid of that," Mark replied.

"You were afraid—"

"Yes," he cut in. "After you left here, I wished I'd told you more about Dirk. But I'm not much for dissecting friends, and Dirk is one of my closest friends, Andi. I suppose I was especially reticent to talk about him. To get into very much about him seemed, to me, to come awfully close to gossip. Women who gossip are bad enough, but men...."

"Let's not be sexist."

He grinned. "I'm glad you still have your sense of humor. To tell you the truth, when Dirk phoned right after his first meeting with you and told me he was satisfied that you were the right person to handle the account, I was staggered."

"Because you knew what a sexist he was?" Andrea asked, irritated. "Mark, you might have warned me...."

"No...not because I thought he was a sexist at all. I did realize that if I offered Dirk a personal preference he'd opt for a man to work with him. But Dirk isn't a chauvinist. He's too intelligent, for one thing. For another, his mother worked very closely with his father in the early years, establishing the bakery business. And again, after Dirk first took over, she came back into the plant to help him. But Gerrit's death took a lot out of her, and her heart isn't what it was, so Dirk tells me. He made her bow out once it became apparent they'd have Marietta's child to care for. Did you meet the little girl?''

Andrea was tempted to tell him that not only had she met ''the little girl,'' but the entire Van Der Maas family felt she had saved Johanna's life. Instead she only said, ''Yes.''

''It wasn't easy for Mrs. Van Der Maas to take on the care of a child at her stage in life. Not that Klaus still isn't a child in many ways,'' Mark added, with a touch of asperity. ''She's had her hands full enough with him...and still does, I'd venture to guess. But it was especially traumatic in the case of Marietta's daughter, because I guess having her around is a constant reminder to Dirk.''

Mark paused as he saw the puzzled expression on her face. ''You don't know what I'm talking about, do you?''

''No,'' she admitted. ''No, I don't.''

''Wasn't anything said to you about Johanna's mother?''

''Klaus told me that Johanna's parents drowned two years ago. Johanna was not quite five at the time. It's left her with some very deep emotional scars.''

"I gathered that," Mark admitted. "I've only seen Dirk once, since Gerrit's death. That was in New York, a year or so ago. Mrs. Van Der Maas had begun to take Johanna to a child psychiatrist."

"Yes. She's still going for consultation on a regular basis. But Johanna has an obsessive fear of the water...even though Klaus says she can swim like a fish."

Mark's reaction to this statement was a sharp one, but it didn't concern Johanna's swimming ability. "Klaus was there? You met him?"

"Of course," she said, surprised. "He works in the bakery offices. He took me on a tour of the bakery, as a matter of fact."

Mark frowned. "That must be a recent development. I'd say it means Klaus has gotten himself in trouble...again. Last I heard he was at Ann Arbor. He was a student at the University of Michigan," he elaborated. "Was he in Holland when you got there?"

"I don't know. I didn't meet him till last Thursday morning, when he took me through the bakery. Then I went to the house for dinner that night, and he was there. He's very attractive, as a matter of fact. He has a very engaging personality. He's not at all like Dirk."

Mark smiled wryly. "I won't quote you on that last remark. I agree, though, that Klaus is not at all like Dirk. In my opinion, Dirk has more character in his little fingernail than Klaus has in his whole

body. He's a twenty-one-year-old teenager, Andi.
A brat who should be getting old enough to know
better and should be thinking about a time coming
when maybe, just maybe, he can take some of the
burden off Dirk's shoulders. Except for his
mother's help, Dirk's had more than one man
should have to deal with for...for the past eight
years, I'd say.''

Andrea clutched at her patience. ''You're losing
me, Mark,'' she warned him. ''I don't know anything about the responsibilities Dirk has had to
shoulder. All I know is that he's head of the Van
Der Maas bakery. I wouldn't think that should
wear him down.''

''If that was all there was to it, you'd be right,''
Mark agreed. ''Though Dirk was never cut out to
run a bakery in the first place.''

''Yes, I'd say that's true enough,'' she agreed.
''He was an architect, after all.''

''He told you that?''

''Precisely that,'' she admitted ruefully. ''That,
and nothing more.''

''Andi,'' Mark said, ''I could use a cup of coffee.
Plain black coffee. None of your pastries with it,
just now.''

''All right,'' she conceded, and went down the
hall to the small kitchenette where coffee could always be had in the agency at any hour of the working day.

She came back with coffee for Mark and a glass

of milk for herself. Her stomach was churning, and she wondered if she was about to experience one of the advertising business's occupational hazards—an ulcer.

She sensed, as Mark stirred his coffee, that he'd been using the short interval when she was out of the room to regroup, and it was clear that he'd come to a decision when he said, "You should know more about Dirk, I can see that, if you're going to work with him, Andi. Okay...yes, he was an architect. Not just an architect, but a brilliant one. We'd gone to college together, you know that."

She nodded yes.

"I was a liberal-arts student, Dirk was enrolled in a six-year program leading to a master's degree in architecture, so when I say we went to college together it's a loose term. Actually, we shared an apartment with two other guys, starting from our sophomore year on. But Dirk and I became very close. I don't want to sound maudlin about it, but to me he was like the brother I never had.

"I got my bachelor-of-arts degree after the routine four years," Mark went on. "After a time I was lucky enough to latch on to a job with an advertising agency in New York. I'd been working there for over two years when I got a call from Dirk one day telling me that he was working as a draftsman in an architectural firm there in the city."

"As a draftsman?"

"Yes. Every state in the union requires that a

man be licensed before he can practice as a registered architect. To qualify for the exam that leads to the license, two years of practical experience in an architect's office is required, if you already possess a master-of-architecture degree—which Dirk did at that point.

"Dirk had only been in the city a couple of weeks when he contacted me. He was living in a hotel. I had an apartment in the East Fifties and my roommate was moving out. She and I," Mark added with a rueful grin, "had come to a parting of the ways. That's what usually seems to happen to me with the women in my life!"

"Oh, come on, Mark," Andrea protested. "Spare me the sob story."

"Consider yourself spared," Mark said agreeably. "Anyway, I was delighted to have Dirk come and share my space with me, and we were apartment mates for the next two years. By that point I was engaged to the girl I married not long afterward. Dirk took his exam, meanwhile, got his license, and was launched on a career that promised to make him famous. I'm not alone in thinking that. I could give you references in the field who'd swear to you that Dirk was destined to do great things. He had a vision. . . ."

"You said once that you considered him a visionary," she remembered.

"Yes," Mark confirmed.

He fell silent, and after a moment she prodded

him. "What happened to put an end to all of this? I gather that there was an end put to it."

"Yes. The Van Der Maases," Mark said slowly, "have always been a family with extremely deep roots. Dirk's forebears were among the first Dutch settlers out there in Michigan."

"Yes, Dirk indicated that," Andrea admitted.

"His grandfather was a large landowner, but the family money came primarily from a flour mill that was a major supplier to the entire area. It was a big operation, it still is, for that matter. The Van Der Maases still own the flour mill. But Dirk's father saw beyond merely operating the mill. He saw the need for a large modern bakery that could service the same area the mill did. So he founded Van Der Maas, Incorporated.

"As I've said, in the early years Monica Van Der Maas worked side by side with her husband. She and Peter—Dirk's father—were a devoted couple. Monica was a local girl. They'd been high-school sweethearts, and she waited for Peter till he'd finished college. Then they married. They had twin sons—Dirk and Gerrit—and the boys were probably about kindergarten age when Peter started the bakery, and Monica went to work with him. She'd taken a secretarial course in high school, so she knew the rudiments of shorthand and typing, but she also had an astute business sense. She was Peter's right hand in many ways. Dirk has told me this, more than once. He has a tremendous admiration for his mother."

"She's a stunning woman," Andrea said thoughtfully. "Artistic, too—at least I'd say so from seeing her home. It's beautifully decorated. But I admit I would have pegged her as a society type...very much involved in civic affairs, but still primarily a social sort of person."

"She may be that, too, but there's no froth to Monica Van Der Maas," Mark said. "The years passed, and she continued to work with her husband, and Dirk thinks that it's because of this commitment they didn't have more children than they did. As it is, it would seem that Klaus must have been an accident. Gerrit and Dirk were fifteen when he was born. There was such a wide age gap that they were never close when Klaus was growing up. By the time Klaus was three the older boys had gone away to college.

"Gerrit went to a small Michigan college and majored in business administration," Mark went on. "I guess it was assumed that in due course he'd go into the bakery business with his father. Gerrit and Dirk were fraternal, not identical twins...."

"Yes, I understood that."

"Well, in my opinion, at least, Gerrit was not as attractive as Dirk. Not physically, nor in personality. In those days Dirk was a very warm person. Outgoing. He had an intensely artistic nature, to be sure, and that was always a rather private part of him. But I've seen him be the life of many parties...."

Andrea shook her head. "I find that hard to believe."

"Yes, I can imagine that you do," Mark agreed. "I'm the first to admit that he's changed a great deal."

Andrea had finished her milk, and now she put the glass aside and stood up restlessly. "I'm interested in all this," she told Mark, "but your preamble is driving me slightly crazy. What happened?"

"Peter Van Der Maas met with an accident one day while he was inspecting some newly installed machinery at the flour mill. It was in the spring of the year, and I remember it very distinctly because Dirk was to have been married just two weeks later, and I was going out to Holland to be best man at the wedding."

Hearing this, Andrea's throat went dry.

"Peter was paralyzed from the waist down as a result of the accident," Mark went on. "For a time his life hung in the balance, so Dirk's marriage was postponed. But then Peter recovered to the point of being confined to a wheelchair, knowing that this was for the rest of his life and, because he had a strong heart, knowing that he could live a long, long time.

"By then Gerrit was working in the bakery offices, but when Dirk came home after being notified of his father's accident his mother told him frankly that she didn't dare put Gerrit in charge...of anything. She'd discovered that he'd been dipping into the till, among other things. It wasn't anything mammoth enough to be called embezzlement, at least Monica didn't think so. But it was enough to convince her that it would be impossible to let Gerrit take over even temporarily.

"At that point Monica must have assumed that her husband would eventually go back to work, regardless of the wheelchair. But it didn't happen that way. One night Peter Van Der Maas managed to roll his wheelchair down the lawn back of the house and out onto the dock. There's a dock right back of the house, which is on a lake...."

"I know," Andrea reminded him.

"Peter rolled the wheelchair off the dock and... and they found his body the next morning."

The shock was profound. "Oh my God!" Andrea moaned. "Water...."

"Yes," Mark agreed. "First father, and then son. Though the circumstances of Gerrit's death were very different. Gerrit was drunk. He had no business being out on Lake Michigan when storm warnings had been posted. And Marietta...."

"Yes?"

"Marietta was probably as drunk as Gerrit was," Mark decided bitterly. "They'd both turned to the bottle...because of their own guilt, in my opinion."

"What guilt, Mark?"

"Marietta was the girl Dirk was going to marry

when his father met with the accident," Mark told her. "Dirk had loved her all his life...literally. They'd been brought up together, went through school together. When we were in college, Marietta used to come east for all the proms. Later, when Dirk and I shared the apartment in New York, Marietta used to come to visit and I would very discreetly move out while she was there.

"Now, when I look back on it, I'm sure that all this time she was sleeping with Gerrit too." He laughed harshly. "She even made a pass at me once. I couldn't believe it, and fortunately she didn't try again. But to Dirk she was an angel, and when a man sees an angel in a woman there's not much even his best friend can do to dispel the vision.

"Anyway, after his father's accident Dirk stayed on in Holland. He got a leave of absence from his office in New York. But then, after his father's suicide, he resigned from the architectural firm he'd become associated with, and one day he walked into the bakery office and ordered everything taken out of the president's office. There were too many memories connected with his father's old desk, and all the other paraphernalia. He installed himself as president, with his mother's sanction, and he put Gerrit in an office down the hall, where he was given enough work to do to keep him busy, without being allowed to get into anything of real importance.

"Gerrit couldn't have cared less. Christmas Eve

he and Marietta walked into the house on Lake-shore Drive and Marietta revealed that she was pregnant—and that the baby was Gerrit's, not Dirk's. Dirk knew this was true, and shortly after that Marietta and Gerrit were married in a quiet civil ceremony.''

Andrea felt her knees giving away, and she sat down very slowly. "What did Dirk do?" she asked finally.

"Dirk? I'd say that he tried to purge every emotion he'd ever felt out of his system, and just go on. The next time we met I was shocked at the change in him. You know what he's like."

"Yes," Andrea said slowly, "I know what he's like."

Unexpectedly Mark smiled. "I think there may be a chink in the armor."

"What?"

"When Dirk called last night he didn't sound at all like the stone man I've become accustomed to," Mark told her. "I'd say something—maybe some-one—has brought him back to life again!"

CHAPTER TEN

As THE WEEK PASSED, Andrea found herself scanning her daily mail with an eagle eye, looking for an envelope that would be postmarked Holland, Michigan. And every time a long-distance call was put through to her phone, she half expected to hear Dirk's voice at the other end of the wire, but it didn't happen.

It was frustrating. Even though he'd made it plain that it would be a while before he'd be ready to really start work on their promotional campaign, there were basics to be gone over, Andrea reasoned. It seemed logical to assume there'd be something he'd need to get in touch with her about.

For that matter, she had a problem of her own in regard to his account, but it wasn't something she was apt to confide to anyone else about at this stage, not even to Mark. The fact was that she couldn't seem to get started in laying out anything at all for the bakery. May merged into June and June into July, and never before had her mind been so blank about anything.

She knew that she wanted, first, to sketch out

some broad concepts about what should be done to put Van Der Maas's Dutch bakery products across to the American public. But ideas totally eluded her. This was especially disheartening, because it wasn't the first time she'd faced the challenge of taking a relatively unknown product and bringing it to national attention. Previously she'd done so successfully, and she had an excellent record in this area. But it was a record about to be broken, she decided dismally as she got to the floor-pacing stage, both in her office and at home, in an effort to come up with something that would launch the stream of creativity that usually flowed so readily for her.

She turned her attention toward trying to create a logo that would make the Dutch pastries instantly recognizable on market shelves everywhere. But all she could think of was a vignette of a Dutch girl in a peaked cap, or maybe a windmill, and both were entirely too cliché.

She was at even more of a loss when it came to wording a slogan that would give a succinct, easy to remember message. She dismissed every phrase she came up with as trite.

It would have been easy to lay the blame for at least some of this at Dirk's door. She could take refuge in the fact that she had no real idea of what he wanted. They hadn't gotten into the matter of a budget at all, either. She had no way of knowing whether or not he was prepared to go into national television, for example.

But it would be copping out to pin it on Dirk, Andrea admitted ruefully. In all fairness, she had to concede that Dirk had suggested she get only the broad strokes in mind and they could then get down to details when he came to Boston.

She was sure that if Dirk was concerned about the way things were progressing, he'd get in touch... with Mark, if not with her. But the summer was passing and there was no communication at all from Michigan. Or if Dirk was contacting Mark, Mark wasn't saying anything about it.

Mark was preoccupied with his own affairs these days. He'd fallen in love again, this time with a model, and from what Andrea had heard of the affair it seemed unlikely it was going to come to any satisfactory conclusion. The woman, for one thing, seemed much too preoccupied with her own career, and from what Mark had said it sounded as if she hoped to go on to Hollywood and a career in films.

Andrea was fond of Mark and hated to see him laying himself open to being hurt again. But she reminded herself that he was a grown man. Once people reached a certain stage in life there was little that could be done to soft-cushion their route. She'd found out about her own vulnerability from personal experience, first with her unhappy college romance and later with George. And she'd been close enough to danger with Dirk. Looking back, she realized it was a good thing she'd left Holland when she had.

Andrea had resumed the handling of her other accounts with her return to Boston, and fortunately all of them were going smoothly. Still, between that and trying to get started on her work for the Van Der Maas bakery, her working schedule was such a full one that she dropped into bed each night exhausted.

This wasn't conducive to getting good, healthy rest, though. She'd long ago discovered that mental fatigue didn't usually lead to a good night's sleep, and she envied more physical types because they could work their bodies to the point where sleep came easily. A tired mind, on the other hand, tended to foment little else but bad dreams.

On the spur of the moment, one day in early August, Andrea asked for a couple of weeks' vacation time. To her gratification, both Carl Saunders and Mark acceded willingly to her request, so she promptly accepted an invitation that had been dangling from a friend of her mother's who had a summer place on a lake up in New Hampshire.

Gertrude Hastings was a widow who'd earned quite a reputation writing children's books, which she illustrated herself. She was a charming person, and a good companion. And most important of all, Andrea thought gratefully after she'd been her guest for a couple of days, she knew when to leave someone alone.

The first few mornings Andrea slept late, to awaken to the sound of birds chirping and the wonderful scent of fresh air. She formed the habit of taking a swim before breakfast, and she lived in either a bathing suit or cutoff jeans.

Gertrude liked to walk in the woods as much as she did, and they took some long rambles together. It seemed to Andrea that Gertrude had discovered every trail in New Hampshire, and their excursions made her feel closer to nature than she had for a long time, a feeling she loved. At moments the thought would come unbidden that Dirk, too, would love this place. Then she reminded herself that she really didn't know that much about Dirk.

Gertrude's books were delightful, and as Andrea browsed through them she thought about how much Johanna would enjoy them. She was just the right age for them. When she mentioned the little girl to Gertrude, the older woman replied promptly that she'd love to autograph some of her books for Johanna, if Andrea would like to send them off to her.

Andrea hesitated. Dirk's silence had stung her pride, and the last thing in the world she wanted him to think was that she was making another bid for his attention. On the other hand, there was no reason why Johanna should be denied the pleasure the books would give her.

One rainy afternoon Gertrude autographed several of her books and Andrea packed them up in a stout cardboard carton and mailed them off to Michigan.

THE LETTER WAS WAITING in Andrea's apartment mailbox when she got back to Boston. Looking at the large, carefully formed script she could imagine the effort Johanna had put into writing it. She could visualize the little girl doing her very best as she leaned forward over a desk, her long dark curls tumbling over a face that would be flushed from her efforts.

"I love the books," Johanna had written. "They're really super. When are you coming back to Holland? Uncle Dirk keeps saying you'll be back. Please hurry! I miss you very much."

"I miss you very much." Tears stung Andrea's eyes as she read that.

She tucked Johanna's little note into the top drawer of her small desk, then went out to her kitchenette and made herself a vodka and tonic. Her apartment took up half of the second floor in an old Back Bay town house and she loved it. The rooms had very high ceilings and long windows in the back that overlooked a little bricked-in garden. But the place was not air-conditioned, and on this late-August evening it was hot and seemed especially airless because it had been closed up for two weeks.

Andrea took her drink into the bathroom and tried to relax in a cool pine-scented bath, but her nerves remained on edge despite her recent holiday. She fervently wished she was back in New Hampshire with Gertrude, to the point where she actually contemplated calling Carl Saunders and telling him she couldn't come back to work the following morning, that she had to have a couple more weeks off.

Chances were, she thought ruefully, that he'd give her the time. She'd paid her dues with the agency, and she knew that both Carl and Mark valued her work. But she'd never before taken advantage of that extra little ''in'' she had with both of them.

She wished that another account would open up, maybe in Alaska or Hawaii or some place a fair distance from both Boston and Holland. If so, she'd make a strong bid for it. Then she'd resign the Van Der Maas account, she'd forget all about Dirk and his bakery and...and....

She sat bolt upright in the tub with a suddenness that caused water to splash over the rim.

Resign the Van Der Maas account!

This was the first time it had occurred to her that she had a viable alternative.

She got out of the tub and reached for her favorite huge, thick Turkish towel. After rubbing herself down she wrapped it around herself sarong fashion and went out into the living room.

Sunday night...it would soon be night, anyway. It would seem too impetuous to call Carl Saunders at home to tell him she wanted out from the Van Der Maas account. Understandably, he would wonder why this great decision on her part couldn't wait until the following morning.

That was another thing, too. She was acting from an emotional base, which was never a good idea when dealing with a business situation. She also wanted to save face. She didn't want either Carl or Mark to suspect that she wanted to be relieved of the bakery account because she couldn't face up to working with Dirk. Their personalities just didn't jibe, that was all there was to it. The potent physical attraction between them didn't negate this in the least. In fact, it only made her contention all the more valid. It would be impossible to work in close proximity to a man as unpredictable as Dirk. Someone who set her afire with his kiss one minute, then was as cool as Lake Michigan's waters the next.

Something Dirk had said to her flashed through her mind. He'd mentioned that he suspected one of their greatest problems would be keeping their blood pressures down while working together. Something like that, anyway.

Well, Andrea brooded, maybe Dirk would be able to hold his pressure down under such circumstances, but she had to face up to the real possibility that hers might fly right out of control.

Right now what she needed more than anything else was a really good excuse for not going on with Dirk's account, and for the next two hours she mulled over this. Meanwhile she opened a can of jellied consomme she'd discovered in the fridge, sprinkled some lemon juice over it and had this for her supper.

It occurred to her that anyone watching her eat lately—even up at Gertrude's, where the food had been very tempting—would have thought she was on a strict diet. Even Gertrude had accused her of dieting, but this wasn't the case. Usually she had a good appetite, and she enjoyed food very much, all sorts of food. Her mother was a gourmet cook, and Andrea had been brought up to try any dish put in front of her before she made a decision about it. She'd been eating escargots—and relishing them— since she was five, and when she thought back on it she had to admit it was miraculous that she'd never had a weight problem. Swimming whenever she had the chance and walking had evidently been just enough to keep unwanted pounds from creeping on.

Now, though, she'd been losing weight. Mark had commented on her appearance before she went to New Hampshire, none too flatteringly, either. He'd said flippantly, "Where are the curves of yesteryear?" and Andrea had taken a long look at herself in the mirror that night, only to realize that the dress she was wearing was too loose to do anything for her at all.

She knew that thin was in, the thinner the better, but she had no desire to be slim to the point of skinniness. And if she kept on the way she was, that was going to be a real possibility.

Nevertheless, on this hot August night she didn't want anything more to eat than the jellied consomme, even though she knew that her meal was virtually noncaloric.

Late in the evening, as she continued to try to conjure up an excuse to present to Carl and Mark, she mixed herself a second vodka and tonic. This was not her usual habit. She seldom drank much of anything and almost never drank alone. But she hoped that once she'd found her suitable "out," the drink might help her get some badly needed sleep.

It didn't, nor had she come up with anything she could be sure would satisfy the agency by the time she went to bed.

It was raining the next morning, but rather than alleviating the heat the rain merely increased the humidity. Usually Andrea walked to work, cutting across the Public Garden and the Boston Common. This morning, though, she called a cab, certain that she'd be unlikely to find one cruising in her neighborhood on this kind of a day.

As she'd sipped her breakfast coffee, her excuse for an out had finally come to her. It had almost literally hit her on the head when she opened her kitchen cupboard to get down a box of sugar and a can of tuna flew out. She'd stared at the design on the tuna wrapper as she picked the can up, and suddenly everything had come clear to her.

She was going to resign from the Van Der Maas account because she'd drawn a blank when it came to thinking up either a logo or a slogan. That was the truth! She'd been more vacant, mentally, about Dirk's bakery than she'd ever been about anything.

In the past she'd heard both Carl and Mark say at staff meetings that there were those times when advertising people found themselves up against the wall... rather like a writer's block, when ideas simply would not flow.

The implication had been that when this happened, it was sometimes wise to turn to something else. In other words, not every account was for every executive.

Well, the Van Der Maas account was not for her, Andrea decided, and there was consolation in remembering that she'd warned Mark right at the beginning, before she'd ever met Dirk Van Der Maas, that it wouldn't be.

As she'd told Mark at the time, she didn't even like to cook, probably because cooking had always been one of her mother's passions. It had been much easier, growing up, to sit back and enjoy the marvelous meals her mother prepared than to try to scrounge around the kitchen and experiment on her own.

She hadn't changed now that she was on her own, either. She did tire of even gourmet TV dinners, yet she was grateful for them, and she seldom bothered preparing a real meal from scratch, never for herself. She had a couple of standbys she made when she had guests in for supper. But it had been a long time since she'd had a guest, she realized now, not since before her trip to Michigan. Over the summer she simply hadn't been in the mood to entertain.

But that would change, she promised herself. Once she'd gotten the Van Der Maas account off her back, everything would change. She'd be her old self again.

The decision made, Andrea wanted to get the whole thing over with as quickly as possible. She'd never been able to stand putting off something that had to be done, no matter how distasteful a task it might be.

And this task, she knew, wasn't going to be easy, at least not where Mark was concerned. She knew that Mark would never entirely believe that a part of her reason for giving up the account was not personal.

Well, in that case, he'd just have to believe what he wanted to believe.

Andrea walked into the agency ready to state her case, preferably to Carl Saunders. Briefly she wished Mark hadn't fallen in love again, because if he'd asked her to go out with him that night, this was one time when she would have said yes.

Trina, the pretty redheaded receptionist who presided at the outer desk, looked up with a smile, and Andrea wasted no time in asking, "Is Mr. Saunders in yet?"

"No," Trina said, and made a face. "He won't be in, Miss Campbell. He just phoned. He's got poison ivy. They had a family picnic yesterday and I guess he sat down in a nest of it."

Andrea winced, but persisted. "Is Mr. Terrence in?"

"Yes."

"Hold any calls for me, will you, Trina," Andrea requested. "I'm going in to see Mr. Terrence before I go to my own office."

Despite her outward air of calm, Andrea was quaking internally as she knocked on the door of Mark's office and then entered when he called out, "Come in."

The cast had been taken off his foot before she'd left for New Hampshire, and he was sitting behind his desk rather than in the armchair with his foot propped up on a hassock. He looked very much the smart young executive in a pin-striped pale-gray suit with a light-yellow tie, and he also looked happier than she'd ever seen him. Andrea fervently hoped that the happiness was valid, and that Mark's model wasn't going to let him down. From the way Mark put it, a fair number of women had let him down through the course of his life—yet he always seemed to go back for more punishment.

"Hey, gorgeous," he greeted her, and then paused to survey her narrowly. "Hell," he commented, "you don't look as if you've been on a vacation! If you ask me, I'd say you're still a candidate for a rest cure!"

"I didn't ask you," Andrea said rather shortly, and took the chair by the side of his desk without being invited.

He was continuing to inspect her, and she was beginning to feel very uncomfortable. "You must have been burning both ends of the candles up there in the boonies," he finally concluded.

"Oh, come on, Mark!" she protested irritably.

His grin widened. "The truth hurts, does it?"

"Whatever I did or didn't do in New Hampshire isn't relevant," she told him flatly. "I came in because there's something I have to discuss with you."

She hadn't intended to sound so serious. She was fully aware that the more she made of her desire to quit the Van Der Maas account, the more suspicious Mark was going to be of her motives.

"Well," he said now, leaning back and still smiling, though the smile no longer reached his eyes, "what seems to be the problem?"

"It isn't a problem," Andrea snapped. "I mean—not that kind of a problem."

"What kind of a problem did you think I had in mind, love?" he asked lightly.

"I don't know. Look, Mark, I was going to talk to Carl first about this but he's out today."

"He's home itching," Mark said, nodding sagely. "And you're arousing my curiosity. What might you have to say that you'd want to confess to Father Carl before you tell me?"

Andrea's nerves were screeching, and she was hard put to sit still. She gritted her teeth as she crossed one leg over the other—negligently, she hoped—and tried to look calm as she said, "I might as well come right out with it, Mark. I've given the whole matter my most serious consideration, I want you to know that. But I've come to only one conclusion. I want you to take me off the Van Der Maas account."

Mark's chair had tilted as he leaned back in it, and now it crashed down as he moved forward. "The hell you say!" he exclaimed, the smile completely gone.

"Please, Mark," Andrea protested. "There's no need to overreact. I'm sure it isn't the first time in your experience that someone's asked to be taken off an account, nor will it be the last. The fact is, I can't handle it. I mean, it isn't even a question of my having gone stale on it. I haven't been able to get started in the first place. That's why I don't look...more rested. All the time I was up there in New Hampshire I couldn't get the account off my mind. I've nearly gone crazy trying to think up the right logo, the right slogan, anything to get me pointed in a direction that could be followed. And I've drawn a blank. An absolute blank!"

She'd gotten up as she was speaking, and despite herself she was pacing the floor back and forth in front of his desk.

"I told you in the beginning I didn't think the account was right for me," she reminded him. "I told you it wasn't my area of expertise and unfortunately, as it turns out, I was right. When you get down to basics, I simply don't give a damn about bakery products, Mark, Dutch bakery products, any kind of bakery products. And I've never been able to work on an account with my tongue in my cheek. I have to believe in what I'm doing, I have to have genuine enthusiasm for it. When it comes to the Van Der Maas bakery, I'm not even lukewarm. I'm stone-cold!''

"It didn't seem that way to me when you first came back from Holland," Mark said slowly.

"I hadn't gotten down to the drawing board when I first came back from Michigan," Andrea countered. "At the time, I think I told you I was worried because my discussions with Dirk Van Der Maas had been so general in context. I think that getting the actual building for the frozen-food division under way was primary in his mind, and he wasn't ready to go beyond it. Personally, I don't understand why he didn't assign someone else in his office to work on the advertising campaign with me, but evidently he's the kind who feels he has to keep tabs on everything himself.''

"It's a feeling that's come about out of necessity," Mark said shortly. "Dirk *has* had to keep tabs on everything himself. The only person he's ever been able to turn to since he took over the bakery is his mother, and he's been doing his damndest these past couple of years to keep her out of it, for the sake of her own health and peace of mind.

"If Klaus was more responsible, it would be different. But it looks as if Klaus is going to be as much of a loss as Gerrit was, where the business is concerned. Klaus has gotten himself into all kinds of trouble...liquor, girls, drugs, you name it. Dirk has bailed him out again and again. When you were first out there in May, Dirk got word that Klaus had flunked out, up in Ann Arbor. There was nothing to do but try to put him to work in the firm, but Klaus has no interest in the business at all.

"Anyway," Mark continued gloomily, "don't blame Dirk for wanting to get the advertising campaign started himself. I think his big hope has been that you could then carry the ball on it, for the most part."

Mark frowned at her. "Too bad this couldn't have happened last week," he observed.

"Why last week?" she asked.

"Because Dirk was here then, and you could have told him how you feel yourself."

CHAPTER ELEVEN

DIRK IN BOSTON? Here in the office? Andrea's knees went so weak that she fumbled her way back to the chair by Mark's desk and sat down shakily.

Her eyes were accusing as she spouted the first thing that came to mind. "Why didn't you tell me he was coming?"

"Because I didn't know," Mark replied simply. "He walked in last Wednesday. He'd been in New York on business for a couple of days and he flew on up here, just as he'd told you he was going to do."

"I know he told me that's what he planned to do, but he didn't say when," Andrea interjected. "You'd think at the least...."

"Yes, I would," Mark said, to her surprise. "But Dirk, as you've probably already discovered, tends to do things in his own way and his own time."

"Yes," Andrea agreed tightly. "He does, doesn't he?"

"He was disappointed when he found out you weren't here," Mark went on, "because he thought his visit would be a good time for the three of us to have a conference. I offered to go over the account with him, but he said there'd be no point in that without your presence."

"I see."

"In any event, it was good to see him," Mark reported calmly. "We lunched together, and I suggested Lila could maybe fix him up with another model that night so we could double-date, but he wasn't interested."

"You should have known he wouldn't be." Andrea couldn't resist the remark. "Certainly you realize Dirk Van Der Maas swore off women a long time ago?"

"Yes, I suppose I should have," Mark agreed blandly. "Andrea, about the account. You don't seriously expect me to say we'll take you off it, do you?"

"I'd like to think that my wishes would have some bearing on your decision," Andrea countered.

Mark shook his head. "Dirk's completely sold on having you handle his account, and I know him. Now that he's made up his mind about you he won't settle for anyone else we can offer."

"But that's ridiculous," Andrea sputtered. "Look, Mark, Dirk Van Der Maas has the outmoded idea that because I'm a woman I must be interested in bakery goods, and in his mind that means I'll be better able to relate to the new products he's planning to put out than a man would."

"So what's wrong with that?"

"I can't believe what I'm hearing," Andrea answered wearily. "Mark, look, you know me. You know I had no interest in the Van Der Maas account from the very beginning, and the time I spent in Holland made me realize I was right in the first place. If Dirk doesn't want to work with someone else from this agency, then he'll have to go to another agency. That's all there is to it!"

An expression of intense pain crossed Mark's handsome face. "I can't believe what *I'm* hearing. This isn't you, Andi. What in hell has happened to you?"

"Nothing has happened to me," Andrea fibbed. "I want out, that's all."

Mark thought for a moment, then gravely shook his head. "I can't give it to you," he informed her, "and I can tell you right now that Carl will say the same thing. I know you looked down your nose when I brought up the matter of our handling a relatively small, Midwest bakery. But with this expansion, Dirk isn't going to be 'small' anymore. He's prepared his advertising budget, and I was surprised myself at what he's ready to spend to put this idea of his across. He'll want prime TV time for his spot commercials, he wants his ads in the best magazines, there will be terrific opportunities to plant media stories about the Van Der Maas enterprises. If you could get over your dislike for bakery products, Andi," Mark concluded somewhat cynically,

"I would say that putting the Van Der Maas account across could be a real challenge to you."

He was right, of course. Andrea knew that. She also knew she couldn't do it.

"Dirk has suggested that the time would be right in about two more weeks for you to go back to Holland," Mark continued. "The addition is coming along very well, and he's ready to start getting thoughts down on paper."

Andrea shook her head. "There is no way that I'm going back to Holland," she said firmly. "No way!"

"It's not your decision, Andi," Mark told her coolly.

She'd been staring at her hands, folded in her lap, wishing that there was a way to steady her trembling fingers. Her head snapped up at Mark's statement, her green eyes blazing.

"Exactly what is that supposed to mean?" she demanded.

"Carl and I talked it over after Dirk left," Mark admitted. "I had a feeling you might come in with something like this. I'm a little bit surprised at you...maybe disappointed would be a better word. I knew what your feelings about the Van Der Maas account were, true. But I thought you were enough of a professional to take on any job that was given to you."

"I *am* enough of a professional, damn it!" she glared.

"It doesn't seem so. I'm sorry the way you feel about this," Mark went on, his voice suitably regretful, "but as I've said, it's not your decision, Andi. Carl and I both insist that you keep on with this account. You know that one of the first rules in the agency business is to please the client...and then to keep him pleased. Whether you like it or not, there seems no doubt that you pleased Dirk initially, regardless of any feelings you may harbor about him...or against him. So it's important that you keep on pleasing him."

"And if I won't?"

Mark grimaced, and Andrea suspected that this time he was feeling a few genuine pangs about what she knew he was going to say to her.

"It's part of the job," he said reluctantly. "It goes with the job, Andi."

"So if I refuse to go back to Michigan I lose my job?"

"Hell," Mark said abjectly, "I don't like to hear that."

"You don't like to hear it? How do you think I feel about it?" she demanded furiously.

"Andi!"

"Don't try to protest too much, Mark," she warned. "It doesn't become you. I might also add that you know damned well you wouldn't try to pull something like this on a man in your employ. I think that galls me most of all."

Mark met her eyes steadily. "You're wrong," he

informed her. "I would pull it on a man. So would Carl. This isn't a question of the sex of the account executive, but of having the right person to handle the job."

"Great!" Andrea said scornfully. "With a philosophy like that you should win the Advertising Man of the Year award hands down!"

"Sarcasm doesn't become you, Andi," Mark said with unexpected gentleness. The brooding quality that crept into his eyes aroused a sudden wariness in her. "You know," he said reflectively, "there was a time, right after the divorce, when I wished something could get going between you and me. I could have gone for you...seriously, Andi. I could go for you."

His confession distressed Andrea. She had to say something. "Have you forgotten Lila?" she demanded.

"No, I haven't forgotten Lila," he said wearily. "She's beautiful, ambitious. There are moments when I'm sure I'm madly in love with her." He took in her expression. "Don't worry, Andi. I know that if I introduced her to the head of a movie studio tomorrow and he was...receptive...she might never look in my direction again. That's the way the cookie crumbles...as they used to say on Madison Avenue a long time ago. But I'm prepared, you can be sure about that. In other words," he added whimsically, "I'm ready to face the worst."

The words burst out from her. "Mark, don't you have any faith in women at all? Doesn't it occur to you that there's someone out there who could really love you, and be loyal to you? You're worse than Dirk!"

That was not at all what she'd meant to say, and she flushed. But Mark only shook his head. "No," he corrected, "I'm not worse than Dirk. Dirk gave his heart and he got smashed in the process. I've never been smashed all the way, Andi. Dented, yes, but not destroyed. Dirk came close to being destroyed, and he patched himself together in his own kind of way. As it happened, the patches stuck together like that glue they feature nowadays that's a thousand times stronger than whatever substance it fixes was in the first place. Dirk came out very strong, Andi. So strong that it frightens me to think he might stand a chance of being smashed again. I don't think I'd want to see that. I'm not sure Dirk could put himself back together a second time if he were ever to love again. But," he concluded, "that's neither here nor there. Andi, I hate being put in this position with you. I don't enjoy playing the heavy-handed tyrant. If you'd rather talk the whole thing over with Carl. . . ."

Andrea shook her head. She knew that Carl Saunders would be even more adamant than Mark when it came to the Van Der Maas account. And the more she thought about it, the less she liked the idea that she was permitting herself to back out of something because she couldn't face up to a challenge.

Dirk Van Der Maas was a challenge. But this time she'd cope, Andrea told herself. She couldn't deny the tug of the attraction between them, but it was purely physical. She could handle it. The important thing was to keep business uppermost in her mind, and not to let things get out of hand again as they had that night on the dunes. She and Dirk had both been swayed by the moonlight, the mood of the moment. There was no need for it to happen again.

She faced Mark resolutely and even managed a faint smile. "Very well," she conceded. "You win. I'll go back to Holland for you."

DIRK HAD SAID there was no point in her flying to Grand Rapids and renting a car again. He'd insisted it would be no trouble at all to meet her at the airport.

He had called the agency two days after Mark had told her flatly that there was no way he'd release her from handling the Van Der Maas account, and Mark had ordered the call transferred to her line. She'd been concentrating on a new approach she was working on for another of her accounts when the phone rang, and she'd been completely unprepared for the sound of Dirk's voice. In fact, she'd nearly dropped the receiver.

He'd been pleasant, polite. . . but formal. It was only when they'd settled the fact that she could rent a car in Holland when she got there, if she felt she really needed one, that he'd gone on to say, "This time you'll be staying with us, of course."

"What?" Andrea had echoed hollowly.

"At our house," Dirk had explained patiently. "Remember, mother invited you when you were here before?"

"Yes, I remember," Andrea had admitted. "But that was just a...a very gracious gesture on your mother's part, Dirk. I couldn't think of staying at your home."

"Why not?" he had demanded bluntly.

"Because...because I'd feel that I was intruding," Andrea had explained lamely.

"Nonsense," Dirk had said crisply. "I've spoken to mother, and she's looking forward to having you as a houseguest. And, needless to say, Johanna is ecstatic."

That had been the end of the matter, and Andrea had hung up the phone feeling as if things had been wrested out of her hands before she'd had the chance to grab on to them in the first place.

Now, as the plane approached the Grand Rapids airport on a Saturday afternoon in September, she found herself at the edge of succumbing to a bad case of jitters.

A fine businesswoman I am! she told herself scornfully. *Remember that you're here to do a job. This is all in the day's work!*

Nevertheless her hands were clammy as she left

the plane, clutching her handbag and a small carry-on tote, and when she saw the tall man waiting for her at the airport gate, her knees started shaking.

Dirk Van Der Maas gave her one long look and then frowned. "What's the matter? Did you have a rough flight?"

"N...no," Andrea stammered. "No. The flight was fine."

"Mark said something about flying not being your favorite form of transportation, but I didn't know it really upset you." He reached over to take her tote bag away from her. "Come on, let's claim your luggage. Then I'll buy you a good, steadying drink."

Andrea was so rattled that her two suitcases swished by her on the luggage belt before she recognized them. Dirk, with another frown in her direction, swooped them off as she finally identified them, then said, "I'll handle these. Can you manage the tote?"

She nodded, not trusting her voice. It was all she could do to keep her eyes off him. He was so damnably attractive! He was wearing camel-colored slacks and a light-brown tweed jacket that came close to the color of his hair. The color—close, also, to the rims of his glasses in tone—made his eyes seem even lighter. She'd almost forgotten what an unusual shade of blue they were. Almost...but not quite.

It would be hard to ever forget very much about

Dirk. A fact that only reinforced her conviction that coming back to Holland had been the wrong thing for her to do. She should have let the agency have her job. She should have gone off...somewhere...and started all over again.

"Seriously, are you feeling all right?" Dirk asked.

"I'm fine," she managed to reply, and followed him out of the airport building and across to the space where he'd parked his car.

As he opened the door of the Mercedes for her his hand brushed hers, and Andrea felt as if she were a sparkler just lit for the Fourth of July, about to explode in a hundred different directions.

She envied his calm as he drove onto the airport exit road. She couldn't equal it, that was for sure, and she couldn't imagine how she was going to handle being a guest in his home in addition to working with him.

Dirk, swinging onto a main road, said, "I'm sorry I missed you in Boston. Did you have a good vacation?"

"It was...very pleasant."

"Johanna loves the books you sent her," he said. "She says the woman who wrote them is a friend of yours?"

"Yes. She's a friend of my mother's, actually. I spent my vacation with her. She has a place on Lake Winnepesaukee."

"You don't look as if you got in much tanning

time," Dirk observed, making Andrea conscious of her pallor. And it was a pallor. It had gotten worse and worse these past couple of weeks since she'd agreed to go back to Holland. She'd felt so inert. She hadn't been able to sleep well at night, and as a result she'd moped around the apartment, even turning down a weekend invitation to go down to Cape Cod with friends.

"I—I tend to sunburn," she said lamely.

"Yes, I imagine you would. You're very fair," he told her.

Dirk himself was deeply tanned, and he looked terrific. She remembered that when Mark had first mentioned Dirk Van Der Maas he'd said they had planned to go sailing together. That was when Mark had intended to go to Michigan to discuss the account with Dirk himself. Now Andrea latched on to this particular recollection and in an attempt to make conversation asked, "Did you do much sailing this summer?"

He glanced sideways at her and said rather shortly, "No." Then he added, more gently, "I don't have a boat any longer, Andrea." He paused. "You've heard about my brother's accident, I imagine."

"Yes," she said, beginning to realize that she couldn't have stumbled onto a worse subject. "I...."

"Gerrit was...using my boat," Dirk said, his voice almost too level. "The boat went down." To her surprise he added, "I love to sail and some time I hope to have another boat. I'd planned to charter one if Mark came out last spring but, as you know, that didn't come to pass. I haven't bought a boat, though, because I was afraid it might upset Johanna too much."

"She's still afraid of the water?" It was the first thing that Andrea had been able to say naturally.

He nodded. "Yes, she is. So far she avoids even going near our swimming pool, and we've been advised not to push her. You know the way she reacted the day she fell into the canal. She didn't even try to save herself."

Andrea nodded. "Yes. But...." She was trying to grasp at something, an elusive idea still unformed. "That day you took us both out to that place along the lakeshore, I'd thought we might go for a walk along the beach."

She felt his glance sweep her face before he turned his attention back to the road. "Yes?"

"You did take us to a place on the water," Andrea went on, "yet I had the feeling that was as close as you wanted to get to it."

"You were right," he said, and added ruefully, "I suppose I keep trying to expose Johanna to water, even the sight of it. But I've hesitated to go beyond that."

The elusive thought took shape. "Dirk," Andrea exclaimed, "out on Windmill Island that day, Johanna had gone very near the water...of her own accord. She was leaning over, looking at one of the black geese...."

"Muscovy ducks," he interrupted absently.

"What?"

"They're Muscovy ducks, not geese," he said. "Not that it matters, especially. Just what are you saying, Andrea?"

"Johanna was so close to the water, leaning over as she watched the goose or duck or whatever it was, that it just took a single slip for her to fall right into the canal. I mean, she was at the very edge of it. I saw her, just before she fell. If she was still that afraid of water, would she have gone so close to it of her own volition, especially when she was all by herself?"

Dirk expelled a long breath and then said slowly, "I don't know. But... I wouldn't think so. Do you know...."

"Yes?"

"Well," he said, "I was very much afraid that Johanna would really be traumatized by that experience. I was afraid we'd lose any progress we'd made with her and that she'd be right back where she was at the time when her parents were... drowned. That's why I was so anxious to have you go to the Tulip Time parade with us. I wanted to divert her, and it didn't prove to be nearly so hard as I'd thought it might be. She took to you immediately. And you were wonderful with her."

"She's a very lovable little girl," Andrea told him.

"Yes, that she is," Johanna's uncle agreed.

"I wonder..." Andrea mused. "It's still warm enough to swim, isn't it?"

"That depends," Dirk said. "Some nights it can get pretty chilly this time of the year, so the water temperature drops faster than you might think it would. It's warm enough to swim in the pool, though, especially on sunny afternoons. Why?"

"I wonder if there might be a chance of getting Johanna to go in the water with me," Andrea ventured. "I wouldn't push her, Dirk. I'm not one to go against expert opinion, believe me. But, just maybe...."

He smiled. "I'd say that if anyone might make a miracle happen with Johanna it could very well be you."

ANDREA REMEMBERED THAT STATEMENT once she'd gotten into bed that night. It stood out especially because it was the only thing of a really personal nature Dirk had said to her.

They'd stopped along the way to Holland at a pleasant roadside lounge, and he'd ordered whisky sours for both of them. As they'd sipped the drinks, he'd concentrated on telling her about the new bakery addition, and his satisfaction at the way it was coming along.

"We're ahead of schedule," he'd reported.

After that they'd spoken about the account without getting into any real depth about it. Andrea had admitted frankly that thus far she'd been unable to come up with anything satisfactory in the way of either a logo or a slogan, but Dirk had been unperturbed.

"It'll come to you," he'd assured her.

Her welcome at the big house on Lakeshore Drive had been warm and genuine, with both Mrs. Van Der Maas and Johanna on hand to greet her. Andrea had thought that Mrs. Van Der Maas looked tired, but she had been charming as she showed Andrea to the beautiful second-floor guest room she was to occupy during her stay. It was furnished in soft tones of deep rose veering to the palest pink, and Andrea was enchanted with it.

Johanna, tagging along, had stated proudly that she'd picked this particular room for Andrea. "We have the blue room and the green room and this rose one," she'd said. "I thought this suited you best, even if you do have green eyes."

"Also, this is closest to Johanna's own room," Mrs. Van Der Maas had laughed. "I think that was quite a consideration when she made her choice!"

Dinner had been a pleasant affair. Klaus had not appeared for it, though, and Andrea wondered if he'd left Holland again, and if that was the reason his mother looked as if she'd been doing her fair share of worrying lately.

Johanna's bedtime on school nights was nine o'clock, and Andrea agreed to come up and say good-night to her. She found the little girl occupying her pretty canopy bed with a dozen dolls lined up precisely, six on either side of her. As she kissed Johanna good-night, unexpected tears filled Andrea's eyes. She brushed them away hastily, so that the child wouldn't see them. There was something so very appealing about Johanna, something so sweet and also so vulnerable. She'd been through so much for a child of her age.

Downstairs again she found Mrs. Van Der Maas alone in the family room.

"Dirk had to go over to the plant," the older woman explained. She sighed. "I keep telling him I wish he'd learn how to delegate responsibility. He tends to take everything on his shoulders. They're strong shoulders, to be sure, but he needs some people he can really rely on. That will be more true than ever once the new division gets going."

Andrea hadn't intended to pry where Dirk was concerned, but she couldn't refrain from asking, "Aren't there any people in the bakery Dirk can depend on?"

"Yes, there are," his mother said firmly. "Jan van der Houten, who is our production manager, is capable of shouldering far more responsibility than Dirk gives him. Then there are two other men in the office who could handle a lot more than Dirk requires of them and would be only too glad to have the opportunity to prove this to him. Dirk has been...let down too often," Mrs. Van Der Maas concluded, reluctantly. "I suppose I can't blame him. He's still young, he can stand it now. But he deserves to lead a life that's apart from his work, Andrea, and that's something he hasn't done for eight years.'' She smiled. ''True, I have one lovely granddaughter. But I'd like to think I may have other grandchildren before I die. Dirk's children.''

Andrea didn't know what to say to this, but fortunately Mrs. Van Der Maas didn't seem to expect an answer.

A short time later Andrea could no longer stop yawning, and her hostess suggested with a smile that it might be an idea for her to go to bed.

''It's the change in pace from the city to the country,'' she said kindly, but Andrea could have told her that her weariness did not stem from that at all. The truth was, the day had taken a lot out of her emotionally. It still seemed impossible to think that she was in Holland again...living in Dirk Van Der Maas's house.

As she drifted off to sleep, her thoughts turned toward Dirk, as they'd been doing most nights since she'd met him. This time, though, she had to face the knowledge that she'd be seeing him again the next day, and she only wished she could get better control of herself before she did so.

She also thought back to what Dirk had said about her being able to work a miracle for Johanna, if anyone could.

If only that could prove to be true.

CHAPTER TWELVE

ANDREA SLEPT LATE that Sunday morning. Awakening, she stretched luxuriously. She couldn't recall when she'd felt so contented.

Swinging her legs over the side of the bed, she conceded that this was, in part, because she'd had her first really good night's sleep in longer than she liked to remember.

She'd dreamed, yes, but they hadn't been disturbing dreams. And Dirk had been in them, she was sure of that. But—maybe fortunately, she thought with a wry smile—she couldn't remember the role he'd played.

She heard something that sounded like a splash and went to the window. Her room was at the back of the house and looked directly over the swimming pool. She saw a man swimming from one end of the pool to the other and she paused to admire his strong, powerful stroke.

As she watched, he turned and swam back to the deep end, and then pulled himself up, clinging to the edge of the pool as he looked up at her.

Dirk. For a moment she'd thought it might be Klaus, his blond hair dampened.

"Andrea?" There was an uncertainty in his voice.

"Yes," she called.

"You have a suit with you, don't you? Come on down," he invited.

She hesitated. There was no one else around the pool, and as she listened the house seemed very silent. Was there a chance that she was there alone with Dirk? She knew she was flirting with danger, but she couldn't resist the idea of swimming with him.

"I'll only be a minute," she called down.

Andrea's vivid green bikini left little to the imagination. Despite her recent weight loss she was still beautifully proportioned, her full breasts swelling the cups of the snug bikini bra, their fullness only emphasizing her slim waist. The bikini bottom was just the right size to cover the contours of her hips. Though Andrea usually paid little attention to the effect her appearance in a bikini tended to have on men, she became very self-conscious as she approached the pool, especially since Dirk had gotten out of the water and was stretched on a lounge chair awaiting her.

He rose slowly and came toward her, and she noticed that he was wearing dark glasses. The morning sun was bright, and she could imagine that his very light eyes were sensitive to glare. The sunglasses were no doubt prescription ones.

As if to confirm this, Dirk said, "I was pretty sure it was you up there in the window, but I didn't have my glasses on. Things are fuzzy without them.''

So that accounted for the note of hesitation in his voice when he'd called her. She'd wondered about that... assuming that maybe he'd called her name impulsively, and then perhaps wished he hadn't.

He took off the dark glasses and put them on a small table by the lounge chair, then started back to the pool, saying over his shoulder, "Come on!"

Andrea only stared after him dumbly. At that instant she could not have moved. Her eyes were filled with the sight of Dirk Van Der Maas in sleek black swim trunks that fit him like a second skin.

The first time she'd ever met him she'd been aware of his well-proportioned body and the easy grace with which he moved. That initial impression had been confirmed many times, but until now she hadn't realized how perfect Dirk really was.

He was broad shouldered, slim waisted, long legged, but it was the way he was put together that caused Andrea's heart to beat a lot harder than it usually did. Dirk was smoothly muscular, every contour of his body firm and defined. He exuded a sense of power and a forceful masculinity. She smiled to herself. His swim trunks left as little to the imagination as her bikini did!

He looked back again, squinting slightly, and Andrea knew with a definite sense of relief that things must be blurry without his glasses. This was a plus as far as she was concerned. Right now she would have hated to have him read the expression on her face.

He dived neatly into the pool from the edge at the deep end, and then treaded water, waiting for her to join him. Andrea had never been great at diving, even from pool sides, and she didn't want to do a belly flop in front of him. She hesitated, then grasped her courage and plunged...right into his arms.

They encircled her, and as he saw her astonishment Dirk laughed, his light eyes sparkling in a way she'd never seen before.

"I wasn't taking any chances with you," he teased. "You just might have sunk to the bottom."

"Are you saying I'm rock heavy?" she accused.

"No. Just right," he said, still holding her and keeping both of them afloat as he tread. His arms were cool and wet, and Andrea would never have guessed there could be anything so sensuous about two people with wet skin touching each other. He was close...so very close to her. And as if it was the most natural thing in the world to do, she tilted her head up and impulsively kissed him.

Their moist lips clung together, Dirk responding to her gesture as if it was the invitation he'd been eagerly awaiting. She felt the gentle thrust of his tongue and touched it with the tip of her own, sending a convulsive shiver through her.

She stilled, though, as he pulled her even closer, their bodies touching in a provocative intimacy erotic in its effect. Andrea had thought herself reasonably experienced, but this was an arousal that sparked a rush of new sensations, and she felt a sudden, driving need for this man who was holding her.

He spoke softly, directly into her ear. "We belong together," he told her huskily.

Their *bodies* belonged together. Dizzily Andrea accepted this much of his assertion, and the caution that was usually such a basic part of her evaporated, as if it had been blown away on the September breeze.

His arms still encircling her, he began to kick his legs in a slow, steady rhythm that propelled both of them until they came to the point where Andrea could just touch the bottom of the pool with her toes. Only then did he release her, to begin a voyage of exploration with those strong, capable, artistic hands she'd noticed the first time they'd ever met.

He traced the contours of her body as if he was studying her, sketching her with pliant fingers. Then his hands moved from her hips to her buttocks and he drew her toward him again, Andrea arching her body involuntarily until they were molded together. She'd never felt so much of a woman as she did when his arousal became manifest to her, and she knew she'd been capable of causing this response in him.

Her bikini bra tied in the back. She felt Dirk loosen it, then his cool hands cupped her breasts, his touch bathing her in an elixir of pure ecstasy.

She felt herself filled with pleasure and desire, and as if to share this gift with him she sought his mouth again, her lips conveying their own message. Slowly she feathered her fingers across his broad, powerful back, then let them trail to his waist, descend to his thighs and continue, as if possessed of their own power, until they rested upon the very center of his manhood, and she heard him groan.

They were drifting back out of her depth, and instinctively she began to tread water, still continuing her exploration of his body. It was like a nightmare suddenly descending to blot out the most glorious of dreams when he released her as abruptly as if he'd been burned and then, turning, swam furiously toward the other end of the pool.

Andrea floundered and felt herself going under, and it was only with a great effort that she rallied. With fumbling fingers she retied her bikini top, then began to swim herself, her strokes slow and steady but nowhere matching his in either style or strength.

But she couldn't have cared less about demonstrating her swimming ability—or lack of it—just then. She was so confused that she struck out blindly, only realizing that she'd gone the full length of the pool when her outstretched hand brushed the far edge of it.

By now Dirk had reversed direction. Holding on to the edge of the pool, Andrea turned to watch him. He was swimming as intensely as if he were in an Olympic race, and she was sure she knew exactly why.

Andrea made her way to the steps that led into the water and sat down, letting her legs trail as she gasped for breath. She could not possibly have found the stamina to swim another stroke and she marveled at Dirk's self-control.

He was coming toward her again, and he pulled himself up on the step alongside her, keeping a cautious distance between the two of them. As she watched, he shuddered, and then to her surprise he looked up at her and smiled.

"Don't misinterpret me," he cautioned. "My mother took Johanna to church, and they'll be back any time. So we couldn't...."

Andrea felt her cheeks go hot with embarrassment and Dirk said quickly, "Don't worry. No one saw us. The kitchen is on the other side of the house, and Hans and Mabel will be busy preparing lunch. We always have a light lunch midday on Sunday, and then we let them have the rest of the day off. Sunday nights we do our own thing," he said. "We raid the fridge, and it's every man for himself."

He got up as he was speaking, moving across the pool apron. When he came back a moment later, he was wearing his dark glasses.

He touched the rims lightly as he sat down next to Andrea again. "I don't do too well without these," he said ruefully. "A wicked case of astigmatism, among other things...."

"Have you ever tried contacts?" she asked. Actually, she found his glasses—both plain lensed and tinted—attractive, yet she would have thought that someone with his looks might have had the kind of vanity that would have made them balk at wearing "spectacles."

He shrugged. "I'm one of those people who can't tolerate contacts," he said. "Something about the shape of my eyeballs. Anyway, the cosmetic aspects of wearing glasses have never concerned me, and I've worn them for a long time. Till I got them, I used to have miserable headaches and they helped a lot, in that respect."

His dark glasses served as a camouflage, Andrea thought, veiling those light eyes that could be so very expressive. At that moment she wished she could see his eyes; she wanted to read his expression. But he was standing, reaching out a hand to help her up.

"Let's stretch out," he suggested.

Andrea nodded. A moment later she was lying back in one of the loungers, watching the sunlight sprinkle gold motes across the surface of Lake Macatawa, just beyond the edge of the sloping green lawn.

The sun was still giving out a lot of warmth, and she was comfortable in her bikini, which was rapidly drying out. But inwardly she was not comfortable at all. Dirk had lowered the back of his lounger so that it was almost flat. He was stretched out full length on it, and it was all she could do to keep from reaching out and touching him. She yearned for him, she wanted to experience the feel of him again, his devastating closeness. . . .

"Could I get you something, Andrea?" he asked. "Maybe some coffee, or perhaps you'd like a mimosa?"

"A mimosa?"

"Champagne and orange juice, half of each."

"Thanks, no. If I had anything alcoholic I'd fall flat on my face."

She saw his lips curve into a smile. "Again?" he asked.

She knew he was remembering the night when she'd tripped as they were about to start up the sand dunes. She was sure their thoughts were running parallel when he said, his voice lower than usual, "Andrea, that night on the dunes. . .do you have any idea how much I wanted you! And. . .the wanting hasn't changed for me. I've done a lot of thinking these past four months, and there've been times when I've wondered if I was losing my sanity. I told myself I'd been crazy to let you go back to Boston. I nearly picked up the phone a dozen times, to call you and ask you to come back. . . ."

"Why didn't you, Dirk?" she asked him. "Why didn't you call me?"

He drew a long breath, then, expelling it, said, "Because you scare the hell out of me!"

It was the last thing she would have expected to

hear from him, and when she saw that he was serious it shook her. Before she could rally enough to speak, Dirk turned on his side, and though his expression remained veiled because of the dark glasses, she was aware he was studying her intently.

When he spoke his tone was almost conversational.

"When I first met you," he said, "I thought you were the most beautiful woman I'd ever seen. No, don't look like that! I haven't changed my opinion. Do you know how unusual your coloring is, Andrea? Those enormous green eyes, with that silvery blond hair? You reawakened a lot of things in me that I'd thought were...dead. And...." He let the sentence trail off.

After a difficult moment, he went on, "I found you overwhelmingly attractive, physically. And of course I also had to admire you on a different level. Professionally."

Professionally! Her smile was wry. "You haven't seen anything I've done on a professional level, Dirk," she reminded him.

"I don't need to be convinced," he told her. "I can tell you're good by the way you talk about your work—even if you hadn't come so highly endorsed by Mark, who, despite that flippant attitude that can sometimes be so annoying, is a perfectionist in his own field. But it isn't the physical you or the professional you I wonder about."

"Oh?"

He nodded. "It's the inner you," he said. "The you that very few ever come to know as I'd like to know you. You're a caring, generous person. I would have seen that the first moment you looked at Johanna, if I hadn't surmised it already. But there's a part of you that stays beneath the surface, isn't there?"

"Yes," she agreed slowly.

"I want to know that part of you," Dirk said, his voice so soft that his words were like a caress. "I want to know your past and your present, and I want to know what you think about when you look toward the future—" He broke off and was silent for a moment, and then he said, "Haven't you ever wished that you could creep inside another person, for just a little while. So that you could look out through their eyes and listen with their ears and speak with their voice? That's what I wish I could do, Andrea, and it saddens me to admit it's impossible. Impossible ever to really know another human being like that. To ever reach out and touch and...and encompass. In one way, I suppose the sex act is the closest we get to it. Two people fuse, and for just a little while they are one. But what I'm speaking about is a different sort of togetherness."

He turned onto his back, lying very still as a silence crept between them that began to make Andrea increasingly uncomfortable. Then he asked, "Am I reaching you?"

"Oh, yes," she told him. "You're reaching me,

Dirk. What you're telling me is that what you're talking about, what you want, is impossible. You're saying that it can never be like that—all the way—between two people. You're saying that the human body can be invaded, but the human mind and the human soul stops short of ever letting anyone else know all its secrets. Isn't that what you're saying?''

"Yes," he said. "Yes. . . I suppose it is.''

It was a beautiful September day, a warm and sunny day, but Andrea felt as if she'd started walking across a very narrow bridge covered with ice. She shivered, feeling its cold, knowing that it would be so easy to misstep entirely with Dirk.

She said carefully, "There has to be faith between two people, Dirk. The richness in a relationship between a man and a woman comes about because of faith, a mutual trust. Two people have to start with trust as a foundation and build from there. . . .''

She heard his impatient exclamation, and with an almost savage gesture he adjusted the lounge chair so that he brought himself into a sitting position.

"Yes," he stated bitterly, staring toward the lake with eyes obscured from her by the dark lenses. "You've got your finger right on my problem, Andrea. I want you. . . I've never wanted another woman as much as I want you. But I'm afraid I don't trust you." Then, almost under his breath, he concluded, "I don't think I have it in me to trust a woman ever again!''

LATER ANDREA DECIDED that life had a way of ordering an interruption whenever a situation was approaching the untenable.

As she listened to Dirk say that he couldn't trust her, the words uttered in an oddly hopeless tone of voice, she'd become engulfed by such a wave of depression that when it receded she felt both bleak and bereft.

She knew only too well that without trust there could be nothing between two people. Nothing of any validity. And Dirk must know that too. Yet he'd committed himself to a philosophy that made the promise of any real future relationship between them next to impossible.

What was he thinking? Andrea demanded silently, and angrily. Did he really believe she'd go to bed with him, knowing how he felt about women, just because this physical side of her that he'd spoken of cried out to him?

She couldn't deny that Dirk's physical appeal to her was tremendous. Yet there was still something deep within her that would prohibit her from ever giving herself to a man purely for the sake of sexual gratification. It seemed to her that Dirk should know that much about her.

No, she could give herself to a man only if she loved him.

If she loved him.

Did she love Dirk?

She found herself staring at her clammy hands,

folded in her lap, her fingers tightly pressed together. And she knew that Dirk was looking at her, she knew that in another second he'd be saying something else and she didn't want to hear it, whatever it was.

Then the blessed interruption came, and Andrea thanked whatever fate had arranged it.

Monica Van Der Maas, standing at the top of the terrace at the back of the house, said, "Ah, there you are."

Dirk's mother was fashionably dressed in a wine-colored two-piece outfit. Poised. Elegant. Suddenly Andrea felt underclad, even flamboyant, garbed as she was only in her brilliant emerald bikini.

Mrs. Van Der Maas walked down the shallow steps that edged the terrace and across to the pool rim, sitting down on one of the white wrought-iron chairs that rimmed a large umbrella-topped table. Andrea noted that she moved as a model might, every gesture she made a graceful one. But she suspected this came naturally to her. In her own way, her son Dirk exemplified the same kind of grace.

Dirk had stood up at his mother's approach. Amazingly he was smiling pleasantly and even seemed relaxed. It was difficult to believe the searing admission that had been wrung from him just minutes before. Andrea sighed, knowing there was a ragged edge to the sigh and hoping that Monica Van Der Maas wouldn't notice. Dirk's statement had been like a stab wound to her, and the pain was still there, a throbbing, terrible pain. She didn't have it in her to anesthetize her own feelings, as Dirk seemed to be able to do his.

Glancing at Monica Van Der Maas, she saw that the older woman was preoccupied. It was unlikely she'd noticed anything amiss between Andrea and her son.

"Where's Johanna?" Dirk asked.

"In her room," his mother said briefly. Then added, almost reluctantly, "I asked her to come out and join us by the pool. I even suggested we might have Mabel bring our lunch out here."

"She wouldn't?" Dirk asked.

His mother shook her head. "No. Not even to see Andrea. She said she had a tummy ache, and she's lying down."

Dirk muttered something under his breath. Then he said, "Does the doctor give you any idea at all, mother, of what to expect? I mean, will Johanna ever get over this? It seems to me...."

"The doctor says that she's doing very well, Dirk," his mother interrupted, her tone faintly reproving. "When I ask him for a more specific prognosis, all he tells me is that it will take time."

"Time!" Dirk said bitterly. "It begins to seem it will take forever."

Andrea, rising, said, "I think I'll go change, if you'll excuse me."

Dirk didn't appear to have even heard her, but Mrs. Van Der Maas nodded. "Lunch will be in half an hour, my dear."

From the top of the terrace steps, Andrea cast a swift backward look at the table by the pool. Dirk had joined his mother, he was sitting close to her, and the two of them were already deep in conversation. Even with the dark glasses on to obscure his expression, Andrea could sense Dirk's agitation, and she wondered about the cause. Were he and his mother still discussing Johanna? Somehow she doubted it.

It occurred to her again that, thus far, no one had said a word about Klaus. It was almost as if Klaus had never been around at all. It didn't seem natural. There was the chance, of course, that Klaus had merely gone somewhere for a visit. Perhaps he'd re-applied to the University of Michigan and was back in Ann Arbor again. But she had the nagging feeling that this wasn't the case.

Dirk and Klaus were so different, she mused, as she went up the stairs and then down the hall to her room. In many ways she found Klaus far easier to understand.

She peered into the clothes closet, wondering what she should wear. Dirk had indicated that Sundays were casual in the Van Der Maas house. Nevertheless, Monica's outfit was quite formal, but then she'd dressed to go to church.

Andrea hesitated over a gold-toned silk dress, so simple in cut that it could be dressed up or down to suit any occasion, and then decided to go for a casual look instead. She slipped into a pair of snug-fitting jeans and topped them with a fuchsia over-sized sweat shirt. Her hair, soaked during her plunge into the pool, had dried out in the sunlight and responded to a good brushing. After a glance at herself in the mirror, she settled for a touch of pale-pink lip gloss, and nothing more in the way of makeup.

Her good night's sleep had erased the shadows of fatigue that had been much too prominent lately. She looked fresh and lovely as she went out in the hall, nearly running into Dirk, who was heading for his own room.

He stopped short when he saw her, and his nearness had a powerful effect on Andrea. She felt something twist deep inside her, the wrench so intense it was physically painful.

She knew her transparent face was in danger of giving her away, but there was no way she could simply brush past him. Inadvertently he was blocking her path.

Slowly, tentatively he said, "Andrea," his voice husky. She was forced to look up at him, and she was startled by his expression. There was a look she'd never seen before in those clear eyes.

She told herself unsteadily that it was insane to think Dirk might be pleading with her.

He said softly, "Mother's in the family room, and I'll be along in a few minutes."

She knew that wasn't what he really wanted to say to her. She hesitated. "I thought I might stop in and see Johanna."

"Yes," he said, his eyes never leaving her face. "That might be a good idea."

Andrea nodded, puzzled by the way he was looking at her. She had the disturbing feeling that there was something he wanted to ask of her, and he didn't know how to frame the question.

She was unprepared when he bent forward, his mouth meeting her lips squarely, his kiss brief but strangely eloquent.

"Thank you," he said simply, and Andrea, more puzzled than ever, wondered what it could be he was thanking her for.

CHAPTER THIRTEEN

THE GIRL was lying on her bed, clutching a doll in either arm. She was wearing the pretty red corduroy jumper with a frilly white blouse in which she'd gone to church, and there was a matching red bow perched in her dark curls.

The door to Johanna's room had been partly open, and Andrea, peering in while trying to be as quiet as possible, felt a wrench at the sight of the child staring fixedly up toward the ceiling.

What sort of visions was Johanna seeing? It was frightening to speculate.

She said tentatively, "Johanna?"

Johanna turned toward her instantly and managed a smile, but the gesture took such an effort that it only tore at Andrea's heart all the more. It didn't seem as if a small child should have to try so hard to smile.

"Is your tummy ache better?" Andrea asked, standing in the doorway, reluctant to enter the room unless Johanna asked her to.

"I think so," Johanna said doubtfully. Then added, "Andi...."

The tone was an invitation and Andrea crossed over. After only an instant's hesitation, she sat down on the edge of Johanna's bed.

Johanna said again, "Andi...."

"Yes?"

"You like to swim, don't you?"

Andrea drew a deep breath. This was the last subject she'd expected Johanna to bring up, and she was desperately anxious to handle it right. Would that she held a degree in child psychology, she thought ruefully. As it was, she had only her basic instincts to guide her.

"Yes, I do like to swim, Johanna," she said. Then added honestly, "Even though I'm not very good at it...not like your Uncle Dirk."

Johanna nodded solemnly. "Yes, Uncle Dirk is good," she agreed. "Uncle Dirk is good at a lot of things. Sometimes he plays cards with me and... you know what?"

"What?"

"I think he'd beat me all the time, except sometimes I think he lets me win," Johanna confessed. Then she said slowly, "I'm afraid of the water, Andi."

"I know you are, darling," Andrea said. "And...I understand why. But you know, Johanna...."

She was painfully conscious of the child's large brown eyes gazing at her face, and she uttered a small silent prayer for guidance in her choice of words.

She said, very carefully, "Johanna, sometimes accidents happen. In a car, or an airplane, or right in your own house, as well as on the water."

"I know," Johanna nodded. "Uncle Klaus had an accident in his car. He smashed the car all up, and he was in the hospital for a while."

Was this recent? Was Klaus still recuperating from a car crash? Was that why he hadn't been around? If he'd been in a car crash, wasn't it odd that neither Dirk nor his mother had mentioned it?

These questions raced through Andrea's mind, and then were set aside as she concentrated on the problem that was haunting this small person looking up at her so anxiously.

"Your Uncle Klaus will still drive a car, won't he?"

Johanna nodded.

"He'll remember his accident," Andrea went on, "but he won't stop driving because of it, Johanna."

Having said this, she sat back, almost afraid to breathe. Had she gone too far? Or was Johanna too young to understand the implications of what she'd just said?

"Uncle Klaus isn't scared like I am," Johanna explained. "Uncle Klaus isn't scared of anything. Andi, do you think I should...should go in the water again? Maybe even out in a boat?"

To Andrea's horror, sudden tears shimmered in the child's eyes as she voiced this question, and then

Johanna shuddered. "I'd be so scared I think I'd just die," she said, her little voice trembling.

Andrea yearned to sweep her up in her arms and console her. She wanted to tell her that she never need go near the water again if she didn't want to. But she knew better than to do that.

Instead she said slowly, "I think maybe sometime you should try, Johanna. Sometime when you feel like it, that is." She hesitated, then managed to force a laugh that sounded reasonably normal. "You know what?"

"What?"

"Maybe you could start out by going in the pool with me just to get your toes wet. All ten toes," Andrea went on, as if outlining a game they both could play. "You and I could stand in the water and look down at our toes and see who could wiggle each toe all by itself. Did you ever try to wiggle your toes separately? Even if you have, they look different in the water. Like plump little sausages."

To her delight, to her infinite relief, Johanna laughed. "Maybe we could try to wiggle our toes right now, and see who can wiggle the most?" she suggested.

"I think it's easier when you have your feet in the water than it is on dry land," Andrea told her. "Anyway, it's a lot more fun."

"Maybe," Johanna conceded, and then she said, "Hi, Uncle Dirk!"

Andrea went weak all over as she turned to see

Dirk standing in the doorway. He was wearing
faded jeans and a dark-blue turtleneck that fit snug-
ly across his broad chest. He looked handsome and
virile, and he was smiling in a heart-stopping way as
he surveyed his small niece.

"Hi, beautiful," he greeted her. Then he added,
"May I come in?"—and Andrea had the funny
feeling that he was addressing this question to her.

She answered before Johanna could, her tone
stiffer than she'd intended. "Of course," she said.

Dirk sauntered over to the bed, coming to stand
much too close to Andrea to do anything toward
steadying emotions that she felt were about to go
out of control. She caught a whiff of the faintly
spicy after-shave he favored, and between the sight
of him and the scent of him and this recent, emotionally tense conversation with Johanna, she felt
her nerves fraying at the ends. . . again.

A dull ache arose within her, an ache that had a
peculiar sweetness about it despite its pain. Being
here with Dirk, with Johanna, gave her the dangerous misconception that they were almost like a
family unit.

The mere thought of this was devastating, and
she stood suddenly and walked over to the window,
glancing out blindly as she fought back threatening
tears. It wouldn't do to cry right now, for Johanna's sake. It was vital to keep things on a happy,
even keel.

Slowly her vision righted. Johanna's room was

on the opposite side of the hall from the guest room
Andrea was occupying and looked out over the
front of the house. The flower beds were ablaze
with annuals, yet to be touched by the first frost of
the year, marigolds and zinnias and dahlias flaming
in a riot of differing colors.

The huge trees along Lakeshore Drive were in
their fullest leaf, rich green with only an occasional
hint of the tawny tones of autumn. Everything was
full and rich and beautiful now, in September, Andrea found herself thinking, and she yearned for
her love to be equally full, equally rich, then sadly
knew that this could never be so. A long time ago,
the mother of this lovely child who lay on her bed,
still cuddling her dolls, had destroyed something in
Dirk, and the destruction had been awesome in its
scope. Even the best surgeons, Andrea found herself thinking dully, could not rebuild a totally shat-
tered heart....

She heard Dirk's low laugh, and then Johanna
called out, "Andi," and she forced herself to rally
so that she could turn and face them with a smile on
her lips.

"I was just suggesting to Johanna that after
lunch maybe we could drive down to Saugatuck and
go for a dune-schooner ride," Dirk was saying
casually.

The word schooner leaped out at Andrea, and she
wondered at his suggesting such a thing. She and
Johanna had touched on the subject of water and

boats earlier, but to suggest she take a trip on a schooner....

Johanna said excitedly, "Will you go, Andi? Will you?"

Andrea, not sure she'd ever been invited, looked across at Dirk uncertainly, and he smiled encouragement. "I think you'd enjoy it."

"Uncle Dirk's been promising," Johanna went on, putting her dolls aside and sitting up. "But all summer he was so busy with things."

"It will be even better now that it's cooler," Dirk said. "And on a day like this the colors should be terrific. Will you come along with us, Andrea?"

"Yes," she said. "Yes, I'd like to very much." And she was rewarded by Johanna's crow of delight.

Johanna, her "tummy ache"—whether real or mythical—forgotten, slid off the bed and, without even being asked to do so, went into the adjoining bathroom and washed her face and hands in preparation for lunch.

It was a pleasant luncheon. They had chilled cucumber soup, sandwiches, iced tea and a delicious blueberry cobbler for dessert. Although Mrs. Van Der Maas still seemed preoccupied, her pleasure was genuine when she heard about the forthcoming expedition to Saugatuck. Dirk, too, seemed to be in a very good mood, again puzzling Andrea... as he had so many times before.

Lunch over, she, Dirk and Johanna started out,

Johanna sliding into her customary place in the back of the Mercedes. She'd brought one of her dolls along with her, the boy doll Andrea remembered. He was a Dutch boy, dressed in an authentic costume right down to the miniature wooden *klompen*. He looked disconcertingly like Dirk, except that his hair was blond, rather than that almost golden, nut-brown shade, and he made Andrea think of Dirk as he must have been as a little boy. She wondered if he'd dressed in a costume like this for special occasions, such as the opening of the Tulip Time festival. If so, what a little Dutch delight he must have been!

A Dutch delight. The phrase lingered, and she turned it over, appraising it. A Dutch delight! Dutch delights! It was an incongruous time in which finally to be able to give thought to the upcoming Van Der Maas advertising campaign, but she liked the ring of the phrase and filed it away in her memory for subsequent study.

Saugatuck was just a few miles down the road, and during the course of the drive Andrea exerted all her willpower, forcing herself to put aside her perplexed thoughts about Dirk, her concerns about Johanna, her curiosity about Klaus and anything at all to do with business. She concentrated on the beauty of the day and . . . just being there.

When they reached the station from which the dune schooners departed, she discovered promptly that she was not going for a boat ride after all. The dune schooners were specially constructed vehicles made for rugged overland driving. They were strictly "open air" and looked like combinations of Land Rover four-wheel-drive vehicles and pickup trucks, and each could accommodate upward of two dozen persons.

At this time of the year business was slacking off, so there were only a dozen or so on the trip Dirk had booked for them, two of them children about Johanna's age. Johanna was delighted when these two elected to share a seat with Dirk, Andrea and herself.

They roamed over the giant sand dunes that edged Lake Michigan in this part of the state, and it was an exciting and spectacular safari. Some of the dunes seemed incredibly steep to Andrea, and she felt as if she was riding on a roller coaster. A couple of times she squealed aloud. Sometimes they'd come out on top of a dune and the views were fantastic...sparkling blue water, stubby green pines, then vast expanses of beautiful beige sand.

"I feel as if I could be in the Sahara," Andrea whispered at one point, when they seemed engulfed by sand.

There was a wonderfully wild and natural beauty to this whole area, and the climax was reached for Johanna when a deer followed by two babies darted across in front of them, to disappear into a thicket of pines on the far side of the sandy trail.

"I should have brought a camera," Dirk said regretfully. "I'd have liked to have caught the expression on Johanna's face."

Johanna, chatting away with the two children sitting next to her, didn't hear his comment, and he went on under his breath, "Sometimes she seems so normal."

"She is normal," Andrea returned softly. "And very close, I think, to getting over all her fears."

She could feel Dirk's eyes on her, but when she looked up at him the sunlight was glinting off his glasses, making his expression difficult to read.

"You really care about her, don't you?" he asked, his voice husky.

"Very much," Andrea told him, her own voice not entirely steady. He'd reached across to take her hand, and there was something so comforting about having her hand held by him. This, she thought wistfully, was what it must be like to feel safe and loved.

If only I were his love! The hopelessness of the wish brought pain and a small visible grimace.

"What is it, my sweet?" Dirk asked quickly, and Andrea shook her head, sure that her ears must be deceiving her. Then, to her horror, tears brimmed, and she reached frantically in her small tote bag for a handkerchief.

"Andrea!" Dirk began urgently, but she shushed him angrily with a warning glance in Johanna's direction, and he subsided, frowning.

The dune-buggy ride lasted about an hour, and

despite her brief lapse Andrea enjoyed it thoroughly. Johanna was ecstatic, promptly asking if they could come back the next Sunday, a question to which Dirk gave a cautious response.

On the way back to Holland, Dirk stopped at a specialty ice-cream stand where they all indulged in giant Oreo-flavored cones. This topped the day off for Johanna, and there was no doubting the little girl's happiness. Once they were home, when her grandmother reminded her gently that she had some homework to do for school the next day, she made no protest at all.

"Remarkable," Mrs. Van Der Maas observed, as Johanna obediently trotted toward the stairs to go up and get her schoolbooks. "She isn't usually so compliant about doing homework, especially when it involves math!"

They were in the family room, and Dirk was making them daiquiris.

"Later," he promised, "I'll conjure up some omelets."

Andrea was standing at the window wall overlooking the terrace while he was speaking, not far from the bar where he was mixing their drinks. She was watching the sun making its nightly pilgrimage through the evening sky, painting Lake Macatawa in the process with beautifully glowing colors.

She grinned at his comment about making omelets and could not resist the tiny thrust. "You can cook too!" she teased.

His beautifully arched eyebrows rose, clearing the rims of his glasses, and he said in a significant undertone, "Later, I may ask for an elaboration about that 'too.'"

She felt herself flushing. She knew that her cheeks must be turning red, and there was no chance of camouflaging them. Dirk's chuckle was low and decidedly wicked, and when she looked at him again, his eyes shone with a gleam of amusement.

It took a quick reassembling of her own inherent poise to calmly accept the daiquiri from him. It was smooth, delicious, and went down very well. It would be easy to drink too much of something that tasted so good, she warned herself, and that would not be the thing to do tonight, given her already mellow mood.

Johanna came back with her homework and curled up on the couch alongside her grandmother, and Andrea noted that although Mrs. Van Der Maas was willing to help Johanna, she first made the child figure out as much as she could by herself.

Dirk, glass in hand, asked, "Want to stroll down to the lake and watch the sunset?"

He was referring to Macatawa rather than Michigan, she knew, but even though this involved a relatively short distance she was almost afraid to walk with him, honestly shaken at the thought of being alone with him. Her emotions were running perilously close to the surface. All he'd have to do was look at her. . . .

"Andrea?" he prodded gently.

"Yes," she said quickly, and followed him out onto the terrace.

They descended the steps side by side, walking around the swimming pool and on down the flower-bordered path that led to the lake. There was a faint breeze, just enough to cause the boats at anchor to bob slightly. Watching them, Andrea was especially aware of the vacant space by Dirk's dock where in earlier years there would have been a sleek sailing yacht tied up.

Maybe one day there will be again, she thought optimistically. *Johanna's getting over her fears. I'm sure she's getting over them!*

They walked out onto the dock and stood sipping their drinks, and Andrea felt as if she were being washed by the glorious sunset colors, as if the colors, the drink and everything else were going to her head. . . especially the tall attractive man at her side.

"About this morning. . ." he began.

The glow faded. She wasn't ready to go back to the morning, she didn't want to hear anything else about. . . about. . . .

"Andrea," he said gently, but so definitely that she was forced to turn and look up at him.

"What I want to say about this morning," he told her steadily, "is that I was an idiot. I don't

know what in hell made me blurt out something
so... extremely stupid.''

"Your subconscious, maybe?" she suggested.

"No," he contradicted her emphatically.
"Look," he went on, "I don't know what Mark
or...or anyone else has told you about me,
but...."

Anyone else. By that he almost surely meant Klaus.

"Not knowing," he continued, after a moment,
"puts me at a disadvantage."

"Yes, I can see that," she allowed.

His smile was bitter. "I wish I'd had the opportunity to tell you my life story myself before you
heard it from anyone else. And I can tell by your expression that you've been fully filled in on my
past." He sighed. "My problem is that confession
isn't something that comes naturally to me. What I
wish...."

"Yes?"

She could sense his struggle to find the right
words. In the meantime she tried to prepare herself
for whatever they might be. She was not at all sure
she could cope if he got on to the subject of Marietta. She was not sure she could bear to hear him
speak of his feelings for another woman, even
though that woman was dead.

"What I wish," he said slowly, "is that we could
let the past be past. I wish we could close the door
on the day before I met you and take it all from
there.

"What I'm trying to say," he went on, only too aware of the uncertainty mirrored on her face, "is that I don't want to go back, where you're concerned, Andrea. I don't want to remember anything that was. Above all else I don't want to make comparisons...."

She stiffened. He didn't want to make comparisons! Was he afraid to compare her to Marietta? Was he afraid that he would find her lacking? How could she ever hope to measure up to the true love of his life? And she was not prepared to take second best.

Dirk was watching her closely, and she was not about to meet those discerning eyes. She forced herself to concentrate on the sunset. The sunset was so beautiful! How could a world so essentially imperfect go on presenting a perfect spectacle like this day after day after day?

"I don't think you're hearing me," Dirk said finally.

She found her voice. "Oh yes, I'm hearing you," she retorted wryly. "I know what you're saying. But you're asking the impossible, Dirk. There's no way to close the door on yesterday, because yesterday is a part of what we're made of, just as today is and as tomorrow will be. You don't need me to tell you that."

There was a long silence between them. Then he said reluctantly, "No, I don't need you to tell me that. You're right, of course."

After a moment he added heavily, "If I'm going to make dinner, we'd better get back to the house."

ANDREA SET THE TABLE and tossed a salad and got out wineglasses and some chilled chablis. Under other circumstances there would have been joy to all of this, a bliss, in fact, in lighting the candles on the Van Der Maases' dining-room table and sharing this intimate Sunday-night supper with Dirk and his family.

The omelets he made were as delicious as the daiquiris had been, but it was all she could do to eat even a portion of hers.

They hadn't quite finished their supper when the phone rang and Dirk went to answer it. He looked tired and disgruntled when he returned to tell them that the night shift had run into a problem at the bakery, and he'd have to go over.

His mother muttered something impatiently, but Dirk turned her protest aside.

"Sorry not to help out with the dish washing," he said lightly, then kissed his mother briefly on the forehead, gazing, as he did so, toward Andrea.

"Good night," she replied, hating to have their day end like this.

Johanna was permitted to watch one television program before going to bed. While she did so, Andrea and Mrs. Van Der Maas tidied up the few dishes, Andrea washing while Monica did the drying, then put the things away.

"Dirk must do something about turning over some of his responsibilities to others," Mrs. Van Der Maas said as she worked, almost echoing words she'd used to Andrea previously.

"I should think he'd realize that," Andrea agreed, a bit tautly.

"I don't know," his mother said sadly. "He's become a workaholic, and I can only see the situation getting worse instead of better once the frozen-foods division is in operation." She was standing at the stove as she spoke. "There's still some coffee in the pot. Will you join me in a glass of iced coffee?"

"Yes, please," Andrea said, scrubbing out the pan in which Dirk had made the omelets and turning it upside down on a rack to dry.

Mrs. Van Der Maas fixed their coffee and took it over to the big, round kitchen table, where Andrea joined her. There was an intimacy to sitting there in the kitchen together, and it was not surprising when Mrs. Van Der Maas began to talk about Dirk. "Dirk has taken entirely too much on himself, I'm sure I've said that to you before. A problem is that he's laid so much guilt on himself in the process. Dirk should never have come home when he did."

"But he had to, didn't he?" Andrea blurted. "I mean...Mark mentioned that your husband had suffered a very bad accident and...."

"That's right, he did," Mrs. Van Der Maas said. "Perhaps your mutual friend Mark has also told you that Dirk was with an architectural firm in New York when it happened, and he had a brilliant future ahead of him?''

"Yes," Andrea admitted.

"My son Gerrit—Dirk's twin brother—had majored in business administration at the University of Michigan, and he'd been out of college for quite a while when my husband met with his accident. Gerrit was working in the bakery offices. My husband was grooming him to eventually take over, as a matter of fact.''

Mrs. Van Der Maas nodded. "Gerrit and Dirk were not at all alike," she said flatly. "Dirk was the brighter of the two, there was no doubt of it. We'd also always fostered the thought that he was the older...by all of five minutes," she admitted bitterly. "The time came, believe me, when I wished I'd never mentioned that! Incredible though it may seem, Dirk took it seriously...probably because he'd been encouraged to be the leader, where the two boys were concerned, all his life.

"When his father was injured, Dirk took a leave of absence from his firm in New York so that he could be here with me," Mrs. Van Der Maas said. "In the early days we were not sure my husband was going to live. Then, once he was out of danger, we knew the recovery period was going to be long and hard and, eventually, we learned there was no hope of a full recovery. Peter had to be told that he'd be in a wheelchair for the rest of his life...and he was not a man who could tolerate that kind of confinement. And so, as you may know, he put an end to his own life.''

Andrea shuddered. When she'd been standing out on the dock with Dirk watching the sunset, she'd forgotten that that very spot must be the one where his father had chosen to meet death.

What a terrible memory for Dirk! How many terrible memories he must have!

''We'd all hoped Peter would be able to go back to the bakery,'' Mrs. Van Der Maas continued, ''that his business would occupy him again so that he could. . . well, live with his own infirmity. I think I knew better than anyone else that he could never accept it. By the time of his death, though, it was Dirk who had taken over, and what had started out as a temporary solution to a problem became permanent.

''Gerrit resented it terribly, though few people realized that. Gerrit covered things up well, but I can see now that he'd always resented Dirk. . . over the years he'd tried to get even with him in so many ways. Did your friend Mark tell you that Johanna's mother was Dirk's childhood sweetheart, and that their wedding date had been set at the time my husband met with his accident in the mill?''

''Yes,'' Andrea admitted reluctantly, wondering if it was going to seem to Mrs. Van Der Maas as if she and Mark had done a great deal of gossiping about Dirk.

"In due course Gerrit laid another guilt trip on Dirk," his mother said now. "Dirk has always been generous with anything he owned, and Gerrit used his boat more than Dirk did. Gerrit, of course, should not have taken Marietta and Johanna out sailing on an afternoon when there were storm warnings posted, especially since Marietta was a very poor swimmer. Ever since, Dirk has felt he should have been able to stop their going, and he's wrong, of course. But it has been impossible to convince him so.

"I think he also knows, now, that he should have gone back to New York and let Gerrit take over the bakery," Mrs. Van Der Maas added. "I would have worked with him, and between the two of us we would have kept things going. Gerrit did not have Dirk's flare or his imagination. If he were at the helm, we would not be in the throes of an expansion that Dirk hopes will make Van Der Maas nationally known. But there would have been enough for everyone."

What could she possibly say to all this, Andrea thought, but Mrs. Van Der Maas made it plain that she didn't expect her to reply. She rose slowly, carrying her empty glass to the sink.

"Thank you for listening, Andrea," she said. "I don't usually unburden myself in this way."

Andrea could believe that. She was discovering many similarities in nature and character between Dirk and his mother.

Monica Van Der Maas flashed her a smile that was also reminiscent of Dirk. Then she said, to Andrea's surprise, "Don't give up on him, my dear."

CHAPTER FOURTEEN

THE CHANGES THAT HAD TAKEN PLACE at the Van
Der Maas bakery in less than five months were
startling. The new building that would house the
frozen-foods division had been translated from
Dirk's architectural rendering to near reality, and
the neighborhood transformation it had already ef-
fected was startling.

Andrea, having been shown over the site by Dirk,
said, "You're going to upgrade the whole area!"

He nodded. "That's what I hope will happen. I'd
like to see our buildings spur a revitalization around
here. For example, I'd like to see the vacant lots
cleaned up and converted into miniparks. That's
what we intend to do with some of our own adjoining land. I see no point in leaving ugliness where
there could be beauty, even temporarily. What I
mean by that is that we have to keep in mind the
thought we may need to use the land at some future
point for further expansion. But there is no reason
for it not to be enjoyed both visually and actually
until—if—that happens."

As she listened to him, Andrea was looking toward the front of the bakery. The office addition Dirk had pointed out to her that day in May when he'd shown her his sketches was now going up. She could visualize the way it was going to look when it was finished, now, something she hadn't been able to do then. She felt a surge of admiration toward Dirk. His ideas were bold in concept, functional, yet beautiful at the same time. Though she still veered toward the traditional in architecture, she had to admit that Dirk Van Der Maas made the contemporary singularly attractive.

He took her by the arm and said, "Come on. We have to use a side entrance because of the office-unit construction."

They entered on the bakery side of the building, circumventing the core of the bakery as they went around an outside corridor. As they stepped through the connecting door into the small reception area, Andrea was forcibly reminded of the first time she'd ever come to the bakery, the first time she'd met Dirk.

She'd felt herself up against a man made of stone. Sometimes she still did. But in those relatively short intervals over the past few months when she'd been with him, Dirk had also shown many other sides to his nature. He still puzzled her more than anyone she'd ever met. She wished, wished to the depths of her being, that this was a puzzle she could one day be sure of solving.

At her side he was saying, "Hi there, Gretel." He

was addressing the receptionist, a different woman from the one who'd been at the desk last May. Then his voice changed slightly as he said formally, "Van der Houten."

Andrea glanced up to see the production manager standing by the receptionist's desk, and she caught an odd expression in the man's deep blue eyes.

"Dirk," he said, equally formal as he nodded to his employer. And then, "Miss Campbell. Nice to see you again."

She sensed Dirk's surprise at the man's greeting. But then it had been Klaus, rather than Dirk, who had shown her through the bakery last spring.

"How are you, Mr. van der Houten?" she said.

"Fine, thank you. Am I going to have the pleasure of showing you around again?"

"I don't think so...not today, that is," she said with a smile.

Dirk had been speaking in a low tone to the receptionist, but now he turned away from the desk. "I'd like to see you later, Jan," he told the production manager. "Maybe around midafternoon. Give the office a call first to be sure I'm free."

Van der Houten nodded, but his eyes lingered on Andrea and she had the strange feeling that he wanted to tell her something. In fact she thought he was about to speak, but then his mouth tightened and he nodded and went back into the bakery through the door they'd just used.

Dirk, Andrea was sure, had been unaware of this

brief interchange of glances between his production manager and herself, which was just as well. But the memory stayed with her as she walked up the long flight of stairs to the executive offices. Her curiosity was provoked. There'd been something disturbing about the expression on Jan van der Houten's face. But why should anything that was bothering him concern her?

Evelyn Bleeker was at her desk. She was very friendly as she greeted Andrea. Dirk, leading the way to his inner office, said over his shoulder, "Hold all calls for the next hour, will you, Evelyn? Andrea, would you like coffee?"

"Not just yet, thanks," she told him.

"Maybe about an hour from now you could get us some coffee," he suggested to his secretary, and she agreed with a smile. Andrea suspected that she'd agree to anything Dirk said.

She noticed at once that Dirk's office was as stark as ever, and the observation left a sense of disappointment. She didn't know what she'd expected to find as far as Dirk's private office was concerned. Now she realized she'd been hopeful that he had made a few changes, maybe added a few personal touches that would make the setting less bleak. This would have been a visible indication that he had softened a little, mellowed a little.

As it was, when he sat down behind that almost-barren desk, he seemed so much the way he had

been the first day she'd met him that it would have
been easy to imagine they were back in May.

He was wearing a dark-blue suit with a white shirt
and a conservative tie striped in tones of blue and
dark red. The suit was exquisitely tailored, as were
all his clothes, and it could not have fit more perfectly. But it made him look even more austere than
he usually did.

He could be the model for a magazine cover featuring the Young Executive of the Year, Andrea
thought, and the perverse stirred in her. She
yearned to rumple that smoothly coiffed nut-brown
hair, to take off his glasses so that she could see
deep into those eyes, to bring a flush to his cheeks
and to... to make love to him.

The force of her need for Dirk was a shock. Unable to resist glancing at him, she surprised an extremely aware look in his eyes. She turned away,
annoyed at herself because all of those resolutions
she'd framed so carefully before leaving Boston
seemed to have taken wing. She'd come back to
Holland so determined to live up to her own philosophy about client relationships. She'd convinced
herself that she'd be able to handle this insidious attraction Dirk had for her with no particular effort.
And so far she'd been stumbling every step of the
way.

Dirk reached into a desk drawer and pulled out
two folders, one of which he handed to her.

"Preliminary thoughts about my advertising

budget, just what it is I'd like to accomplish, and so on," he told her. "I think this is something you might prefer to go over by yourself, first time around, and then you and I can get together and talk about it."

"All right," she agreed.

"I haven't yet determined a launch date for the advertising," he went on. "It depends in part, of course, on whether the construction stays on schedule. We're somewhat ahead of schedule at the moment, but before we start advertising, I want us to be in production. Not full production, but right at the edge of it."

Andrea nodded. Ever since she'd seen Johanna's Dutch-boy doll her thoughts had been stirring, and now she said, "How about a launch date that ties in with the opening of the Tulip Time festival?"

Dirk's smile was skeptical. "I don't delude myself that our Holland festival is so world-shaking it reverberates around the globe. What would the advantage be?"

"It could be considerable, in my opinion," she said rather tartly, feeling that in a quiet way he'd just put her down. "I think we could sell national TV on the idea of giving the street scrubbing and the *klompen* dancing some play. Some shots on news programs, perhaps, but maybe they'd go a step further if we lay our groundwork right. I can picture a segment on one of a number of national programs devoted to Holland and the festival."

"I give you points for optimism," he said, picking up the gold pen that was the single loose thing on his desk top aside from the leather appointment pad and rolling it between his long slender fingers.

"And I say if you don't have faith in what you have to sell, you're never going to make it in the market," she returned somewhat hotly.

"The old nothing-ventured, nothing-gained concept, right?" he challenged.

"Right!"

He flung the pen down on the desk and said, "Okay. I'll go with the opening of the Tulip Time festival. I can see no problem right now, as far as being ready is concerned. I take it your intention is to see that Holland gets into national focus with Tulip Time, and then maybe to back up with a Van-Der-Maas-bakery spot?"

"You're getting there," Andrea ventured, and was relieved when Dirk grinned at her.

"We Dutch are not so slow," he teased.

Andrea, wishing that her face wasn't quite such a giveaway, tried to muster all her professional aplomb as she said, "About Tulip Time. . . ."

She was unable to resist looking at him as she spoke and she saw that there was nothing at all cold about those very light-blue eyes at this moment. He was leaning back in his chair, and as she watched he loosened his tie, and there was something endearingly casual about the action.

"I was about to strangle," he explained. "Yes. . .

you were going to say something about Tulip Time?"

"Holland is identified with Tulip Time," Andrea said, "and I think we should capitalize on that fact. I think the logo should feature a tulip...a rather stylized tulip. I'd like it to be a bright red tulip, a really clear, vivid shade, against an opaque white background. The tulip should be surrounded by a circle, and I see the circle being bordered in a bright blue. That same shade of blue will be used for the slogan, which will curve around the inside of the circle...."

Dirk was reaching into a desk drawer again, and he brought out a pad of paper and a drawing pencil. As she watched, he sketched swiftly, then held the pad out to her.

"Like this?" he suggested.

He'd captured her concept so quickly and so perfectly that Andrea was staggered. "You're quite an artist," she stammered.

"Most architects—even ex-architects—have a certain amount of drawing skill," he told her. He gestured toward the sketch he'd made. "Is this something like what you have in mind?"

"Very much so," she said, nodding. "I visualize the colors as being very simple, pure and bright. They will stand out—as will the opaque white background—against any sort of wrapping on a bakery product, even clear plastic."

"Excellent thought," Dirk complimented.

"The red tulip will be quickly identifiable. And the name Van Der Maas is not only pleasant sounding, but very Dutch...."

"Isn't it, though?" Dirk remarked with a grin.

She ignored his comment. "I think it will catch on," she said. "As for the slogan itself, I've been mulling around with the phrase 'Dutch delights.'"

"Van Der Maas's Dutch Delights?" he offered.

"No, I don't think so. It's too hard to say." She paused. "Maybe," she said slowly, "Dutch Delights by Van Der Maas." She repeated this, holding on to each syllable as she did so, then nodded with satisfaction. "Yes, I think that's it. Dutch Delights by Van Der Maas."

"I like it," Dirk approved. "The word 'delights' could cover the whole gamut, as far as products go. It doesn't limit the thought to cakes or pies or any specific items. Matter of fact, if we wanted to go into the souvenir business one day we could put out mini windmills and wooden shoes and all sorts of things and call them 'Dutch Delights.'"

"Dirk!" she protested.

He laughed. "Just trying it on for size." Then sobering, he added, "I like your thoughts, Andrea. I can visualize this, I can see it working out."

"We can go 'Dutch' on your TV commercials," she told him. "I think we should go for authentic local scenes, though. Maybe a girl in costume with De Zwaan in the background. Maybe, for a complete contrast, a scene with some people in one of the dune schooners holding up Van Der Maas bakery products. There are a lot of possibilities. I just want to be sure that we don't become cliché 'Dutch,' if you know what I mean. That's one reason why I like the red, white and blue colors for the logo. It gives an American as well as a Dutch connotation.''

He smiled. ''The Netherlands flag is also red, white and blue,'' he told her.

''I didn't know that,'' she admitted, chagrined.

''Well, don't look so crestfallen,'' he said. ''No one would expect you to. Holland's flag, though, has three broad horizontal stripes. The top one is red, the middle one white, and the bottom one blue, but a lighter shade of blue than that of the background for the stars on our flag. You're quite right when you say that, generally speaking, using red, white and blue on the logo will blend an American emphasis with the Dutch, and I like that concept. For those who do know the colors of the Dutch flag, we'll score twice. It's a nice touch to think that we can unite the two nationalities by their use of the same colors on their flags.''

Dirk stretched. ''I think we're coming along very well. Incidentally, I was sorry to have to walk out on you last night.''

''Quite all right,'' she said politely. ''Was there much of a problem?''

''No. It was a personal matter that was easily solved. A case of ruffled feelings.''

"You do get called out for all sorts of things, don't you?"

"What makes you say that?"

"The first time I came here you'd been called away from the office for a problem concerning the yeast, if I remember rightly," she told him.

"You remember rightly," he said, surprised. "And that was quite a problem. We were trying out a new supplier for our yeast and we got a bad batch. Whew, but you've got a memory!"

"It was rather unusual," she replied, "so...it stuck with me, that's all."

He picked up the gold pen again and studied it as if he was seeing it for the first time. Then he asked, unexpectedly, "Ever want to play hooky?"

She was startled. "What?"

"When you were a kid, didn't you ever play hooky from school?" Dirk asked her, then confessed, engagingly, "I did. I remember once my parents found out, and they were so dumbfounded they didn't know how to deal with me. They thought it was completely out of type for me. Gerrit—my twin brother—was the one who usually did things like that. Sometimes I see a streak of him in Johanna. But I was the serious student, the one who always did his homework without having to be pushed.

"So when I cut out it was a shock to everyone concerned," Dirk added with a smile that tore at her heartstrings. "I haven't felt like cutting out for years, but I do right now. Today. I'd like to play hooky with you. I'd like to go off someplace where no one would find us.''

Andrea stared at him. Was this Dirk? She was in the process of discovering yet another facet of his character, and she wondered how many-sided one person could be?

Dirk flashed her a wry grin. "Don't worry," he assured her. "I know it's impossible. At least it's impossible today.'' He glanced at his slim gold wristwatch. "I have an appointment with the contractor in an hour, and one thing after another on the agenda after that. But believe me, Miss Andrea Campbell, it's not a notion I'm discarding. I may have to put it on the back shelf temporarily, but one of these days I'll put it out again and take action!''

She laughed. "Is that a threat or a promise?''

"Which would you like it to be?''

She took the plunge. "I think,'' she said, "I'd like it to be...a promise.'' She saw something flash in those eyes that she couldn't quite decipher. Triumph?

With an effort she brought her thoughts back to business. "Where do we go from here, Dirk?'' she asked him. "About the advertising campaign, I mean,'' she added quickly.

"When you went back to Boston last spring, I gave you a few of our products, with the recipes for them,'' he reminded her.

She nodded. "Yes.''

"You'll be meeting the people involved with our products," he said. "Once the new plant is in operation we're going to have some impressive test kitchens, laboratories, a complete research-and-development staff. I've spent a fair bit of my time for the past year scouting out the right people for these jobs. Meanwhile we have some very capable people on our staff who've been with us for years, and they've taken the first steps in selecting heirloom Dutch recipes that can be adapted for mass production and will lend themselves well to freezing. I think the more you know about every phase of our operations and the products we intend to put out in the frozen-foods division, the better. Your own ideas will spring from what you see and what you hear."

"True," Andrea said, but she said it cautiously. From what he'd just told her she could envision a series of interviews with plant employees involving those already on the scene and those who'd be arriving as the frozen-food plant neared completion. To do what Dirk was asking of her obviously would require her presence there for quite some time.

When she'd flown back to Holland the previous week there had been no specifics given her about how long she'd be staying. Now she quickly tabulated the time that remained until the campaign would be launched with the beginning of the Tulip Time festival.

Nearly eight months! There was no way she could

stay away from Boston for anything like that length of time. She had other accounts that were in capable hands for the moment, but she didn't want to rely on others to carry her work load any longer than was strictly necessary. Andrea had put a great deal into every account she'd ever handled. She had given lavishly of her own time and attention, and thus far she'd never had a dissatisfied client. She wanted to keep her record that way.

"Dirk," she said, "we'll have to map out a time schedule. I'll want to start as soon as possible to talk to the people who are on the scene now and will be involved in the frozen-food division. Then, once you've gotten your full staff together, I can come back and take it from there."

"Come back?"

"Yes."

"I thought it was understood that you'd be spending most of your time here between now and the launch date for the campaign."

"That won't be necessary," she answered. "I can cover everything locally within the next week or so, I'd think. If I need any specific details, I'm sure I could get them on the phone, from Boston. If there were something of sufficient importance to fill in, I could always fly back for a couple of days. I think, for that matter, we can certainly go with what I'll be able to get right here, now, for openers. That will give me new territory to explore with your people for our next wave of copy."

Dirk's face was expressionless as he looked across at her, and when she saw this, her heart sank. His tone was aloof, as aloof as it had been the first time she met him, when he said, "That's not the way I see it, Andrea."

"Then just how do you see it?"

"I can't expect this project to be as important to you as it is to me," he said coldly. "But when I agreed to let Saunders and Terrence handle my account it was with the understanding that the executive in whose hands they placed it would give it undivided attention for as long as necessary."

"That's exactly what I plan to do," Andrea pointed out, her need to keep a tight rein on her patience mounting. "I will have everything I need to start work with by the time I leave here. As I've said, if anything else is necessary I can fly back for a conference, or perhaps you might wish to make a trip East yourself."

"Not necessarily," he said, infuriatingly.

"Dirk, really, you're being very stubborn about this."

"I don't agree," he said stiffly.

"Come on!" she protested. "Look, you can't seriously expect me to stay in Holland for the next eight months!"

Only a slight twist of his lips betrayed any emotion. "Would it be that difficult for you to stay here for eight months?" he asked her.

"No, it wouldn't be difficult at all," she sputtered before she realized that she had, in a sense, fallen into a trap with her answer. Hastily she plowed ahead. "This isn't a question of my personal feelings," she said. "I have a job to do, and my office is in Boston. I frequently go out in the field to consult with clients, but it's understood that the main volume of my work must be accomplished in Boston, where I have all the facilities with which to do it."

"What facilities?" he asked abruptly.

"My own office, my own secretary, my own things!"

"All of which could be provided to you here—with the exception of the 'things,' perhaps," he said, his tone laced with irony.

She glared at him. "You do know you're being unreasonable, don't you?" she challenged.

He didn't answer her. Instead, he switched on the desk intercom and leaned forward to speak into it.

"Bring in the coffee, will you please, Evelyn?" he asked his secretary.

They were both silent until Evelyn Bleeker appeared with a tray on which there was not only coffee but a plate of cookies.

"*Stroop Koejes,*" she said. "Fresh from the oven. They sent them over so you could try them, Dirk."

"Thanks," he said absently. "Keep holding the calls a while longer, will you, Evelyn?"

She nodded, but warned, "You're going to have quite a few to answer."

"That's okay," he replied, nodding. "I'll get to them later."

With Mrs. Bleeker gone, he poured out the coffee, then offered the plate of cookies to Andrea. They were a rich brown in color and absolutely delicious, she discovered, once she'd taken a bite.

"*Stroop Koejes* translates as syrup cookies," Dirk told her. "I suppose that sounds as if these are made with maple or some other kind of syrup, but actually it's molasses that is used. I think we should use the original Dutch names for the cookies. Of course there will be the usual list of ingredients on the label for those who want to check."

"You're right," she agreed. "The Dutch names are colorful. They definitely enhance the products. But we want to be sure to translate sufficiently so people know what they're buying. A lot of that can be done through the advertising."

A thought struck her. "Incidentally," she began, "there's one thing I should take care of immediately."

"Oh? And what might that be?" he asked.

"I need to rent a car." She'd driven to the bakery with Dirk that morning and hadn't thought about needing further transportation later.

He frowned. "Is there someplace you want to go?" he asked.

"Well...yes," she said. "Back to your house,

eventually, for one thing, probably long before you'll be ready to leave here. You said you have a day-long conference ahead of you.''

''You can use the Mercedes.''

She hesitated. ''I'd rather not, Dirk. You need to have your own car available, after all. And....''

''If I need a car, I can use one of the bakery ones,'' he told her shortly. ''We keep several cars to be used both by company executives and our salesmen.''

He reached in a pocket and brought out a key chain, tossing it across to her. ''Be my guest,'' he invited.

''Dirk, I'd rather...'' she began.

''Andrea, do you have to argue about everything?'' he asked impatiently. ''And do you have to go to constant lengths to prove your independence? I know you're perfectly capable of renting a car, if that's what you insist on doing, but it seems stupid when the Mercedes will just be sitting out on the lot all day. Go where you wish, do what you want with it. I can use a company car to get home in.''

''Very well,'' she said somewhat ungraciously, knowing that it would be both easier and wiser to give in to Dirk. She'd have enough arguing to do, she told herself, once they got back on to the subject of how much time she was going to be spending in Holland.

CHAPTER FIFTEEN

ANDREA WAS ON HER WAY OUT of the bakery building when she heard someone calling her name.

"Miss Campbell?" It was the receptionist. She'd propped the door that led into the stairwell open and evidently had been on the alert for sounds of anyone descending.

Had Dirk called to give instructions that she should return to his office? Andrea hoped not. Just now she didn't want to get into any further discussion about her schedule over the next eight months.

The receptionist glanced upstairs, as if verifying that Andrea had come down by herself, and then said in a near whisper, "Mr. van der Houten asked me to stop you. . .if you were alone, that is."

Mystified, Andrea repeated, "Mr. van der Houten?"

"Yes. He's in his office. You go into the bakery section and take the first corridor on the right, and it's the second door on the left."

"He wants me to come to his office?" Andrea asked, puzzled.

"He said he'd appreciate it if you would, and he

asked you not to say anything to anyone until you've talked to him.''

Andrea glanced at her wristwatch. It was just after eleven, and she had no prescribed place to go and nothing urgent to do for the balance of the day. Dirk had said he would set up some appointments for her with his employees starting the following morning. He hadn't mentioned having lunch, so at the moment she was very much on her own.

She nodded briefly to the receptionist and opened the door that divided the bakery from the offices. She found Jan van der Houten's office without difficulty, especially since the man himself was waiting in the doorway for her.

''Miss Campbell.'' He drew her inside hastily and closed the door, while she stared at him in bewilderment. Only then did he relax. He took the chair behind a battered old oak desk and motioned to her to sit down on the only other chair in the room, a straight-backed one.

''Gretel called and told me you were on your way,'' he said. ''Thanks for coming.''

''You're quite welcome, Mr. van der Houten,'' she told him. ''I don't understand the apparent secrecy over this visit, though.''

''You will,'' he promised. ''You see, Klaus told me you'd be coming back to Holland shortly, and he asked me to try to contact you. He wants very much to talk to you.''

Andrea frowned, every nerve in her body suddenly vibrant and apprehensive. "Where is Klaus?" she demanded.

The production manager hesitated, then sighed and said, "At my house. And that would be worth my job if you let it get back to Van Der Maas."

He was referring to Dirk, she knew, and the knowledge only caused her apprehension to mount. What had happened between Dirk and Klaus that required this kind of back-alley dealing?

"Van Der Maas kicked Klaus out two weeks ago," Jan van der Houten told her bitterly. "Just a couple of days after he got out of the hospital. The kid still has his leg in a cast. He's still on crutches. When he showed up on my doorstep, I couldn't turn him away, Miss Campbell. I've known Klaus since he was a little kid."

Andrea swallowed hard. Then she said, "You're going to have to fill me in, Mr. van der Houten. I have no idea what happened to Klaus that caused him to wind up with a leg in a cast—"

She broke off, remembering what Johanna had told her about her Uncle Klaus having had an accident. But after thinking it over she'd concluded it must have been an accident that had happened a long time ago. Well...she'd been wrong.

Jan van der Houten said slowly, "I don't enjoy telling tales out of school. I think very highly of Dirk. I want you to know that before I say anything else. Also, he's my boss, and I'm loyal to him, Miss

Campbell, when it comes to most things. But in this case...."

"Yes?"

He shook his head. "This is harder than I thought it would be." He gave her an abashed grin, and Andrea felt a stirring of empathy for him. He was a pleasant, straightforward man, the kind of man, she imagined, who would like to keep the peace, who would hate dissension.

She posed a direct question. "What did Klaus do that was so terrible, Mr. van der Houten."

"One thing too many, I'd say," he told her ruefully, "which is what makes it so tough. Klaus is so much younger than Dirk. Fifteen years. It's a big gap. Dirk was out of college by the time Klaus was in elementary school. Later Gerrit was home, but he always led his own life anyway. He and Klaus had even less in common than Klaus and Dirk. Then Mr. Van Der Maas died." Andrea realized the production manager must be referring to Dirk's father when he said this. "By then Dirk had come back here and he took over. He had his hands full, he didn't have time to supervise a kid. And Mrs. Van Der Maas, for all she's one of the smartest ladies I've ever known, never has been able to keep Klaus in line."

Jan van der Houten sighed. "I know how that goes. My wife's dotty over our youngest. I keep thinking of Klaus, and I tell her she'll spoil the kid to death if she isn't careful, but I might as well talk to the wall. She was never like that with the three older ones.

"Anyway...Klaus has always been wild, and everyone in Holland knows who the Van Der Maases are, which has only made it harder on the family. Klaus was arrested for smoking pot when he was in high school, and I thought his mother was going to have a heart attack. Then he was arrested for driving under the influence of alcohol. He came out with a suspended sentence on that one, thanks to Mrs. Van Der Maas talking the family lawyer into handling the case. Klaus has always had brushes with the law, not because he's a bad kid, understand, but just because he lacked... hell, I don't know how to put it...direction, maybe."

Andrea nodded.

"A couple of times he's cracked up one of the family cars. Then he got his own jalopy. . . .''

Andrea remembered the venerable hardtop Klaus had been driving when she met him.

"Well, a month ago he was in a bad smash. He crashed into a tree a few miles out of town. Fortunately there was no other car involved. But the girl in the front seat with Klaus was hurt seriously. They were afraid at first she wasn't going to live. There was another couple in the back seat, and they got off with minor injuries. The girl, Julie Kuiper, is still in the hospital, but she's going to be okay. Klaus got a job done to his leg, though. The doctors have told him he'll probably have a limp for the rest of his life.''

Andrea thought of Klaus, so young and blond and good-looking, and she shook her head sadly. ''What a pity!''

''He's lucky he's still got the leg,'' Jan said bluntly. ''Anyway. . . the lawyer was able to get a court continuance because of Klaus's injuries, so he hasn't had to face up to the music with the law. . . yet. The case was continued to the first part of October. Meanwhile, Klaus got out of the hospital and Dirk took him back home with him, but after a few days they must have had a hell of a fight. About midnight one night Klaus came to my house in a taxi. He told me Dirk had thrown him out.''

''And what did Dirk say?''

Jan looked at her, pained. ''We haven't talked about it,'' he said.

''You mean that Klaus has been staying at your house all this time and Dirk hasn't said anything to you about it?'' Andrea demanded, incredulous.

''He doesn't know that Klaus is with me.''

Andrea had never seen Dirk angry, but she knew in her bones that she'd hate to be the subject of his fury. That intense control of his hadn't come about without need. He'd learned to keep his feelings under wraps because he'd had to.

''Mr. van der Houten,'' she said simply, ''you're playing with fire.''

"Tell me about it!" the plant supervisor agreed morosely.

"Also," she added, both curious and perturbed, "why did Klaus ask for me?"

"I don't know," Jan van der Houten admitted. "Klaus only asked me to try to talk to you if I could get a chance, and to tell you he wishes you'd get in touch with him. He said he knows it's a big favor to ask, but I think the kid's desperate at this point."

Andrea sighed, mulling this over. It was one thing to tell herself she didn't owe any loyalty to Dirk, but another thing to contemplate doing something behind his back. And if she contacted Klaus in an atmosphere of such secrecy, she didn't see how her actions could be construed otherwise.

She could, of course, get in touch with Klaus, talk to him, even go see him. . . and then tell Dirk all about it and risk his rage. But she was sure that Klaus would try to extract a pledge of silence from her.

Of course she didn't have to give it to him. She didn't have to do any of these things. In fact, she found the thought of being used as a pawn between the Van Der Maas brothers both annoying and dismaying, and she couldn't help but wish that she'd gone back to Boston before she'd become involved in their problems.

She'd intended to call Mark later in the day, to put the matter of her return before him. He should be able to convince Dirk that there was no point in her staying in Holland indefinitely.

"Look," Jan said suddenly, "my house is only five minutes from here. My wife works in the Sears store in town, and my kids don't get home from school until at least three o'clock, usually later because they're involved in sports. Why don't you go see Klaus yourself and hear what he has to say? Then you can make up your own mind." Again he gave her that abashed grin. "I don't like playing middle man," he confessed.

"Neither do I," Andrea told him, "and that's exactly what I'll be doing if I go see Klaus, Mr. van der Houten."

He shrugged. "It's up to you, Miss Campbell," he said, but he couldn't keep the regret out of his voice. "I'll tell Klaus anything you want me to tell him."

She had a sudden vision of Klaus on crutches, cast out of his family home, and the pang of sympathy she felt was an intense one.

"I can't let it happen like that," she admitted, and made her decision. "I'll go see him."

As Andrea crossed the bakery parking lot toward Dirk's Mercedes, she felt as jittery as she ever had in her life. She was afraid to look back, afraid that somehow, some way, she might see Dirk watching her.

She tried to tell herself that she was being unduly

apprehensive. When she'd left Dirk he'd had a full quota of appointments scheduled for the balance of the morning. And the man didn't have eyes in the back of his head, after all! She warned herself to stop giving in to an imagination that was sometimes entirely too fertile.

Jan van der Houten had given her explicit directions to his house, and she found it without difficulty. It was on a shaded street close to Holland's downtown district, a square, two-story frame house with a wide front porch.

As she climbed the steps to the porch, Andrea had some serious second thoughts about being there. That old saying about fools rushing in where angels fear to tread kept repeating itself inside her head like a broken record that wouldn't be turned off.

She was startled when the front door swung open as she approached it, then caught her breath with relief when she saw Klaus standing in the doorway leaning on his crutches.

He looked thinner than he had when she'd last seen him, and he was much too pale. But he flashed her an engaging grin that reminded her of Dirk, and despite herself her heart went out to him.

"Jan called and said you'd be over," he told her. "It takes me a while to answer a doorbell these days, so I thought I'd get a head start."

He stood back to allow her to enter the long hall that ran from the front to back of the house, then quickly closed the door behind her as if he, too, was afraid of spying eyes. Remembering the distinctive Mercedes parked at curb side, Andrea was tempted to tell him that their die was pretty well cast, as far as her being there was concerned.

"Want to come on back to the kitchen?" Klaus invited. "I brewed us up a pitcher of lemonade."

There was something endearingly simple about this statement, and tears stung Andrea's eyes. Her pity was further elicited by the sight of Klaus struggling along on the crutches. He was anything but agile with them.

The van der Houten kitchen was decorated in cheery bright blue and white, and although Klaus protested he yielded to Andrea's suggestion that he take a place at the pretty blue enameled table while she poured out the lemonade.

"One of the worst things about using crutches is that you can't carry anything around," he told her, as she put a tall frosty glass of the pale-yellow liquid in front of him.

"I know," she agreed. "I sprained my ankle once when I was a teenager, and I had to use crutches for a time." She hesitated, then she said sincerely, "Klaus, I'm sorry about this."

He nodded, tight-lipped, and Andrea suspected that he wasn't very far from tears. Then he muttered hoarsely, "I was a damned fool. Julie could have been killed, Andi. And if that had happened... I wouldn't have wanted to live any longer."

"You and Julie are close?" she ventured.

"Yes," he said, his voice low. "Very close. We're like... like Dirk and Marietta used to be."

Andrea flinched visibly at this, and hoped that he was sufficiently preoccupied so that he didn't notice.

"Julie and I went all through school together. Right from kindergarten through senior high. Andi—" he turned, intent deep-blue eyes on her "—she's the only one who's ever really understood how I feel... about a lot of things."

The self-question was inescapable. Had Dirk also felt that way about Marietta?

"Julie's blasted me out more than anyone else about drinking and driving too fast," he confessed. "I wish now I'd paid attention to her. They won't let me see her, Andi. Her parents have left orders at the hospital not to let me go near her."

Even a stone, Andrea thought, could not have failed to be moved by the torment in his voice.

"Klaus," she said, "you can imagine how frantic with worry her parents must have been until they were sure she was out of danger."

The blue eyes seemed to sear her face, darker than Dirk's yet still so much like his. "Jan told you about that?" he asked.

"Yes."

"Did he tell you that I—that I'm going to be lame?" he asked, his voice so low now that she had to lean forward to hear him.

"I don't accept that," she answered. "I'd say at this stage you're jumping to conclusions, and I think any good orthopedic specialist would agree with me. You're young, you're strong, you have all the pluses in your favor."

"I don't know," he said doubtfully, staring down at the heavy cast on his right leg. "The leg is pretty much of a mess."

"Look," she encouraged, "they can do fantastic things today if you'll play the game, especially when it comes to therapy."

"I intend to play the game," Klaus said levelly. "I've gone against the rules long enough, Andi, and I'm paying for it. The trouble is, I'm not the only one who's paying for it. Julie. . . ."

"She's going to be all right, Klaus."

"Yes, I know," he said. "Jan swore that to me, and I believe him. But it's going to be a while, a long while, before she'll be strong again, and in the meantime she's having to fight her battles alone."

"So are you," Andrea pointed out.

"True, but I'm the one who caused all the trouble," he said wryly. "Julie and the other two friends with us were just drawn in. . . by me. Thank God the other two are okay. . . ."

"Klaus," Andrea said firmly, "you've got to stop dwelling on what might have been and take it from here." She braced herself for the question she had to ask. "What happened between you and Dirk?"

"A couple of nights after I got back from the hospital I was going crazy, not so much from pain as from my own thoughts," Klaus confessed. "There's a downstairs bedroom at the back of the house. They fixed it up after my father's accident, and most of the time it isn't used. They moved me in there, and the night I'm talking about I couldn't sleep, so I decided to go out in the family room and watch TV.

"It was late, my mother and Johanna were both in bed, and I thought Dirk was, too. But as it turned out he'd been working over in that studio of his."

"What studio?" she asked curiously.

"He has the whole second floor over the garage fixed up as a studio. Drawing tables, all that kind of stuff. Anyway, I went out to the family room and turned on the TV, and I decided to make myself a drink—just to take the edge off things. I had no intention...believe me...of getting drunk.

"I was pouring some whisky on the rocks when Dirk came in. He took one look and he turned on me and started giving me hell. I was on medication, and he started telling me that I was even a bigger fool than he'd thought I was to be drinking alcohol at the same time."

"He was right," Andrea said soberly.

"Yes, he was right," Klaus admitted. "The thing is, I hadn't even thought about the effect of the medication. I wasn't going anywhere, that's for sure. What I'm saying is that I wasn't about to become a public menace by putting myself behind the wheel when I was loaded with both booze and drugs.

"I tried to tell Dirk that all I intended to take was one drink. Just one drink. And to sip it while I watched an old movie on TV. Then he made me so damned mad I decided I wasn't about to explain anything to him even if he'd listen...which I was sure he wouldn't. So I told him he could go to hell, and words led to more words. Dirk took the drink away from me and he was so furious he threw it in the fireplace. When he heard the glass shattering, I guess he kind of came to himself. He told me to go to bed, and he waited until I'd gone down the hall and was back in my room. After that he switched out all the lights and went upstairs."

Andrea stared at Klaus, puzzled by his rendition of what had happened. "What did you do?" she asked.

"I waited until I was pretty sure Dirk would be asleep, then I went to the library and called for a cab. I told the cab to meet me in front of the gate at the next house along the road, and I said to make it in half an hour. I knew it was going to take me a while to walk that far."

"Klaus!"

"All right, I was an idiot," Klaus agreed glumly. "I had a tote bag, I put a few things in it and slung it over my shoulder, because that was the only way I could carry anything. I had some money...not much, but some. Enough for cab fare. I'll never know how I made it down to the next house. I was in worse shape then than I am now. But I did, and the cab came and...."

"Yes?"

"The only person I could think of to turn to was Jan—he and his wife, Trudy. They've always been good to me, they've always seemed really...interested in me. I can't say that for too many in Holland. Between the local problems I've gotten myself into and then flunking out of college not once but twice, I don't exactly have the best reputation. I've known for a long time that the guys who work in the bakery don't have much...well, much respect for me. Jan's always been different, though."

Klaus fell silent, and after a moment Andrea prodded gently, "So you went to Jan's."

"Yes. I scared the hell out of him appearing on his doorstep in the middle of the night like that... but he took me in. He also went along with it when I asked him not to tell Dirk where I was."

"I can't help but think Dirk must know you're someplace where you're safe," Andrea said suddenly. "Otherwise he'd have the troops out beating the bushes for you by now."

"He does know I'm safe," Klaus admitted. "I wrote him a note and told him I was okay and that I was leaving town, and that I—I wouldn't be bothering him anymore."

"And what about your mother?" Andrea asked softly.

Klaus's mouth twisted, and he said with difficulty, "That's been the hardest of all. When I start to think about it, I...I hate myself for what I've done to my mother, Andi. Somehow I got off on the wrong foot...way back. Once you get out of step, it's so easy to keep getting farther and farther away from...everything. I wanted to call my mother, I wanted to tell her myself that I was okay. But I knew if I heard the sound of her voice I'd...go all to pieces. So I asked Dirk to tell her for me in the letter I wrote him."

Andrea nodded. Then she said slowly, "Then Dirk didn't really kick you out at all?"

"No," Klaus admitted, and she'd never seen a person look more miserable. "To compound my crimes I told Jan that he had. I was afraid if Jan knew I'd left of my own accord he wouldn't let me stay here, or he'd tell Dirk where I was."

Andrea faced Klaus squarely. "That was pretty terrible," she said bluntly.

"Don't you think I know that?" he retorted hoarsely. He pushed away the glass of lemonade he'd barely touched and put his head in his hands. "God," he asked, and it sounded almost like a prayer, "where do I go from here?"

Andrea had no ready answer to this, but there was something else she had to know.

"Why did you want to see me?" she asked.

"Because I know Dirk thinks a lot of you," Klaus told her simply. "He'd listen to you, and maybe you can make him understand—and then he can make my mother understand—why I'm going to do what I'm going to do."

She felt a swift pang of alarm. "And what is that?"

"I really am going to leave this time," Klaus told her. "I have my plans made."

She was aghast. "That's the most ridiculous thing I've ever heard of. Aside from the difficulty you're having just getting around, what are you going to use for money?"

"I had money in a couple of bank accounts," Klaus confessed. "Enough to get me where I want to go and to keep me until I'm strong enough to get a job. Jan. . . well, he cashed in the accounts for me. I gave him written letters of authorization. He took a chance. If Dirk ever found out, it could mean his job. That's why I don't want Dirk to ever connect Jan with me, Andi. He'd fire him in a minute if he knew Jan had been letting me stay here, or that he'd gotten my money for me."

"I doubt that," Andrea said. "Dirk's a fair person, Klaus, whatever else you may say about him. I can't believe that Dirk would fire a trusted employee simply because he gave you shelter."

"Don't be so sure," Klaus cautioned. "I agree that Dirk's fair. But he demands absolute loyalty from his employees, and if he knew Jan had helped me, he'd put him down as a traitor to the company."

"I can't quite believe that," Andrea persisted. "Anyway... I suppose your plan is for Jan to drive you somewhere so that you can get a plane to wherever you're going, and then your family and the whole town will be rid of you, is that it?"

"Yes... that's just about it," he admitted.

"Klaus Van Der Maas... that's the most stupid plan I've ever heard of in my life! Till now I'd thought highly of Jan van der Houten, but he must be an idiot if he'd go along with you on something like this."

"Jan thinks that Dirk threw me out, remember."

"Then don't you think it's about time you straightened him out?" she demanded angrily. "Jan works for your brother, he has a very important job in the bakery, he's devoted his adult life to his work. I think he's the kind of man who has to respect the person he works for. Do you think he can go on respecting Dirk much longer if he feels you've been forced out of town while you're stumbling along on crutches with your leg in a cast?"

"I... I hadn't thought of it that way," Klaus mumbled.

"If you ask me, you haven't thought anything through," Andrea said heatedly. "What you've been doing is making yourself feel so guilty about everything that now you think the only way you can put things right for the people you love is to leave entirely. Well, you're all wrong about that. You'd break your mother's heart if you left here. As it is, you should see her. She looks twenty years older and totally tired out." This was a slight exaggeration, but justified under the circumstances, Andrea told herself.

"As for Dirk. . . he loves you, too."

Klaus shook his head. "I've always been a thorn in his side," he said bitterly.

"That's what you think!" Andrea exploded. "And I'm giving you credit, Klaus, in allowing that you actually do any thinking at all!"

She saw him flinch, but she went on. "You're not only messing up your own life but you're also causing a lot of grief to the people who care for you the most. . . your mother and Dirk and Jan van der Houten. To say nothing of Julie, who's going to need you while she's convalescing, and Johanna, who needs all the family love and support she can get and. . . and me," she finished, and by this time tears were running down her cheeks.

CHAPTER SIXTEEN

"ANDI," KLAUS SAID, shaken, "I'm sorry. I didn't mean to put you through anything like this."

Andrea wiped her eyes. "It's okay—no, it isn't okay. You shouldn't be doing any of this to the people who love you, Klaus."

"What would you suggest I do?" he asked her, and he looked so pale, so desperate, that she wanted to take him in her arms and console him instead of castigating him. But someone had to tell Klaus how wrong he was. It wasn't a job she'd asked for, but it appeared she'd been elected.

"You've got to face up to Dirk."

Klaus looked as if she'd hit him below the belt. After an intense moment he said, "I can't. That's the one thing you might ask of me I can't do. There's no way."

"There's always a way," Andrea said wearily. She reached for the pitcher of lemonade and refilled her glass, then asked Klaus, "Do you want some ice cubes in yours?"

He shook his head. "No. No, thanks."

"Drink it up, Klaus. You need the energy," she advised. "Have you eaten anything?"

"Not yet."

"Not yet? It's almost noon. Look, shall we drive out someplace and get some lunch?"

His grin was lopsided. "In Dirk's car? Come on, Andi," he protested.

"Sooner or later Dirk is going to have to know about this," she warned. "I mean, he's going to have to know that I came here and saw you. I don't want to keep secrets like this from him, Klaus. It's not fair."

She saw the growing apprehension in his eyes and hoped she hadn't said the wrong thing. At least she had an open line with Klaus right now, and she didn't want to cut off their communication.

"You promised," he said simply.

"Yes, I know I promised, and I'm not about to break the promise," she assured him. "What I'm hoping is that you'll ask me to go tell Dirk."

She saw some of Dirk's steely determination in the way Klaus looked at her. "I'm not about to do that, Andi," he said. "I'm sorry but, like I said, there's no way."

"Klaus. . . are you afraid of Dirk?"

He stiffened, and she saw a flash of anger in his blue eyes, but then he relaxed and shook his head slowly. "No," he said, "I'm not afraid of Dirk. Not, at least, in the way you might think. I've let

Dirk down not once, but many times, and that's what hurts. And this last time was the worst of all. I'd never injured anyone before...except myself, maybe."

Andrea settled for a direct approach. "Was the accident your fault, Klaus?"

She flinched at the pain stamped on his young face. "I'm not sure," he said unsteadily. "I hadn't been drinking a whole lot, if that's what you mean. I'd had a couple of beers. Julie was at me not to drink the second beer, and to tell you the truth I didn't even finish the bottle. But maybe it was enough." He shrugged. "I guess I'll never know."

"Do you want to tell me what happened?" Andrea ventured.

"We'd been at a place maybe twenty miles south of here," he said. "It was Saturday night. They have a live band for dancing Saturday nights. It was late when we left, and like I said I'd had the better part of two beers. But...." He paused. "I swear to you, Andi, that's all I'd had! Anyway, I decided to come back on a side road instead of going over and taking the highway. That was a mistake. It was foggy, and I was kind of...upset. Julie and I had been talking, she wanted me to go back to school. I told her it was too late to reapply for this year, and she insisted that if I'd go up to Ann Arbor and talk to the people there I'd have a chance. It wasn't that my grades were that bad it was...just me," Klaus said lamely. "Call it my attitude."

"All right," Andrea said, nodding. "So you and Julie had been quarreling about this?"

"Not exactly quarreling," he said. "She kept wanting to talk about it and...I didn't want to listen. I had on the stereo in the car. There was some good music. I wanted to keep things laid back. I said to her something like, 'Let's just listen to the music, Julie,' and she said, 'You never want to face up to anything, Klaus.'

"A minute later I went into the tree. It loomed up out of the fog and...I couldn't get away from it. I wasn't zooming, Andi. I don't think I was even going over the speed limit. Even so...."

"Even so," Andrea said, "it sounds to me like a genuine accident." And it did. "What I'm saying is that you may be blaming yourself more than you need to, Klaus. There's the chance that what happened to you could have happened to anyone driving in that particular place at that particular time.

"Look," she went on, "when you have your day in court tell them what you've just told me. Tell them like you told me, calmly, without trying to whitewash yourself. I think if you do that they'll listen to you."

He smiled ruefully. "I don't exactly have a spotless record, Andi."

"Never mind," she said stubbornly. "You deserve a fair hearing. If you're honest with the court and yourself, I sincerely believe you'll get one."

She stood. "Klaus, I'm going out to get us some pizzas, okay?"

"You don't need to do that," he protested.

"You've got to have something to eat," she told him firmly.

She came back with pizzas, plus some fresh fruit and some candy bars for Klaus to munch on later in the day. They sat at the kitchen table and ate the food, and she was gratified to see that Klaus latched on to his pizza, finished it, and then obligingly ate half of hers, as well.

The lunch finished, Andrea said, "I'd better get going." The thought of the Mercedes parked out in front of the house was making her increasingly nervous. It was unlikely that Dirk would suddenly come driving down the street in the company car, but stranger coincidences had happened.

"Klaus," she said, "I promised you I wouldn't tell Dirk about seeing you without your consent. Now I want you to promise me something."

There was a touching sadness to his smile. "I think I know what you're going to ask. You want me to promise I won't run off, right?"

"Right. It would be pointless for you to run away, Klaus. You couldn't escape, I think you know that. None of us can ever really escape...and none of us can keep running forever."

"Maybe," he said doubtfully. "But I feel I have to go somewhere, Andi. I've imposed on the van der Houtens long enough as it is. This is a strain for both Jan and his wife. He knows it would mean his job if Dirk found out he'd been letting me stay here."

"I can't think that Dirk would be that unfair," she said. "Besides, it's not going to make that much difference if you stay here for another day or so. I'll get back to you tomorrow, Klaus."

"Look," he started, and then hesitated.

"Yes?"

"Could you try to find out how Julie is? How she really is?"

"Yes," Andrea promised. "Yes, of course."

She said this calmly, but as she drove off in the Mercedes the calm began to give way. She'd gotten herself into a lot more than she'd bargained for.

She didn't want to go back to the Van Der Maas house yet. Johanna would still be in school, so only Monica would be home, and Andrea didn't want to risk being alone with this astute woman. It would be very hard not to try to erase some of those lines of worry that shadowed Monica's eyes by telling her that she'd just seen Klaus.

On an impulse she took the first road out of town she came to and drove toward the south, reflecting that everything looked so very different now than it had in May. She hadn't realized how much corn was grown in the area...there were acres and acres of tall corn, stretching in some places all the way from the edge to the horizon.

This part of Michigan was fruit country, too.

There were both pear and apple orchards and extensive blueberry plantations. The gently rolling terrain was pleasant to the eye, and the trees were magnificent—stately elms, maples and oaks, and tall, thick pines. But although Andrea knew she must be fairly close to Lake Michigan, there were no glimpses of water to be seen. She suspected that some of the dirt side roads she was passing must lead down to the lake.

This was a very rural area, interspersed with small villages, and every little hamlet had its share of antique shops. Andrea browsed in a couple of them but found nothing she really wanted.

She'd wondered at the many "party stores" around Holland and Grand Rapids and discovered that this was the local name for what otherwise would be called a package store or a liquor store. She also learned that when a waitress approached a customer in Michigan with the question, "Do you want a drink?" it was coffee that was being referred to, not an alcoholic beverage.

It was these regional differences and the varying ethnic backgrounds in different sections of the country that made the United States so fascinating, Andrea decided.

After a time she started back toward Holland, but it was still too early to return to the Van Der Maas house. On an impulse, she drove through town and out onto Windmill Island . . . the first time she'd been there since that fateful afternoon when she'd dived into the canal to rescue Johanna.

The parking lot was almost deserted, and there were only a few late-season tourists wandering around. Everything looked so different and Andrea tried to reason why. Then she realized there were no tulips at this time of year. The flower beds in which the tulips had been blooming now blazed with bright annuals.

The black, red-faced Muscovy ducks and the white geese were still swimming in the canal, and Andrea could almost imagine that she was seeing Johanna standing on the bank.

Thank heaven history wasn't about to repeat itself in that department! she told herself shakily.

She wandered into the large coffee-gift shop to find that this, too, was almost deserted. She browsed and found a couple of souvenirs, including a key ring with small wooden *klompen* suspended from it and another with figures of a Dutch boy and a Dutch girl.

She paused to talk to the woman in traditional costume who was presiding at the cash register. "Where do all the tulips go?"

The woman laughed. "They're dug up at the end of the blooming period and immediately replaced with annual plants," she said. "Soon the annuals will die down, and then it will be time to plant the tulips again."

"I was here in May," Andrea confessed. "I've never seen anything more beautiful than those tulips in bloom. There must be thousands of them."

"Ninety thousand," the woman nodded. "That's to say ninety thousand tulips are planted each fall. But it's estimated that if you count the Windmill Island bulbs there are more than three million tulips in bloom around Holland at one time."

"Incredible!" Andrea said. "But I can believe it, having seen the tulips for myself!"

Andrea accepted the offer of a cup of coffee and, as she stirred cream into it, said, "I suppose you'll be closing up soon, here on the island?"

Andrea observed the woman as she replied. She was perhaps in her early fifties. Her hair was an attractive blond merging with silver, and she had the biggest, bluest eyes Andrea had ever seen.

"Yes," she told Andrea, "our season is coming to an end. I can't say I'm sorry. Starting with Tulip Time, when we're jammed with visitors, we have a busy time throughout the summer. Our parking lot is filled with cars and tour buses that come from everywhere, and the traffic is back to back. Students from Hope College come over to help us out or we'd never be able to take care of the crowds."

Andrea smiled. "I suppose this is a question asked wherever there are tourist attractions, but. . . what do you do in the winter?"

The woman laughed. "My husband and I pack up and go to Florida," she confessed. "We used to stay in Holland all year round, but once we got the chance to make the change we took it! We don't like cold weather and snow, and we get plenty of each here. Matter of fact, there's apt to be snow well into April." She smiled. "We both had enough of that when we were younger."

Andrea was thinking about what the woman had said as she drove back toward Lakeshore Drive and the Van Der Maas house. She wondered if Monica Van Der Maas might feel the same way, if she might enjoy getting to a warmer climate over the winter and shedding some of the responsibilities that must hang heavily on her shoulders there in Holland. She had Johanna, Dirk and Klaus to think of, to say nothing of a mansion of a house to run. Possibly Monica saw no way to escape, or maybe she didn't want to. Yet if Dirk was so concerned about his mother's health that he didn't want her involved in the bakery's operation any longer, it seemed strange that he wouldn't find a way to buy some time in the winter sun for her.

Andrea could imagine, though, that Monica might very well be as stubborn as her older son. And as long as she felt she was needed in Holland, she was probably going to stay on the scene, regardless of what she might like to do.

ANDREA FOUND MONICA VAN DER MAAS in the drawing room, crocheting an afghan in glorious tones of blue and turquoise. Johanna was seated at the nearby concert grand piano, laboriously fingering one octave in the key of *C* while her grandmother monitored her.

"I wondered who played the piano," Andrea confessed, sitting, at Mrs. Van Der Maas's invitation, on an antique armchair beautifully upholstered in ivory brocade.

"Uncle Dirk," Johanna said, swinging around on the piano bench. "Can I stop now, grandma?" she pleaded.

"All right," Mrs. Van Der Maas conceded.

"Can I go get a glass of milk?"

Her grandmother nodded with a smile, and Johanna lost no time in running out of the room.

"Dirk plays the piano?" Andrea asked, once the child had left them.

His mother nodded. "Very well," she said. "Or at least he used to. I haven't heard him play in a long while. But then he doesn't have much time for any of the extras these days.

"Dirk is the artistic one in the family," she added. "He gets it from my husband's side of the family. My husband's mother was quite an artist, and my husband played the violin. At one time he even thought of going into music professionally, but the family business called. It would seem that the family business has always 'called,' perhaps unfortunately," she concluded.

"I suppose that's so everywhere, where businesses have been built up and the owners try to keep

them in family hands from generation to generation," Andrea observed.

"True," Mrs. Van Der Maas agreed. "And needless to say, the bigger the business the bigger the
tug-of-war it can engender. Ours is a relatively
small operation, but my husband did set aside the
things he really wanted to do in life so that it could
continue, and now Dirk is doing the same thing."

"Do you think Dirk is unhappy heading the business?" Andrea ventured.

"I think he's become reconciled to it," Mrs. Van
Der Maas said, and added, with a sad smile, "And
that, perhaps, is worse than being unhappy. If a
person is unhappy enough, usually they'll do something about it."

She folded up the afghan and said, "Shall we go
into the family room, Andrea? I find it more comfortable than I do this room. My late mother-in-law
had this redone into this rather elegant style, and
it's always been too stiff for my personal taste."
She smiled. "There again, I suppose I've become
reconciled to it. If it really made me unhappy, I
would have had it torn apart long ago."

Once in the family room, Mrs. Van Der Maas
suggested a before-dinner drink. "I'm not up to
mixing things like Dirk's daiquiris," she confessed.
"How about a glass of sherry?"

"That would be fine," Andrea replied, nodding.

"I forgot to mention that Dirk won't be home for
dinner," his mother said as she poured their sherry.

"This is his Rotary Club night. That's another thing about heading a local business. It's felt that you must play your part in civic activities. I'm not saying there's anything wrong with these fraternal clubs. In fact they all do a great deal of good in varying ways. But in the case of someone like Dirk...well, I can't help but feel that there are other things he'd rather be doing. He has so little time to himself."

Johanna reappeared just as Mabel came to announce dinner, and as they ate the child regaled them with an account of her day in school. Then suddenly she said, "I looked for you when I got home this afternoon, Andi. I thought maybe we could wiggle our toes."

Andrea held her breath. Did this mean Johanna was ready to go into the swimming pool with her?

She said carefully, "Maybe tomorrow, Johanna, if it's a warm, sunny day."

"Okay," Johanna nodded, her brown curls bouncing. "I get home from school right after three."

Andrea made an immediate resolve that nothing was going to keep her from being at the house at three o'clock the following day.

She didn't attempt to explain any of this to Monica Van Der Maas, nor did Johanna's grandmother ask any questions. She probably assumed that "wiggling toes" was a game Johanna and she had thought up, Andrea told herself. Anyway, there was no point in getting her hopes up until she was sure Johanna was really going to try to overcome her fear of water.

After dinner she, Johanna and Mrs. Van Der Maas settled down to watch the rerun of a musical comedy on TV. It was almost over when they heard the front door thud, and Mrs. Van Der Maas said, "It must be Dirk."

He looked tired, but he also seemed glad to see Andrea, and a shot of pure pleasure coursed through her.

The movie over, Mrs. Van Der Maas reminded Johanna that it was her bedtime, and at this Dirk turned to Andrea.

"You haven't seen my studio yet, have you?" he asked.

"N—no," she stammered, remembering that it was only today that she'd learned he had a studio, and it was Klaus who had told her.

"Come along," he invited.

"Andi," Johanna protested, "aren't you going to come say good-night to me?"

"Andrea can look in on you when she gets back," Mrs. Van Der Maas said quickly, and Andrea couldn't refute the impression that Dirk's mother wanted her to go over to his studio with him.

She thought, sadly, that if Mrs. Van Der Maas was trying to encourage a romance, a real romance, between Dirk and herself, the odds were very much against her. But then. . . Dirk's mother should know better than anyone else what Marietta had done to him—and, despite this, how he still grieved for her.

She followed Dirk out of the house. There was an outside flight of stairs at the far end of the three-car garage, and Dirk led her toward it. He paused on the small landing at the top and fished in his pants pocket for a key. It surprised Andrea to think that he kept his studio locked when the whole family was so blithe about leaving the front door of the house unlocked in the daytime.

He caught her expression and said, "I guess I just don't want people poking around. Johanna would be up here in a flash if I gave her the green signal. As it is, people come by invitation only."

"I'm flattered," she managed to say lightly as she stepped across the threshold behind him. And then she stopped short, amazed.

The studio was huge, for one thing. Even though Dirk promptly turned on some lights there were still distant recesses that were shadow filled.

There were several drawing tables, two easels, and so much paraphernalia that she couldn't begin to sort it all out. There were two comfortable-looking daybeds, an assortment of chairs and in one corner a full-sized refrigerator.

"Do you have a stove, too?" she asked, seeing this.

He laughed. "No. Though there've been moments in the winter when I've been working in here and wanted something hot to eat that I've thought of putting one in. So far, though, I've settled for an electric hot pot and instant soup.''

He was moving toward the refrigerator, and he called, "How about some champagne?"

"Champagne?" she echoed. "What's the festive occasion?"

He was opening the fridge door as he spoke and drawing out a dark-green bottle. "Having you here," he told her simply, and her heart thumped yet again.

Before opening the champagne bottle Dirk took off his suit coat and discarded his tie with an impatient gesture. Then he opened three buttons down the front of the shirt, and Andrea could see his deep-gold hair, lightly matted.

Something started to spiral inside Andrea, and she didn't try to fool herself when it came to identifying it. This was desire, desire of the purest kind. . . .

She watched him pour pale-gold liquid into two tulip-shaped glasses, and she hoped she could accept the one he was handing her without dropping it. She'd never felt more unsteady. . . all over.

Dirk reached out his own glass and clicked it to hers. "To forever," he said simply.

It was an odd toast, but it had a profound effect on her. She whispered, "I'll drink to that," and she did. Bubbles stung her nose, and she wanted to laugh, she wanted to cry, she wanted to make love. . .not exactly in that order, she thought, with a sigh.

She started to move around the studio, trying to study the various sketches Dirk had tacked to the walls. Some of them were architectural drawings, some of them were sketches of flowers or boats or people.

She turned toward the nearest easel and was stopped by her sheer surprise. She was staring at a large charcoal sketch of herself.

Dirk, at her elbow, asked, "Like it?"

"It's very good," she murmured, the last vestige of her self-possession destroyed.

"I want to do an oil of you," he said, matter of factly. "I've been getting more and more interested in portraiture. Suppose you could bring yourself to be a guinea pig and model for me, Andrea?"

"Model for you?" she echoed vacantly.

"Yes. I'd prefer it to be in the nude, needless to say," he added wickedly, "but right now I'm going to confine myself to head and shoulders painting!"

He put aside his glass of champagne as he spoke, and then he stood stark still, staring at her without moving.

"Oh God, darling!" he said simply, and it was a cry from the heart.

Andrea responded. She couldn't have said later what she did with the glass of champagne. She only knew that somehow she freed her hands and next she was reaching her arms out to him, she was moving toward him, knowing that she couldn't resist him any longer. She wanted him, she wanted all of him, and she wanted to give him all of herself. Nothing else seemed to matter as their mouths met, their lips twisting urgently.

She helped Dirk undress her, shivering with ecstasy as his hands caressed her bare flesh, moving lower and lower as her clothes were removed and tossed. . . somewhere. He groaned as the last wisp— lace-edged, peach-colored panties—followed the rest. And Andrea, consumed by her passion for him, felt herself fumbling with the belt that was holding up his navy-blue slacks, her desire mounting as his hard muscular body was revealed to her.

He was magnificent. She had to tell him so, she had to tell him. "Dirk," she moaned, "you're so beautiful!"

He was caressing her all over, his fingers moving to probe the most intimate parts of her. His touch, in this very core of her being, triggered an unbearable surge of wanting. She was trembling uncontrollably as they moved to the first of the daybeds, sinking down onto the softness of it. While she reached up imploringly, Dirk leaned over her, supporting himself by his elbows as he gazed into her eyes.

Without his glasses his eyes had a hypnotic quality. She felt as if she were drowning in them as she pulled him toward her and he laughed at her urgency, his voice low, exultant. "Can I really believe this?"

Andrea, uninhibited as she'd never been before, showed him her answer. She was past speaking it. Her fingers dug into the flesh of his shoulders as she drew him close, her lips, her hands, feverishly communicating love's special language.

They stroked, caressed, until they'd each explored every inch of the other, and by then Andrea felt as if she was on fire, the flames of her need for him flaring into a blaze of total passion. She felt him enter her, and she moaned with the pleasure he was giving her. She began to move with him, to love him, as they surged upward and upward toward a transcending moment of glory.

Nor did they let it end there. For a time they rested, and then again they were drawn toward each other, and again the miracle happened. Only then did Andrea relax totally within the shelter of his arms and fall asleep.

When she awakened Dirk had left her side, and she saw that he'd drawn a thin coverlet over her. There were lights still on in the studio, and she had no idea what time it was.

She heard Dirk's voice and turned to see him walking across the room toward her.

"I made some coffee," he said, and she accepted the cup he'd brought her gratefully. The hot, slightly bitter brew had a soothing effect. She drank it, staring at him over the rim of her cup. He'd put his pants and shirt back on, he'd combed his hair, and his glasses were in proper position.

After a moment she asked, "What time is it?"

"Slightly after midnight," he said with a smile.

"Oh my goodness!" she exclaimed. "Johanna...."

Dirk's eyes seemed to be dancing with an inner delight. "She'll forgive you," he told Andrea. Then added, mischievously, "But if you hadn't stayed, her uncle might not have!"

CHAPTER SEVENTEEN

DIRK WASTED NO TIME in setting up a series of interview appointments with the bakery employees for Andrea. Tuesday morning they left the house on Lakeshore Drive shortly after eight o'clock, Dirk driving to the bakery in the company car and Andrea following him in the Mercedes.

Andrea had awakened in the early hours of the morning and hadn't been able to get back to sleep. She showed it, she'd thought ruefully, as she'd tried to camouflage the dark shadows under her eyes with careful makeup.

She'd noticed Dirk's frown when she'd gone down to breakfast, and she knew that he'd taken in her appearance and was giving it his own assessment. He didn't comment, though, and she followed his lead. She wasn't up to getting into a discussion about herself—or anything else—with him right now. She only hoped that he hadn't jumped to the wrong conclusion and had decided that she was regretting what had happened between them the night before.

She didn't regret it. She would never regret it...

no matter what transpired from this point on. As she drove into central Holland, keeping the company car in sight, she admitted to herself that she wasn't too optimistic about her future with Dirk, despite what had happened. There were too many things to be dealt with that he wasn't going to like. Klaus, for one. And her return to Boston. In those sleepless hours toward dawn she'd concluded that she needed to go back to Boston as soon as possible and regroup. It was out of the question to go on staying in Holland, tempting though that prospect was. She and Dirk couldn't keep wandering off to his studio and abandoning themselves to each other without others—certainly his mother—catching on to what was happening.

Her feelings toward Dirk were too important to be jeopardized. She didn't want them mistranslated by anyone else. It would be so easy to have what was going on between them branded as an affair and at best that sounded sordid. But whatever else might be said about the relationship between Dirk and herself, there was nothing sordid about it.

And what else might be said about it? Andrea asked herself as she followed along behind him on the way to the bakery.

Last night she had made a committal that could never be reversed. She had given herself to Dirk, and she wondered if he was aware that this was the ultimate gift she could have offered him. He'd seemed to recognize that at the time. But this morning she wasn't so sure.

She wasn't very sure about anything concerning Dirk, she admitted bleakly. He had the same capacity to puzzle her that he'd had the first time she'd met him, even though in the interim they had, in some ways at least, come as close as two people ever can.

Andrea was all too aware that in capitulating to him—yes, she thought wryly, she had capitulated to him—she had violated her own basic professional principles, and she took this seriously. From this day forward how could she possibly walk down that imaginary middle line with Dirk, the line she'd drawn almost at the beginning of her career when she'd realized it was vital *not* to become emotionally involved with clients.

And Dirk was still a client. They were only at the beginning of their business relationship, and in a sense they were at the beginning of their personal relationship, as well. They'd made a new beginning, an entirely new beginning last night.

Can I possibly handle Dirk as both a client and a lover? It was an agonizing question, and Andrea sighed deeply. Her problem was compounded by the fact that in neither her mind nor her heart could she label the miracle between Dirk and herself as an affair.

No, she thought sadly, *I love him. How I love him! And I've let myself in for whatever happens because I know that deep down he's never gotten over what Marietta did to him.*

The bakery loomed ahead. Andrea parked the Mercedes in the space that was reserved for Dirk, and by the time she'd turned the key in the ignition switch he was standing by the car waiting for her. He smiled at her.

"I feel that urge to play hooky coming over me again," he confessed.

"Don't tempt me," she said, smiling back at him, and wondering if her love for him was showing through.

As they started up the long staircase, Dirk said, "Evelyn's set up an office for you, so you'll have privacy for your interviews. Do you want a recorder, so you can tape them?"

"No, I don't think so," she said. "I'm not interested in quotations. I have my own system for taking notes, which'll do, I'm sure. I don't take many of them, because I've found that people tend to become distracted if they see you doing too much writing. On the other hand, lots of people freeze when you produce a recorder."

"Do it your own way," he advised. "This is just background, after all."

"Exactly," she agreed, a little dismayed to think they could get on an entirely business footing so quickly and so easily.

Mrs. Bleeker had selected a large room for Andrea's use. It overlooked a vacant lot. There was a substantial desk with a swivel chair behind it, a comfortable chair for the use of visitors and not much else.

As she waited for the first bakery employee to arrive, Andrea glanced out the window and remembered what Dirk had said about converting vacant lots into miniparks. This one had a minimum of the litter usually seen in such places, but even so she caught the glimpse of a couple of beer cans and watched a wad of crumpled paper being blown about by the gusting breeze. She'd always hated litter and had often said that if she was an enforcing officer she'd impose enormous fines on people caught scattering their rubbish. She totally endorsed Dirk's project for beautifying the land around the bakery, with the hope that others in the area would then follow suit.

Returning to the desk, she noted that Mrs. Bleeker had furnished her with a large pad of blank paper and a gold pen similar to the one Dirk used. There was a phone but no intercom and, she soon discovered, no list of names of the people who were coming to see her. Though not strictly necessary, a list would have been helpful, and she was thinking about going over to Mrs. Bleeker and asking her if it would be much trouble to get one when there was a knock at the door.

Andrea shrugged. So much for the list! She took her place behind the desk as she called out, "Come in."

It had not occurred to her that Jan van der Houten might be one of the people she was to talk to, though she knew now that she should have realized this. As it was, she was startled to see him. At first her only thought was that he was coming to see her about something involving Klaus.

" 'Morning, Miss Campbell," he said, closing the door behind him. "I guess I'm the first."

Andrea sagged with relief. "Whew!" she admitted. "You had me going there." She glanced toward the closed door. Her office was at the opposite end of the building from Dirk's suite, but even so the sense that she must be cautious gripped her. It wasn't a feeling she liked, and she asked almost reluctantly, "How is Klaus?"

"A lot better since he saw you," the plant supervisor told her.

"Sit down, Mr. van der Houten," Andrea said, indicating the chair by her desk. She smiled wryly. "Before I start talking to you about your work here, there are a couple of things I'd like to get into concerning Klaus."

He nodded. "That's fine with me."

"I'm a little appalled to think that you were going to help him leave Holland," she admitted.

The big man nodded slowly. "I can see the way that must have hit you. Klaus and I talked it out, though. It seemed like maybe it was the best thing for him to do. He has a couple of good friends in Detroit, guys he was in college with. They have a place he could share for the time being. He could get the medical attention he's going to need for quite a while to come.''

Van der Houten shook his head. "I guess maybe I let Klaus talk me into believing this was what he should do. Klaus and I both know that every day he keeps staying in my house is like sitting on a powder keg about to blow up. This is a small town. Sooner or later someone's bound to find out he's been staying with me. . . and when that gets back to Dirk, I'll have had it.''

"You're so sure of that?'' Andrea asked.

"Yes, I am. Dirk would feel I'd crossed him, and that's not something he'd forgive,'' the plant supervisor told her.

"All right,'' she said, "I agree. Klaus shouldn't go on staying with you. What he should do, of course, is to go home.''

"I can't see that happening.''

"No, unfortunately I can't, either. Not without a little negotiation first,'' Andrea admitted. "I suppose that what Klaus and Dirk need is a middleman. Someone to present both sides of the story to each of them. If they'd listen, then maybe they'd come together.''

"Maybe,'' van der Houten said doubtfully. "I've known them both since they were kids, Miss Campbell, Dirk as well as Klaus. They're both pretty hardheaded.''

"Perhaps,'' Andrea agreed, "but I still can't believe Dirk is so unreasonable he wouldn't even consider Klaus's side of the story if someone presented it to him."

"I wouldn't want to try," the plant supervisor confessed. "On the other hand, maybe you could."

"No!" Andrea exclaimed, without even stopping to think about it. "I'd have no right to get into anything like that, Mr. van der Houten."

"I don't know about that," he drawled. "Seems to me both Dirk and Klaus think pretty highly of you."

"I don't...I don't even belong here," she protested.

"There's an old saying that it's the new broom that sweeps clean," he told her with a smile. "Sometimes newcomers see things different. They get a fresh eye on a situation. They're not clouded by a lot of stuff that's gone on over the years."

Andrea eyed him narrowly. "Has Klaus suggested to you that I speak to Dirk about him?"

"No," he replied honestly. "All Klaus said was that you told him you'd get back to him today."

She nodded. "Yes. And that's something I have to do. But I don't know any more about how this should be handled than I did when I left Klaus yesterday. I do know, though," she added, "that something's got to be done about it, and soon. I'm staying at the Van Der Maases' house...."

"Yes," he said. "I heard that."

"Well...I feel like such an imposter," Andrea

told him, her agitation making her voice tremble. "I don't like to play one side against the other and that's what I feel I'm doing. Dirk and his mother have been very kind to me. At the same time I admit my sympathies go out to Klaus. But it isn't right for me to...to be in the middle like this. After all, I'm here on business, Mr. van der Houten. As you know, I'm sure, I'm to handle the bakery's advertising account once the new frozen-foods division is in operation."

He nodded.

"If Dirk became as angry about all of this as you think he'd be, I might lose his account for my agency," she pointed out. "And that wouldn't do much for my career."

"I can see that," he said, troubled. "Looks like maybe I got you into something I shouldn't have, Miss Campbell."

She sighed. "All you did was what Klaus asked you to do."

"Yes, that's true enough. But because I stand to get in trouble myself over Klaus is no reason why I should have dragged you into it. I admit I kind of hoped you'd get this off my back...with Klaus and Dirk. That was wrong of me."

"Wrong or right," Andrea said honestly, "I can understand it!" She paused, thinking hard. Then she said, "What we should do is to think of some way we can get the situation off both our backs, Mr. van der Houten."

He glanced across at her skeptically. "How do you figure we could do that?"

"I don't know," Andrea admitted ruefully.

She sighed and pulled the pad of paper toward her. "We'd better get started on business. I don't know how much time Mrs. Bleeker has allowed for these interviews, but I don't want someone else looming up before I've even started talking to you about the bakery."

He nodded reluctantly. "I guess you're right."

For the next twenty minutes they discussed the years Jan van der Houten had spent in the Van Der Maas bakery, the various jobs he'd performed over those years, and his feelings about the business in general.

Andrea had made it clear to Dirk that these interviews were to be strictly confidential. The advertising campaign would benefit from the results, but she wanted the employees to feel free to speak to her without fear of retaliation.

Dirk had seemed amused by her insistence on confidentiality, his lips quirking into a smile as he'd asked, "What do you think I am? Some kind of Simon Legree?" But he'd gone along with the request, and later had explained to Evelyn Bleeker that the employees were to know that whatever they said in the interviews would be for Andrea's ears only.

He'd teased her, saying, "Is that why you don't want to tape the interviews?"

"Of course not!" she'd snapped, and that had been the end of it.

Now as she talked to Jan van der Houten she was reminded of this little scene with Dirk. Jan would have no cause to fear any criticism for the things he was telling her. She had no doubt about his devotion to the Van Der Maases, both as a family and as employers. He touched sadly on the time when Dirk's father had met with his terrible accident. He said that although it was a pity Dirk had given up his career in New York, his brother Gerrit, had he lived, could never have done the things with the bakery Dirk was doing.

"Also," the plant supervisor added significantly, "Gerrit never cared about the people who worked for him like Dirk does. Dirk gives the maximum in benefits to his employees. We've got the best medical insurance money can buy, life insurance, a pension plan, and once the new frozen-foods division gets going he intends to get into a stock-sharing plan.

"Dirk does a lot for this community, too," van der Houten went on, warming to the subject of his employer. "He gives a lot of money to different things, sure, but he also gives a lot of his own time, which, if you ask me, is even more valuable to him. Dirk's put everything he's got into this business and...."

"Yes?" Andrea asked, unaware that she was leaning forward, hanging on the plant supervisor's words.

"Well, I'd like to see him married, with a couple of kids of his own and a life of his own. He's paid his dues, as far as his family's concerned. He stuck by Gerrit when Gerrit started drinking too much even though another brother would have—"

Van der Houten broke off. "I'm talking too much," he said apologetically. "Anyway, you want to hear about the bakery, not the Van Der Maas family."

Nothing could have been further from the truth, but Andrea could hardly have told him so. The interview concluded, she said, "I plan to take some lunch in for Klaus today, Mr. van der Houten, if that's all right with you."

"It's fine with me," he told her. "I appreciate it. My wife's left plenty of food around, but Klaus doesn't seem to care much about bothering with it, and he needs to eat."

"Yes, he does. He also needs to get things straightened out between Dirk and himself," Andrea said firmly. "Didn't you say he's got to face up to a court date next month?"

"That's right."

"I think it would help him a great deal if he had Dirk's support at that time."

"I wouldn't be too sure he can get it," van der Houten warned her. "Dirk's pretty stiff about people driving when they've had too much to drink. He went through enough of that with Gerrit. Gerrit creamed a couple of cars and it was damned lucky no one was killed at the time. Then—and I'm not telling any tales out of school when I say this— everyone knows Gerrit was drinking the day he went out sailing with his wife and little Johanna. And the only thing that could have made that any more of a tragedy would have been if little Johanna had been drowned too. So don't expect Dirk to take Klaus's side, Miss Campbell."

"I don't," she said. "But I don't think drinking was a problem in Klaus's accident. He said he'd had two beers, and that was over a fairly long course of time. I believe him. He's been open enough about everything else."

Van der Houten nodded. "If that's what Klaus says, I believe him too. The question is, though, will Dirk believe him?"

There was a knock at the door and Andrea said wryly, "That must be my next subject." She hesitated, then asked a question she knew she shouldn't ask at all.

"You knew Marietta Van Der Maas, didn't you, Mr. van der Houten?"

Jan nodded. "Yes, I knew her," he said darkly. "And though I don't like to bad-mouth the dead I'll tell you right now I wouldn't have given a plugged nickel for her!"

THE REST OF THE MORNING passed quickly. Andrea found that the people who worked in the bakery were for the most part very interesting and more than ready to talk to her freely.

She heard few criticisms of Dirk Van Der Maas. His employees were loyal to him to the last man and woman from what she could discern, and they were all enthusiastic about the bakery expansion. She had the impression that they felt very much a part of it, and if it meant more work for any of them, they were willing to shoulder the burden.

"When we help Dirk, we help ourselves," one man approaching retirement age told her. "I don't want to be put out to pasture when I'm sixty-five, and Dirk says I'm not going to be. Regardless of the laws about age and discrimination, a lot of companies have a way of forcing out the older people by one means or another. I guess you know that."

Andrea nodded. She knew it very well, and deplored it. Although it was true that the young needed jobs, companies also needed the kind of experience that could come only with the years. In her opinion, it was vital that a working compromise be made between the two, and since she'd seen this done satisfactorily in a number of instances she knew that while it might be difficult, it was not impossible. She'd been made to mentally applaud Dirk many times over the course of the morning because of the things his employees had been saying about him. Now she applauded him once again for dealing positively with issues like keeping on aging employees— such as this particular man—who still had a lot to contribute.

The noon whistle blew as the older man she'd been interviewing left her office, and Andrea picked up her handbag, determined to beat a hasty retreat so that she could buy some food, take it to Klaus and try to talk some sense into him—all in the course of the lunch hour.

She was thoroughly disconcerted when she looked up to see Dirk walking in the door.

"How did it go?" he asked affably.

"F—fine," she stammered, hoping against hope that he had a luncheon date and had just stopped by to be polite.

"Evelyn doesn't have anyone scheduled to see you until two," he informed her. "I thought maybe you might like to drive out to that place on the lake where we took Johanna last spring. I checked, and it's still open."

Andrea wanted to groan aloud. There was nothing she wanted so much as to accept Dirk's invitation, to go to lunch with him and maybe, this time, to walk along the beach that skirted Lake Michigan. She yearned to share this kind of easy camaraderie with him, she longed to simply be with him. But the thought of Klaus, waiting for her, was tormenting. She couldn't go off and abandon Klaus at such a highly critical time. If she was to fail to appear, he just might take it into his head to do something crazy, such as trying to leave Holland on his own. She doubted if Jan van der Houten would help him in any escape plans after their conversation that morning.

"Dirk," she said, "I'm sorry. I . . . I'd love to go with you, but there's something I have to do."

She was painfully aware of how lame this sounded. Dirk knew that she had no friends of her own in Holland, that there'd be no one she'd be apt to have a luncheon date with. Shopping would be a poor excuse... should she offer it, she knew he'd merely tell her with a grin that she could go shopping after she got through with her afternoon interviews. She thought briefly of saying she was going to the library to do some background research, but she knew how quickly he'd dismiss that, too.

Those light-blue eyes narrowed, and though he was still smiling it was a surface smile. "Is this *something* a deep, dark secret?" he asked, and Andrea flinched.

"No," she said, too hastily. "Of course not. It's just that I...."

"That you don't want to have lunch with me, Andrea?" he suggested a shade too politely.

"No, it's not that at all. It's just that I...."

"I see," he said, and withdrew without another word.

Andrea sank in the desk chair wanting to shout after him that he didn't see anything at all! And she felt a sudden surge of anger toward Klaus for getting her into this. He'd had no right to put her in the middle between Dirk and himself.

Her mouth was set in a taut line and she was simmering as she started down the stairs. To add to matters, she was going to have to use Dirk's Mercedes to keep this rendezvous with Klaus, and that seemed particularly ironic.

The day before she'd noticed a deli not far from the van der Houten house, and she'd fixed its location in her mind, so that she had no problem finding it now. She ordered three supersize sandwiches, two for Klaus and one for herself, had a couple of kosher dill pickles tossed in with them and then, wondering what to have to drink, settled on a couple of cold root beers.

Jan van der Houten had told her that the door to his house would be unlocked, and he'd suggested she go right in, to spare Klaus the need for extra walking. She did so, feeling a little strange about it as she called out Klaus's name.

He appeared in the kitchen doorway, and the smile that crossed his face was so intense it made her glad she'd come, despite the scene with Dirk.

"Andrea!" he exclaimed. "I wasn't sure you'd make it."

If she'd yielded to her own feelings, she wouldn't have, she thought grimly. But she forced a return smile, then chattered about nothing in particular as she spread their lunch out onto the table.

Klaus grinned when he saw what she'd brought. "That looks good," he said, and attacked the first of his sandwiches without any further invitation.

Andrea wished she could share his enthusiasm for the food. The sandwich was delicious, true, but it was all she could do to swallow, her throat felt so tight and dry. Even repeated sips of the tangy root beer didn't help.

Klaus was almost through his second sandwich, and she'd barely finished a quarter of hers, when she knew she couldn't hold off getting into the nitty-gritty any longer.

"Klaus," she said, "I'm going to tell Dirk that I've been seeing you."

He'd been about to take another bite, but now he paused with his hand in midair.

"Andi," he protested, "you can't do that!"

"Yes, I can," she told him flatly. "I can, and I'm going to. This situation can't go on any longer, and don't tell me you're going to put an end to it by running away."

There was something else she had to tell him. "While the sandwiches were made up, I used a pay phone at the deli and called the hospital."

"You found out something about Julie?" Klaus gulped.

"I talked to Julie," Andrea told him.

"What?"

"You heard me. When I asked for information about Julie Kuiper, they switched me right through to her room, and she answered the phone herself."

"My God!" Klaus said, his face so pale that his eyes seemed a brighter blue than ever. "What did you say to her?"

"I told her the truth," Andrea said steadily. "I told her I'd been in touch with you and you were very concerned about her. She couldn't say much in return. I suspect her mother, someone anyway, was probably in the room with her. But she did tell me that she's doing fine. In fact she's going home tomorrow. And she said, 'Thanks a lot,' and then, 'Lots of love.' I think it's pretty plain that was a message meant for you.''

To Andrea's horror, Klaus's eyes filled with tears. He pushed the sandwich plate aside, then lowered his head into his arms, sobbing brokenly.

Andrea wondered why it always seemed so much more terrible when a man cried than when a woman cried. She felt as if her heart were being torn out of her, and there was no way she could have kept herself from going to Klaus and throwing her arms around him.

Then she straightened, patting his hair gently, as she said, ''Klaus, don't. Please don't. It's all going to work out.''

She was completely engrossed in Klaus's suffering, and was totally unprepared for the voice that came from the doorway, speaking in tones so cold they would have frozen the hottest fire.

''How touching!'' Dirk Van Der Maas observed caustically.

CHAPTER EIGHTEEN

ANDREA FROZE. Then fury took over, wiping out everything else.

"You followed me!" she choked, enraged.

"Yes, I certainly did," Dirk admitted coldly.

She straightened, confronting him, her green eyes blazing with scorn. "You had no right to do that!"

"I think I had every right," he contradicted her. "I had a strong feeling you were meddling in my business, and it seems I was correct."

How could you love a man and hate him at the same time? Andrea glared at Dirk, despising his coolness, his aloofness, the arrogant tilt of his head. He looked so damned *proper*. That smooth hair was neatly combed, not a strand out of place. Everything about Dirk Van Der Maas had to be perfect. He couldn't tolerate imperfection, either in himself or in others...which was just too damned bad, she concluded furiously.

Klaus was staring across at his brother in such a state of shock he couldn't speak at all at first, and finally managed only a helpless, "Oh my God!"

"You might try praying," Dirk advised, the

irony heavy in his voice. "Though I'd say it's a little late in the day." He laughed shortly. "Maybe I shouldn't blame you," he told Klaus. "Maybe it's a matter of genetics."

"What are you saying, Dirk?" Klaus demanded.

"You remind me of Gerrit," Dirk said, the coldness of his tone matched by the silvery glint in his eyes. And Andrea knew exactly what he was saying. He was equating Klaus and herself with Gerrit and Marietta.

"Dirk," she began, frantic to convince him that he was making a terrible mistake. "You mustn't...."

Dirk's mouth tightened. "Would you leave, please, Andrea?" he suggested, his words clearly a command rather than a request. "I want to talk to Klaus alone."

"No, I certainly will not leave! Dirk, you're jumping to conclusions. There's no validity at all to the things you're thinking."

"Have you suddenly acquired the ability to read my mind?" he inquired, the irony of his tone making her wince.

"Perhaps I have, in this one respect," she told him steadily.

His retort was curt, abrasive. "You flatter yourself, Andrea."

Each word hurt, and she flinched visibly. But then anger came to block the tears that otherwise would have threatened. Andrea said indignantly,

"Perhaps you flatter *yourself*, Dirk. Just who do you think you are? Do you really believe you can get away with bursting into a person's home and riding roughshod over everyone in it? It's a shame I can't keep you from taking out your miserable spite on Jan van der Houten—who certainly doesn't deserve it—as well as on Klaus, who doesn't deserve it, either. But I'll tell you one thing right now. You're not about to take anything out on me, because I won't stand for it!" She was warming to her subject, flinging out the words as if they were explosives set on target to destroy him.

"You can have your damned bakery and...and your well-ordered life and your gloomy absorption with a woman you should have had the sense not to love in the first place. And...and you can live with that marble facade of yours till eternity, for all I care," she raged.

She hated the caustic smile that curved his lips. "My," he said, "you do have a way with words, don't you!"

"Not enough of a way, perhaps," Andrea said, forcing herself to calm down. "Not enough to suit you, that is, but it doesn't matter. I'm resigning your account, Dirk."

He raised a quizzical eyebrow. "Is that to be considered a threat?" he asked with deceptive mildness.

"No," Andrea said, knowing that the tears couldn't be held back forever. "It's a promise, if that's what you're worried about. I'm *through*, Dirk. I'm going back to Boston as soon as I can get packed and get out of here.''

His face was impassive. He said, his tone cold as a winter chill, ''If that's the way you want it, Andrea, there isn't much I can do about it. Mark will be disappointed, I know.''

''I really don't give a damn whether Mark's disappointed or not,'' she said evenly. ''The situation's untenable. You know it and I know it and Mark will have to accept it.''

She turned to Klaus, her voice shaky as she said, ''I'm sorry. I'm really sorry! If your brother wasn't such a damned coldhearted snoop, nothing like this need have happened. I wanted to help you, I wish I could have helped you. But—'' She broke off helplessly as she looked down at Klaus.

''This isn't your fault, Andi,'' Klaus told her, his own voice trembling. But then it steadied, and he looked Dirk right in the eye. ''Don't blame the wrong people,'' he said, with remarkable control. ''I'm the one who's at fault and I'm ready to pay for it.''

Dirk didn't answer. His eyes were fixed on Andrea. He watched her as she picked up her handbag from a nearby chair, her fingers shaking as she searched through its contents. He ducked instinctively as she threw something at him that had a metal glint to it. A key ring with a single key on it clattered to the floor.

"You can take back your damned Mercedes!" Andrea told him, stabbing out the words. "I wouldn't drive any car of yours again if I had to walk for the rest of my life!"

Impulsively she reached down and kissed the top of Klaus's blond head. "Take care," she murmured brokenly. "I'm...I'm so sorry, Klaus."

Then she stalked across the kitchen, prepared to wrestle the tall man in the doorway if she had to, but he stepped aside and let her pass.

The tears started long before she reached the front door, and it was with a desperate effort that she tried to stanch them with a tissue when she heard footsteps behind her. Measured, even footsteps, a man moving without any particular hurry...yet with the capacity to quickly overtake her, even if she should start to run.

"Andrea!" Dirk said abruptly, and she had to turn to face him.

He was pale, his eyes Arctic in their coldness, but for all of that she sensed a quiet desperation about him and yearned to respond to it. Regardless of her hurt pride, her own anger, she wanted nothing so much as to feel his arms about her. She wanted him to hold her very close to him until she could cry out all the tumultuous feelings that were plunging her into a chaotic state that threatened to be dangerous. Dangerous, because she was almost certain to do something she was going to regret later. She'd already done something she was going to regret, she told herself, remembering all the things she'd just said to Dirk.

He said coldly, "You're acting like a child, Andrea. Are you *trying* to prove my conviction that women are too emotional by nature to function satisfactorily as business executives?"

He could not possibly have chosen anything worse to say to her under the circumstances. Andrea was already painfully conscious of the fact that the way in which she'd flung her resignation at him—to say nothing of the keys to his car—had been highly unprofessional. This was something she regretted, and the thought of calling him later and asking him for a strictly business appointment at his office so they could discuss matters involving the account sanely had already formed in the back of her usually well-ordered mind.

But his statement made it impossible for her to do anything like that. It would be groveling, and at the thought her wounded pride surged to the surface.

She drew herself up to her full height, holding herself so rigid that she felt as if she could easily snap into several pieces. She said levelly, "You've never wanted a woman to handle your account, Dirk, you know that. You should have been more honest at the outset, instead of giving in simply because Mark Terrence is a friend of yours."

"My friendship with Mark had nothing to do with my agreeing to have you handle the account," Dirk informed her tautly.

"No? Well, it doesn't really matter," Andrea told him. "I think we both know that after today there's no chance for either a business or a personal relationship between us, Dirk, despite the way things may have seemed to...to be going." She hesitated. "I'm not about to tolerate sexist put-downs in my business relationships. I'm good at my job. There's no reason why I should. And as for our personal relationship...."

"Yes?" he asked, the one word a challenge.

"I know the impossible when I stumble over it, Dirk. There's no way I can ever hope to overcome your distrust of women. It's far too deep-seated for me to cope with, and I suppose you can say I'm not much of a crusader at heart. There's no way I'm going to try to compete with your love for a dead woman."

She saw his nostrils flare and his mouth tighten to a thin line. A muscle twitched at the side of his lean jaw. Then he said between clenched teeth, "All right, Andrea. If that's what you truly think...if that's the way you really want it!" He turned on his heel, heading back to the kitchen.

The silence was heavy behind Andrea as she covered the rest of the distance to the front door, then stood at the top of the steps on the front porch. Her knees were trembling so badly that she wasn't sure she was going to be able to navigate her way to the sidewalk without falling down.

Sheer determination made her get a grip on herself, and once on the sidewalk level she headed toward Main Street, walking as quickly as she could without actually breaking into a run. She was possessed by the urge to put distance between herself and the van der Houten house, distance between herself and Dirk. She feared that at any moment he might come after her, his car following her alongside the curb.

Well, he could follow her all the way from there to Boston, and it would do him no good at all!

She spanned the distance from Jan van der Houten's house to Holland's Main Street in very little time, and then ducked into the nearest coffee shop because she desperately needed a chance to think.

The hot coffee was bracing. She finished one cup and ordered another, and only then did she sit back in the small rear booth she'd chosen, some of her anger slowly evaporating.

She began to wish she hadn't left the house so hastily. For one thing, she'd abandoned Klaus to fight his battle with Dirk, and she was very much afraid that Klaus wasn't up to it. Dirk was in both a mood and a position right now to trample Klaus and she was certain he wouldn't hesitate to do so. No, she thought bitterly, Dirk would never consider that what Klaus needed was not condemnation but a little understanding, a little help, the feeling that someone cared.

How could he possibly think there could be anything between Klaus and herself other than friendship? Friendship and the kind of affection a woman might be expected to have for the kid brother of the man she loved.

The man she loved. That was the worst part of all. Deeply though he'd hurt her in making such a ridiculous allegation about Klaus and herself, she still loved him.

I always will love him, she thought dismally. *But there's no chance for us. No chance at all. Dirk's made that as clear as anyone possibly could. And he was right, of course. I was about as unprofessional as anyone could be today, and if that's confirmed his opinion about women executives, I have only myself to blame.*

She closed her eyes wearily, opening them only when she heard the waitress say, "Can I get you something else, miss?"

"Thanks, no," Andrea said. "Just the check."

She finished the last of her coffee and slowly stood up. At first she'd thought she'd find the nearest agency and rent a car, but that seemed pointless. She was going to need transportation just two more times while she was in Holland—once to get back to the Van Der Maas house, and once to get to the airport. A taxi would do in both instances.

The driver of the taxi she selected for her first trip was a man who reminded her faintly of Jan van der Houten and he spoke mostly in monosyllables, for which Andrea was grateful. She was in no mood to get into a running conversation.

He pulled up in front of the entrance at the Lakeshore Drive house, and she paid him and got out. Then she suffered a bad moment. If Monica Van Der Maas was at home, all of this was going to be very difficult to explain.

She glanced at her watch. It was just after two, and in another hour or so Johanna would be home. It was imperative that she leave before then.

She turned back to the cab driver, who was just about to pull away.

"Would you be able to come back and take me to Grand Rapids in about half an hour?" she asked him.

He blinked. "Grand Rapids?"

"Yes," Andrea said impatiently.

"I don't usually make out-of-town trips like that," he mused. "We'd have to set a price."

"Whatever you think is fair will be all right with me," she assured him.

He nodded slowly. "All right, then. Half an hour, you said?"

"Yes." She glanced at her watch again. "In fact, if you'll be here at two-thirty I should be ready. Or, at least, I won't keep you waiting long."

Andrea pushed open the front door and sped up the stairs. There was always the chance of running into Mabel or her husband, which would be a lot easier than facing Monica Van Der Maas. But Andrea wanted to avoid them, too, if possible. Chances were, though, that Mabel and Henry were either out or else upstairs resting in their third-floor apartment.

The house seemed very silent, for which she was profoundly grateful. Mrs. Van Der Maas was probably out, but if she was in she was probably resting in her room at the opposite end of the house from the guest room Andrea was using.

Fortunately Andrea had not brought many things along with her on this trip to Michigan. She didn't want to leave anything behind if she could help it. It was imperative, in her mind, that she sever her connection with the Van Der Maases totally and permanently. A sudden image of Johanna came to haunt her, and this hurt. She was letting the little girl down, something she hated to do.

Klaus and Johanna, she thought sadly. The two innocents. They were certainly getting the worst of the deal.

She couldn't bear to dwell on thoughts of either of them, because to do so would only be to cause her to think twice about what she was doing. She was definitely abandoning Johanna, and maybe Klaus too, for that matter, though she reminded herself that he was old enough to stand on his own feet.

Johanna. She'd promised her little friend that they'd go down to the pool that afternoon, and she knew what a terrific implication it would have if Johanna actually followed through and put her toes in the water.

Well, she thought resolutely, it couldn't be helped. Once she was back in Boston she'd write Johanna a letter and explain why she'd had to leave, or maybe she'd even call her up. She'd call at a time in the afternoon when Johanna was just getting home from school, and there'd be no danger of Dirk being in the house to intercept anything she might say. She'd explain why she'd left as well as one could explain such a thing to a seven-year-old. Anyway, somehow she'd make Johanna understand that it had been impossible for her to stay....

She went into the bathroom to get her toothbrush and a few cosmetics she'd left on the vanity, then with a final glance around her, concluded that she'd gathered up everything that belonged to her. Glancing at her watch, she saw that it was nearly two-thirty. Her cab had probably already arrived or would shortly.

She had zipped up her suitcase and was fastening the buckle that covered the zipper closing when the thing she'd been fearing the most happened.

A small voice spoke from the doorway. "Andi? Where are you going?"

Andrea swung around to see Johanna, dressed in jeans and a red T-shirt with a green frog on it, instead of her usual school clothes.

"Johanna?" she gasped. "What are you doing out of school?"

"There's a teacher's meeting this afternoon so we got out at noon," Johanna reported, slowly advancing into the room. "I forgot about it, or I would have asked you last night if you could come home and have lunch with me. Andi...where are you going?"

Andrea felt as if her heart was flipping over. She said carefully, "Darling, I've got to go back to Boston. No, Johanna, don't look like that. You and I are going to keep in touch with each other. We're always going to be friends. I think you know that, don't you?"

Johanna nodded, but she said, "Is that why the taxi's down in front of the house?"

"Yes," Andrea admitted. "And I must hurry. I have a plane to catch."

This was only half a fib, she consoled herself. It was true that she had a plane to catch, though she had no idea when she was going to catch it. She hadn't stopped to check an airline schedule. She'd thought only of getting away from Holland and had decided that if she missed the last flight of the day from Grand Rapids to Detroit, or anywhere else she might connect with a plane for Boston, she would simply stay overnight at a motel and take the first flight out in the morning. In fact, the more she thought about it, the better it seemed to stay overnight in Grand Rapids anyway. She wasn't prepared to face Boston just a few hours from now. She wasn't ready to face either Mark or Carl Saunders. She needed to buy herself a little time, and an overnight rest would help a great deal.

She heaved her suitcase off the bed and was about to pick it up when Johanna's voice arrested her. "Aren't you going to wait to say goodbye to Uncle Dirk?" Johanna asked her.

"I've already spoken to your uncle," Andrea managed to reply—and that was the truth!

She picked up the suitcase, her tote bag and her handbag and started for the door, almost afraid to ask the next question. "Is your grandmother home, Johanna?"

Johanna shook her head. "No. This is her bridge afternoon. Sometimes it's here, but I think today she's playing at Mrs. Ter Horst's. You could phone her there," she added hopefully.

"No, darling, I won't interrupt her game," Andrea said quickly. "Johanna, say goodbye to her for me, will you? Tell her I'll be in touch as soon as I'm settled in Boston again, and tell her that I thank her so very much for everything she's done for me."

Again she started for the door, but Johanna's voice halted her in her tracks. With that odd perception children sometimes seem to have, she said, "You're not coming back, are you, Andi?"

"Please, Johanna," Andrea protested.

She knew that in another instant she'd be in tears, and so would Johanna.

Her voice very small, Johanna asked, "Can I help you carry something, Andi?"

"Thank you, darling, but no," Andrea said,

heading out into the hall and starting toward the stairs. "The bags sort of balance each other."

She forced herself to move a step at a time, wondering how she could possibly make it down the beautiful curving staircase with this small solemn figure trailing along behind her.

Then, when she'd reached the bottom, she was again stopped by Johanna's voice.

"Andi!" Johanna called, and Andrea turned to see that the little girl had paused on the lowest step.

Johanna's lower lip trembled as she said, "I don't want to watch you drive away so I'll...I'll say goodbye to you here." And then the tears brimmed.

Andrea dropped her bags and ran over to the staircase to embrace Johanna's small figure in her arms, her own tears streaming down her face.

"Darling, Johanna, you mustn't cry!" she managed between sobs. "This is just goodbye for a while, I promise you. You can come visit me in Boston when you're a little bit older. Maybe your grandmother might bring you for a visit, meantime. And...."

"Yes?" Johanna wavered.

"You've got to promise me something. Promise me that you'll get your grandmother to play our game with you and that you'll go into the pool and wiggle your toes with her. Promise me that, will you, Johanna?"

Johanna shook her head. "No," she said resolutely. "I don't want to play that game with anyone but you, Andi."

"But you must," Andrea persisted. "Oh, Johanna, you can't go on being afraid of the water, don't you see? There's no reason for you to be afraid of the water! You have to be cautious about it, just as you have to be cautious about almost anything you do, but that doesn't mean you need to be afraid! Try to remember that, will you, darling?"

Johanna nodded solemnly. "Yes, Andi," she said. "I will. I...I'll try. Oh, Andi...I love you so much!"

Andrea gave Johanna one last fervent embrace and then forced herself to break away, almost running through the doorway and down the front walk, refusing to look back once she'd gotten into the cab.

Before they'd turned onto the Interstate Highway on the outskirts of Holland, she'd soaked through the two tissues she'd found in her handbag, and the tears were still streaming down her face. She was conscious of the cab driver's occasional, concerned glances reflected in his rearview mirror, and finally he asked, "Would you like me to pull over into a rest area, miss? Is there anything I can do for you?"

"No, no," Andrea said, "I'll be fine. It's just that...well, sometimes goodbyes are very difficult."

"That they are," the man agreed.

To her relief, he didn't pursue the subject, and

they continued on through the warm September afternoon, the sun casting its golden benediction on fields where the corn was ripe, harvest time almost at hand.

Her awareness of the day's beauty only increased Andrea's sense of sadness. She was glad when they came to the outskirts of Grand Rapids, and she could concentrate on what she was going to do next.

Definitely, she was too weary emotionally to go back to Boston today, regardless of flight schedules. This decision made, she said to the cab driver, "Could you suggest a motel fairly near the airport?"

"There are a number of them," he told her. "The Marriott and the Hilton both run free buses over to the airport, or there's...."

"Either the Marriott or the Hilton will be fine," she told him.

Fifteen minutes later she was settled in a spacious room that featured all the amenities from both indoor and outdoor swimming pools to a sauna, tennis courts and even a private nine-hole golf course...none of these interesting Andrea in the least. Her throat felt parched, and she decided to order up some ginger ale from room service. She knew this wasn't the time to indulge in anything alcoholic. She was much too tense.

After she'd sipped some of the ginger ale, she took a refreshing shower, and then slipped into a pale-pink terry lounger. Though she seldom watched daytime television, she was willing to try anything that might prove to be a diversion. She badly needed to get away from herself, and her own thoughts.

She found an old John Wayne movie being shown, which ordinarily would have offered a good escape. But it was impossible to shut the memory of Johanna's sad little face out of her mind. Or of Klaus, much too pale and much too worried. Or of Dirk.

Why did Dirk have to be so cold, so unyielding? How could a man who could make love to a woman as he had to her last night turn to stone only a few hours later?

But then, she had to admit, there had been nothing very stonelike about Dirk at the van der Houtens. He may have looked calm outwardly, but she'd been thoroughly aware of his contained rage. A rage whose intensity had matched her own fury when she'd realized he'd been spying on her.

It still seemed incredible to her that Dirk had followed her. She wondered if someone in the bakery had discovered that Klaus was staying at Jan van der Houten's house and had passed the word along to Dirk, and if maybe Dirk hadn't been spying on her after all, but had merely gone to the van der Houtens to confront Klaus.

But no, she remembered. He'd admitted that he'd followed her. She recalled the contempt in his voice as he'd observed, "How touching!" when he'd come upon her bending over Klaus, stroking his hair. In retrospect it occurred to her that Dirk had sounded as if he was jealous.

She tried to force her attention back to the TV movie, but it was impossible to concentrate on it, and she'd already lost track of the plot.

Finally she switched off the television and then tried to practice some elementary meditation she'd started to study a few months back after the traumatic experience she'd gone through with George Cabot.

Her mind was so fertile, though, and her imagination so active that it had always been close to impossible for her to block out straying thoughts. She'd often become impatient with herself because she lacked the kind of concentration to meditate. She'd concluded that with someone like herself it would take a great deal of practice to focus on a single word and hold it to the exclusion of everything else.

Now the problem was that the only word she could think of focusing on was "Dirk," and all the wrong images started to crowd in on her.

Although she didn't succeed very well when it came to meditation, the effort of trying to block her own thoughts did make her begin to feel sleepy after a time, and she drowsed off as the afternoon waned, shadows coming to replace the sunlight filtering through the filmy curtains at the windows.

It was dark when she became conscious of a pounding at the door, the sound startling her so that her pulse began to race. She switched on the bedside light, reason coming to take over temporary fright. No one knew she was there, so it had to be the room-service waiter come to take back the tray and glass he'd brought earlier with her ginger ale.

It didn't occur to her to hesitate before flinging open the door. But then, as quickly as she opened it, she slammed it again.

A moment later she was ready to believe she'd been hallucinating. Dirk Van Der Maas couldn't be standing outside in the hallway. He couldn't be. She must have imagined him.

But there was nothing imaginary about the pounding that resumed again, or the angry voice that was calling, "Open up, Andrea, or so help me God I'll break the door in!"

CHAPTER NINETEEN

ANDREA OPENED THE DOOR and stood aside so Dirk could enter, her fury mounting as she hissed, "Quiet down, will you! You'll have the management calling the police."

"Then they may only be saving me the trouble," he retorted, turning on her, his eyes blazing with an anger that more than matched hers. "What have you done with Johanna?"

"Are you crazy?" Andrea demanded. "What makes you think I've done anything with Johanna."

Dirk was peering around the room as if he expected to see the child, and Andrea shook her head, thoroughly exasperated. "Why don't you look under the bed?" she demanded.

"Perhaps I should," he snapped. He ran an agitated hand through his hair, mussing it. "Don't play games with me," he advised her tersely. "If Johanna isn't here, where is she?"

"Dirk, be reasonable," Andrea began, her voice rising. With an effort, she lowered it. "How would I know?" she asked him, and hoped he'd recognize a logical question when he heard one. "The last time I saw Johanna she was standing at the foot of the stairs in your house."

"When was that?"

"Several hours ago, I suppose. What time is it?"

"Nine o'clock," he said shortly. "It took me a while to find out where you'd headed."

"What did you do?" she asked nastily. "Hire a team of private detectives?"

"Thanks," he said, the word dripping sarcasm. "Believe it or not, I was able to figure it out for myself." He added reluctantly, "The cab driver said you didn't have a child with you, but I had to make sure."

"You do have a lot of faith in your fellow man, don't you, Dirk?" Andrea flung the question at him. "You don't merely distrust women, you distrust everyone."

"I'm not going to get into anything like that with you," Dirk said disgustedly. To her surprise, he took off his glasses and rubbed the bridge of his nose wearily. Without the glasses, the lines of fatigue on his face seemed much more noticeable. He looked older, haggard.

"Dirk," she began uncertainly.

"Look, Andrea," he interrupted, "I'm saying it again. Don't try to play games with me! The only person Johanna would have gone off with is you. She trusts you more than she trusts anyone else... including my mother and me. That's why I consider it so rotten of you to have taken advantage of her...as you obviously have."

It would have been easy to let her anger dominate again, but Andrea sensed the ring of desperation in Dirk's voice and her tone was almost gentle as she said, "Dirk, believe me, I'm telling you the truth. I left Johanna in your house. If she isn't there now, I have absolutely no idea where she is.

"Furthermore," she added, hurt by his ready assumption that she could use the child both of them loved as a tool, "I think I'd give up my own life before I would do anything to undermine Johanna's faith in me."

The minute she'd finished this sentence she realized how intensely dramatic it must have sounded to him. Yet it had an effect. He turned away from her, his tenseness manifest in the rigid way he was holding his shoulders.

"Do you have something to drink?" he demanded.

"No. I had some ginger ale, but...."

"I want something a hell of a lot stronger than ginger ale," he said roughly. "Do you mind if I call room service?"

"No, of course not."

He put his glasses back on as he went to dial the telephone, and it struck her that in this one area, the matter of his eyesight, Dirk Van Der Maas was not entirely perfect, and somehow this made him all the more appealing. Andrea's senses stirred treacherously.

"Will you drink Scotch?" he asked her abruptly, and any softening she might have felt toward him dissipated swiftly.

"Yes," she said.

She heard him give the order for a bottle of Scotch, club soda and ice, and when he'd hung up she asked, "Did you have to order a whole bottle?"

For the first time he looked at her in a way that was almost human. "If we don't drink it all, it'll keep," he said laconically.

He sat down and stretched his long legs out in front of him. He was wearing faded jeans and a rumpled gray T-shirt, and he looked as if he could use a shave. Andrea, who had never seen him like this, felt a sudden wave of fear pass over her.

"Dirk," she asked, "don't you really know where Johanna is?"

He glared at her. "Do you *really* think I'd have come storming in here like a madman to accuse you of kidnapping my niece if I knew where she was?" he flared. "What do you take me for, Andrea?"

He got up again, further rumpling his hair as he ran agitated fingers through it. "What did you tell her when you left?" he demanded.

"When I went back to the house after leaving Klaus," Andrea said slowly, "I thought Johanna was still in school. But there'd been a teacher's meeting scheduled for this afternoon, so she'd gotten out early."

"I know that," he put in impatiently.

"I was packing. I'd just finished when she walked in on me," Andrea continued, finding it unexpectedly difficult to tell Dirk all this. He was watching her closely, and the ragged pain she saw in his eyes was having an adverse effect on her self-control.

"It . . . it was the last thing in the world I wanted to have happen," she said in little more than a whisper.

"I can imagine!" Dirk retorted bitterly.

"Dirk, don't you know I wouldn't do anything in the world to hurt Johanna?"

He drew a long breath. Then he said, "Yes, I do know that, Andrea. I'd thought maybe you'd try to use Johanna in an attempt to get back at me. But . . . it was an unfair assumption. I admit that."

The question had to be asked. "Are you sure she really has disappeared, Dirk? Couldn't she simply have gone to visit someone?"

He shook his head. "No. At least it's highly doubtful."

"She said that your mother had gone to play bridge at a friend's house," Andrea remembered.

He nodded. "Yes. At the Ter Horsts'."

"Couldn't Johanna have gone over there to meet her grandmother, perhaps?" Johanna, Andrea remembered, had been terribly upset when she'd left her. It seemed reasonable to think that the child might have tried to find someone close to her, at such a time, and Monica Van Der Maas was a likely candidate.

"I thought that at first myself," Dirk admitted. "I got home shortly after five, and Mabel was just beginning to start dinner preparations. She said she'd had a bad headache earlier and she went upstairs to lie down for a while and fell asleep. She had no idea where Johanna might be, but like you, she remembered that it was my mother's bridge day. Henry had gone into town for some supplies, and so he hadn't seen Johanna at all.

"After I checked and found that Johanna wasn't anywhere around the house, I called the Ter Horsts. My mother had already left. She walked in just a couple of minutes later. She hadn't seen Johanna. She thought maybe you'd come home and Johanna had gone off somewhere with you.

"I knew better," Dirk admitted. "At least I was afraid I knew better. You'd made yourself plain enough, there in Jan van der Houten's house. But. . . I thought maybe once you'd left you'd cool off and at least decide not to go back to Boston until you and I had talked again."

His eyes met hers levelly. "I should have known better, shouldn't I?" he asked quietly. "I should have known that you don't make idle threats. You say what you mean, even when you're angry, and you follow up with action."

Andrea could find no answer to this.

"Anyway, I went up to your room," Dirk continued wearily. "Your things were all gone, of course, and it didn't take much snooping ability, as you might put it, to figure out what had happened. You didn't have a car, though, having returned the keys to my Mercedes to me so graciously, so I realized that the logical way for you to have gotten to the airport would have been by cab. I started calling the cab companies in town. There aren't that many of them, so in a relatively short space of time I connected with your driver.''

"You should be in the CIA,'' Andrea said caustically.

"Maybe I should be. Anyway, I phoned Mark...."

"What?"

"I phoned Mark. I thought you'd have been in touch with him by then.''

"Damn you!'' Andrea moaned. "You do butt into everyone's business, don't you?''

"You're saying that to *me*?''

The knock at the door was a welcome reprieve. Dirk relieved the waiter of his tray and, bringing it back into the room, set it on top of a chest of drawers.

"If you don't mind,'' he told Andrea, "I'm going to make myself a drink. I can't remember when I've needed one more than I do right now. Will you join me?''

She nodded. "Yes. Don't make mine too strong, though. If you do, I'm apt to fall flat on my face.''

"I suppose you've eaten practically nothing all day?''

She was surprised that whether or not she'd had anything to eat would matter to him, but she only said, "I...wasn't hungry."

Dirk shook his head at this. "I'll order some food sent up later. Right now...."

He doled ice cubes into two glasses, splashed whisky over the ice, added a generous amount of club soda to Andrea's and very little to his. "Here," he said, handing the glass to her.

"Thank you, Dirk." It was an automatic response, but it elicited a quizzical expression.

"How polite you can be, even under trying circumstances, Andrea," he observed.

"There's no need to be snide."

"Let's say that it has been a hell of a day, and you've had a lot to do with causing it," he accused.

She bristled. "In your opinion, which isn't necessarily valid."

"Oh?" He'd sat down and stretched out his legs again, and he prodded an ice cube with a long finger. "What's your opinion, Andrea? What kind of a game were you playing with Klaus in Jan van der Houten's kitchen?"

The chair Dirk had chosen was one of a pair, placed on either side of a low round table. Andrea, feeling as if her legs were about to give out on her, sank onto the other chair and put her drink, yet untouched, down on the table.

"I wasn't playing any kind of a game, Dirk," she

said steadily, and she knew it was very important to her that he believe this.

"The scene I interrupted was touchingly affectionate."

"That was your interpretation of it. I'd just told Klaus something that affected him...strongly. I felt very sorry for him. It was a natural impulse to put my arms around him."

"I see." Dirk took a hefty swig of his drink, then asked, "Do you always yield to your natural impulses, Andrea? Or shouldn't I ask that question. Or should I, perhaps, trust the voice of my own experience where you're concerned. Was it a natural impulse you were giving in to when you were with me in the studio the other night? Are you always so impulsive when you're with a man?"

She reached toward her glass of Scotch, ready to throw the liquor and the ice cubes right in his face, but he raised a weary hand and said, "Don't bother. It would be a waste of good whisky."

Her pulse was pounding, and she felt as if he'd torn something deep within her. The ragged edges of whatever it was—her heart, maybe?—were hurting so much that she could hardly breathe.

She found the strength to say just two words. "Please leave."

This was plainly not something Dirk had expected to hear, and there was scorn in the way he surveyed her as he said, "I'm not about to go anywhere until you and I settle a few things, dear Miss Campbell."

"I disagree, Mr. Van Der Maas," she told him icily. She found the strength to get up and to move across to the telephone. She was reaching for the receiver when a lean tanned hand intercepted her.

Dirk held her wrist so tightly that it made her wince. But his voice was level, emotionless, as he asked, "Just what were you about to do?"

"Call the desk," she told him defiantly, managing to free her wrist, "to have you evicted."

He stared down at her for a long moment, his face blank. Then he said slowly, "You'd actually do that, wouldn't you?"

"Yes, you're damned right I would!" Andrea assured him. "And will, unless you get out of here...or beat me to a pulp trying to stop me!"

She added bitterly, "If you're so concerned about Johanna, shouldn't you be out trying to find her instead of here, making my life hell?"

She thought for a moment that Dirk was going to strike her. Then he expelled a long breath, a very long breath, and said in that same toneless voice, "You're right, of course. You and I should both be out looking for Johanna."

Her reaction was swift. "Leave me out of it, Dirk," she warned him. "I don't have your snooping abilities. And even if I did, you know far better than I where Johanna might be found."

He shook his head in disagreement but he only said, "May I use your phone?"

"Why ask?" she taunted. "You'll use it anyway if you want to, won't you?"

"At the moment, yes."

Andrea's mind was whirling and she felt sick, bruised... and terrified when she thought of Johanna.

Was there a chance that the child could have been kidnapped? It was not beyond the realm of possibility. The Van Der Masses were wealthy, although they were not at all ostentatious about it. And if Johanna hadn't been kidnapped, where could she be? She'd been so upset... Andrea didn't like the thought of her wandering off in such an unhappy frame of mind.

Her speculation came to an abrupt end as she heard Dirk say, "Klaus?"

She stiffened, wondering what was about to happen next, and was surprised to hear Dirk speaking in a reasonably normal tone of voice to his brother.

"I'm with Andrea here in Grand Rapids," Dirk was saying. "She decided to stay over for the night.... No, Johanna isn't with her. I'm going to order up something for both of us to eat, and then we'll be heading back to Holland. In the meantime I think you'd better call the police."

After a few monosyllables in answer to something Klaus said to him, Dirk hung up the phone, and Andrea flinched as she saw the expression on his face. He looked as if he was just about spent, both physically and emotionally. But then he straightened, staring across at her coolly as he asked, "What would you like to eat?"

She marveled that he could even think of food at such a time.

"Nothing," she told him shortly.

"Then I'll order soup and a dessert for both of us," he said firmly. "Dessert, because you'll need the energy."

Watching him, Andrea tried to convince herself that she hated Dirk Van Der Maas. She almost succeeded when he turned away from the phone, having placed his order, to say, "You might as well pack up your things while we're waiting for room service. I want to get back to Holland as soon as we've eaten."

"We?" she asked.

"You're going with me," he said firmly.

"I am not going with you anywhere, Dirk. I think you'd have a rather difficult time dragging me out of here by brute force without someone noticing. And I can assure you that's the only way you could manage it."

He shook his head. "You're going with me!"

"You're out of your mind, Dirk!"

He rose by way of answer and fixed himself another drink. Then he turned, glass in hand, to say, "I'm not suggesting that you come back to Holland because of me, Andrea. I've got enough sense to know that at this point you wouldn't do anything for me...nor is there any reason why you should. But I do ask you to think of Johanna. Wherever she is, she must be very lonely and frightened about now, and she's already had a severe enough problem with fear. This can only add to the trauma...so it's imperative we find her as quickly as possible, and that's going to require a united effort.''

''You plead very well,'' Andrea told him, ''but not well enough.''

''Look,'' he said, his voice edged with desperation. ''Can't you see that this isn't a time to get into a war between the two of us? Declare that later, if you want to, but right now let's do what has to be done first, and that's to find Johanna. I don't know how we're going to find her or where we're going to find her,'' he added heavily, ''or even if she'll be alive but—''

''Dirk!'' Andrea intercepted sharply.

''Something may have happened to her, Andrea. That's a possibility we have to face.''

Her anger toward him dissolved, everything in her centering upon the thought of Johanna out somewhere in the dark...alone.

She remembered something else. ''Where was Klaus when you spoke to him?'' she asked.

''Where? At home,'' he answered, seeming surprised by her question.

''Your home?''

"Our home," he corrected. "It's as much Klaus's home as it is mine."

He added slowly, "Klaus has told me that he told Jan van der Houten I'd thrown him out, and Jan subsequently told you this. So I can understand both Jan's shock and yours, to think that anyone would do such a thing to another person under such circumstances, let alone to one's own brother."

"It was wrong of Klaus to have said that, and I told him so," Andrea admitted.

"Yes," Dirk agreed carefully. "He said you had. Andrea...."

She looked pale and tired and frightened, and her green eyes were enormous. "Yes?" she asked.

"Please," Dirk said. "Please come back to Holland with me."

Again, a reprieve came for both of them with the arrival of the room-service waiter.

Dirk had ordered beef stew for both of them instead of soup. It was hearty and nourishing, and he didn't have to convince Andrea that she really needed to eat something. But she balked when it came to the chocolate cake he'd chosen for dessert.

"I can't," she protested.

"All right," he said. "Coffee, though."

"Yes, please."

They hadn't spoken at all while they were eating. Andrea had been trying to think, trying to come to a logical decision about what she should do. But it was almost impossible to be logical with Dirk sitting just across from her, so close she could easily reach out and touch him.

There were so many things to think about. Johanna, first of all. And Klaus, too. She marveled that Dirk had been able to persuade Klaus to go back to the house on Lakeshore Drive, and thinking about this she asked abruptly, "What is going to happen to Jan van der Houten?"

Dirk had been toying with his chocolate cake and she sensed he had no more appetite than she did. He put down his fork and looked across at her as if he was wondering whether he'd heard her correctly. "What?" he asked.

"Jan van der Houten. What is going to happen to him?"

"He'll be leaving Holland shortly," Dirk said.

Andrea's green eyes blazed with scorn. "Then you really are going to get rid of him, aren't you?" she asked bitterly.

"Get rid of Jan?" Dirk echoed, perplexed. "He'll be leaving Holland to go on a tour of some of the major bakeries around the country that have large frozen-food divisions," he explained. "They've been kind enough to agree to let us share their expertise. Jan will be assuming new duties as supervisor of our frozen-food division once we open. He'll be taking a few university-level courses over the winter and spring. I want him to learn all he can learn before we get into operation. He'll have men working with him who've had experience in this field, but I want Jan to be in charge. He's a quick learner, and he has a very level head. He's also been loyal to the Van Der Maases for a long, long time. He deserves to profit.''

He paused then asked, ''Did you really believe I was going to fire him?''

''Jan felt, as Klaus did, that he wouldn't stand a chance with you if you ever learned he'd harbored Klaus in his house,'' she said carefully, knowing that this was hurting him.

''I see,'' Dirk nodded. ''Well. . . I can't say that I blame either of them. I suppose if I'd been in their position I might have thought the same thing. I might have hoped that they had a slightly higher opinion of me, but—''

''They both have a very high opinion of you, Dirk,'' she interrupted. ''So do all the people who work with you. All the people who know you.''

He didn't reply, and looking at him, Andrea surprised an odd expression in his eyes. Briefly Dirk looked first hurt, then moved. She almost fancied that she saw a glint of tears, then told herself that wouldn't be Dirk. That would never be Dirk.

He pushed back his chair and stood up. ''Please,'' he said, ''come with me, Andrea. I'm so damned tired and wrung out I don't think I have the strength left to argue with you about it. But it would mean an awful lot to Klaus and my mother to have you with us tonight.''

Andrea wished he could have found it in his heart to add that it would also mean a great deal to him.

CHAPTER TWENTY

THE TRAFFIC WAS LIGHT, and they made good time on the trip back to Holland. They spoke only in monosyllables, and until they pulled up in front of the Lakeshore Drive house and Dirk slumped back in the seat, dropping his hands from the steering wheel, Andrea did not become fully aware of how exhausted he was.

She said reproachfully, "I could have shared the driving, you know."

"It wasn't much of a drive," he told her, and then smiled, a lopsided smile that had a very disturbing effect on her. "Anyway," he said simply, "you're more done in than I am."

He glanced toward the house, blazing with lights. "Keep your fingers crossed," he said. "Maybe Johanna's back home!"

But Johanna wasn't back home.

Klaus and his mother were in the kitchen. Monica Van Der Maas got to her feet swiftly when she saw Andrea and embraced her warmly.

"Thank God Dirk found you!" she said.

Andrea, who had been dreading this reunion, returned Mrs. Van Der Maas's embrace with equal fervor, and then met Klaus's blue eyes.

"Thanks for coming back, Andi," Klaus said simply.

"Have you had any word about Johanna?" Dirk interposed.

Klaus shook his head. "Nothing. The cops are out beating the bushes, they've called in the state police to help. They've made inquiries at houses all up and down the road. Nobody's seen her."

Dirk shook his head. "I can't see how she could wander away without someone spotting her," he said. "A little girl her age...."

He turned to his brother. "No phone calls?" he asked, a strange note in his voice, and suddenly Andrea knew what he meant. He was thinking of a possible ransom demand.

"No," Klaus said. "And...Dirk...."

"Yes?"

"If Johanna's been kidnapped," Klaus said steadily, "I think we would have heard from someone by now."

Dirk turned to Andrea. "Do you remember exactly what time it was when you left here this afternoon?"

"Yes," she said. "The cab came for me at two-thirty, or very close to it. I...I stopped to say goodbye to Johanna, but I'm sure I was on my way before a quarter to three."

Dirk glanced at his watch. "And it's almost midnight," he said. "Nine hours." His mouth tightened. "Where in hell could she have gotten to in nine hours without anyone seeing her?"

Andrea had thought of something terrible. Something so horrible she shrank from even mentioning it. Then she felt Dirk's eyes sweep her face and he asked impatiently, "What is it, Andrea?"

"Dirk," she protested, moistening her lips nervously, "I don't like to even bring it up...."

"This is no time to hedge!"

"Well, I...I can't help but wonder if she could possibly have gone down to the lake."

"Johanna?" Monica Van Der Maas echoed. "She's terrified of the water, Andrea."

"I know," Andrea said unhappily. "But we'd been talking about it lately. She'd agreed to go in the pool with me. We were both going to stand in the shallows and...and wiggle our toes."

Dirk caught his breath. "She agreed to do that with you?"

"Yes, she did. Then today, when I was leaving...." Andrea couldn't go on.

Dirk's voice was sharp. "Yes?"

"I suggested that she ask you to go with her instead, Mrs. Van Der Maas," Andrea admitted. "She...she told me she wouldn't do it with anyone but me. I told her then that she...that she mustn't be afraid of the water," Andrea went on, each word becoming more difficult to utter.

Dear God, what had she done!

She glanced at Dirk and felt as if she were being burned by the pure blue of his eyes. Then she heard Monica Van Der Maas urge, "Go on, Andrea. Please, dear!"

"Well, I told Johanna that you had to be careful with...with water, as you had to be with just about everything. But that there was no reason to fear water more than...than anything else. And I had the feeling she was listening to me, that she believed me."

"So you think she might have wandered down to Lake Macatawa to test out your theory for herself?" Dirk asked so coldly that she flinched.

"I...I don't know," she stammered.

"Of course you don't know," Mrs. Van Der Maas said gently. "But even if Johanna did go down to the lake, that doesn't mean anything... happened to her."

Andrea had the impression that Monica Van Der Maas was trying to convince herself about this... and not succeeding very well.

"Dirk," Mrs. Van Der Maas suggested now, "why not tell the police that there's a chance she could be...wandering somewhere along the lake front."

"For nine hours?" Dirk asked caustically. "Come on, mother! I agree, though, that the lake area will have to be searched. Excuse me. I'll use the phone in the library."

As Dirk strode out of the room, Mrs. Van Der

Maas said, "Andrea, sit down before you fall down, will you? You look absolutely exhausted!"

Andrea obligingly pulled out one of the kitchen chairs and sank onto it gratefully.

"May I get you a cup of coffee?"

"No, thank you. Dirk and I had some just before we left Grand Rapids. Mrs. Van Der Maas...."

"Yes, dear?"

"I am...so sorry."

"Don't blame yourself needlessly," the older woman said. "Too many people around here have been blaming themselves needlessly for a lot of things. You had every right to pack up and go back to Boston under the circumstances. Both Klaus and Dirk have told me what happened, and I can imagine how you must have felt when Dirk appeared at the van der Houtens this afternoon."

"I got you into this," Klaus said abjectly. "I should have had the guts to handle things myself without drawing either you or Jan into my mess."

"I'm going to give you the same advice I just gave Andrea," his mother said tartly. "Don't heap blame on yourself, Klaus. Accept guilt for those things you may be guilty of, if you must. Personally I don't think we know yet how guilty you really were of anything. But it was a natural impulse for you to leave here and go to Jan. You've known him all your life, you trust him."

"He's...a very good friend," Klaus said.

Andrea, touched by the misery in his eyes, had to tell him what Dirk had told her.

"Dirk isn't going to fire Jan van der Houten," she said. "As a matter of fact, he's going to promote him, Klaus."

"Yes, I know," Klaus said, to her surprise. "Dirk told me about it this afternoon."

Monica Van Der Maas's tired face mirrored her surprise. "Did the two of you actually think that Dirk would fire Jan because he'd taken you in, Klaus?" she demanded.

"I did," Klaus admitted, "and I told Andrea so."

"Dirk would never do such a thing!" his mother said staunchly.

"What would Dirk never do?" The subject of their discussion slowly walked back into the kitchen.

"We were talking about the mistaken idea that you might have considered firing Jan," his mother told him.

"I see." He glanced toward the trio sitting at the table, and this time Andrea had no problem reading the expression in his eyes. Both she and Klaus had hurt Dirk deeply because they'd assumed he would fire the plant supervisor for his interference in the Van Der Maases personal affairs. His reaction was a revelation to her. She'd thought Dirk far too autocratic to be concerned about what others might think, especially of his business actions.

It was strange, but this sudden insight into him had an almost therapeutic effect on her. All the resentment, all the anger she'd felt toward Dirk began to evaporate, and what was left was what had been there all along, surviving in the face of everything else. Her love for him.

The impulse to go over to him and try to console him was almost overwhelming. The urge to try to make him understand that she knew how wrong she'd been in her assumptions about him was so intense it became impossible for her to sit still any longer.

Andrea got to her feet so suddenly that both Klaus and his mother looked up, startled.

"Couldn't we try to find Johanna?" she demanded. "I know you can't move around, Klaus, and you should stay here, Mrs. Van Der Maas, in case there are any phone calls. But Dirk and I...."

Dirk and I. She saw his beautiful mouth twist with irony, she sensed his pain, and she wanted to cry out to him, to reassure him. But before she could speak he asked, skeptically, "Where would you suggest we start looking, Andrea?"

"I don't know," she admitted. "But there must be places where Andrea might have gone. Places, maybe, where she thought she could hide, though I don't know why she would have wanted to hide from any of you."

A thought struck her. "Did Johanna take anything with her?"

"The police asked us that same question," Monica Van Der Maas admitted. "All I could tell them was that as far as I know, she didn't. But Johanna has so many dolls I've never been able to keep count of them. She might have taken a doll with her..."

"Would you mind if I look in her room, Mrs. Van Der Maas?" Andrea asked. "She's shown me some of the things she treasures. I might be able to spot it if she took any of them with her."

"Of course I don't mind," Mrs. Van Der Maas said quickly. "I'll come with you if you like."

"I'll go with her," Dirk volunteered quickly, and Andrea's pulse began to quicken when she heard this.

All the way up the long curving flight of stairs she was intensely conscious of Dirk, just behind her, moving with steady, silent strength. He'd turned on the lights in the upstairs hall, and once inside Johanna's room he flicked on the ceiling light.

Looking around, Andrea felt a terrible wrench. The pretty canopy bed, the parade of dolls, all of Johanna's things there, yet there was such a sense of emptiness.

All of her things? Andrea looked more closely. Then she began to scan the dolls, one by one, and when she'd finished she said triumphantly, "She took the Dutch boy with her."

Dirk had gone to stand by the window, staring out into the darkness as if he couldn't bear to look at Johanna's possessions. He swerved now to ask, "What?"

"The Dutch-boy doll," she said. "I think it's her favorite of all. It...it looks like you," she finished lamely, "except it has blond hair like Klaus."

He came to stand over her. "You're sure of this, Andrea?"

"Yes, Dirk, I'm sure of it. He always sits right there," she said, motioning to a bench alongside the wall where there was a conspicuously vacant space.

"Couldn't she have left the doll somewhere around the house?" he demanded.

"Yes, I suppose she could have. But we can find that out easily enough, can't we?"

As she spoke, Andrea was going into Johanna's spacious closet, which had an overhead light of its own.

She remembered that another favorite possession of Johanna's had been a tote bag someone had sent her from Disney World. It didn't take long to find that it too was missing. A survey of the pretty painted dresser in which Johanna's underthings were kept also revealed that a pair of pink pajamas Johanna had proudly shown Andrea—explaining that they'd been a birthday gift from Mabel and Henry and had real lace on them—were also gone.

"I think Johanna's gone off on a small safari," Andrea reported, as she told Dirk what she'd discovered. "I wonder if she took anything to eat with her."

"What?" he asked incredulously.

"Little girls like to have pajama parties and things like that," Andrea said, remembering her own childhood. "I have a feeling that Johanna set off on a kind of pajama party of her own, with her Dutch-boy doll for company. I think she had a motive. . . ."

"And what do you suspect that motive could have been?" Dirk inquired dryly.

Andrea bit her lip, not daring to look at him as she said, her voice very low, "I. . .I think she wanted to bring all of us together, Dirk."

He didn't answer her. He turned and moved across to Johanna's dresser, and only his rigid back and the uncompromising tilt of his head betrayed his tension.

He picked up a small music box with a clown on top of it and put it down again. Then he asked tonelessly, "Well. . .now that you've deduced all of that, what next?"

Andrea stiffened, determined that she was not going to be swayed by his attitude. She said firmly, "If you want to follow my hunches, I'd say Johanna isn't far from here. Isn't there someplace nearby where she might go if she just wanted to hide out for a while?"

Dirk shrugged. "I can't think of any place."

A memory came to Andrea, suddenly and vividly. "Klaus told me once about an old stone hut he used to play in when he was a boy," she said. "Down near the lake, I think."

"That was years ago," Dirk said. "I imagine it must have tumbled down long ago, and, anyway, I doubt Johanna would have known anything about it."

"Children do explore around the places where they live," she reminded him.

"True," he said, finally turning to face her. "The stone hut was down on the lakefront. Our property extends for quite a distance along the lake. We've left most of it in its natural state. My mother always said that when my brothers and I married there'd be enough land for us to build our own waterfront houses, if we wanted to."

When my brothers and I marry. Gerrit had married. He'd married the woman Dirk loved.

Andrea shied away from this topic and directed her thoughts back to Johanna.

"Let's check out the kitchen," she suggested. "Maybe Johanna took some food along with her."

Downstairs they soon discovered that Johanna had indeed taken along some supplies, exactly the sort of supplies one might expect a child to choose. The jar of milk-chocolate bars Mabel usually kept on hand for a special dessert she liked to make had been seriously depleted.

"I'd say she's been into the cookies, too," Dirk concluded as he helped in the inventory they were making of the kitchen's contents. "Andrea...."

"Yes!" she said quickly, reading his mind in this instance. "Let's go!"

That the Van Der Maases had left the balance of the property in a natural state had been an understatement, Andrea soon discovered, as they laboriously made their way through tangled undergrowth with a powerful flashlight to light their way. Then she heard Dirk mutter something under his breath, and she asked quickly, "What is it?"

"Someone's been through here fairly recently," he said. He flashed his light on the ground. "You can see that twigs have been broken off, and the grass matted."

"Quite a short person," Andrea added, as she snagged the fabric of her blouse on yet another bramble. "Up at our level nothing's been touched."

Regardless of this encouraging evidence, it seemed forever to her until they came upon a small stone structure, and Dirk said, "I can't believe it's still intact!"

At the same time they heard a plaintive voice calling, "Uncle Dirk!"

Dirk flashed his light toward a hole in the side of the building, and they saw Johanna crawling through it. Her face was streaked with dirt, her clothes were torn, and her hair was tangled with briars and twigs, but she was smiling through her tears.

"Oh, Uncle Dirk!" she said. "You've brought Andi back!"

"I DIDN'T KNOW whether to spank her or kiss her," Dirk said. Johanna had been put to bed, and the adults were sitting at the kitchen table, relaxing with a drink.

He added dryly, "Remind me to make a generous contribution to the Policeman's Benevolent Association, or whatever it is they call it. What a wild-goose chase we sent them out on!"

"It couldn't be helped," his mother pointed out to him. "We had no way of knowing what had happened to Johanna."

"But Andrea figured it out," Dirk said, casting an enigmatical glance in her direction. "It would seem that she can read the Van Der Maas mind better than a Van Der Maas can."

His mother laughed and said, "Sometimes the women who marry into the family know you Van Der Maases better than you know yourselves."

Andrea felt herself flushing scarlet. How could Dirk's mother make such a blatant statement?

"Johanna's safe, anyway," Dirk said, unperturbed. Then his voice grew serious. "I'm very grateful to you, Andrea. We all are."

Andrea had been wondering what she should do next. She was so exhausted, mentally, emotionally and physically, that it was difficult to think about doing anything at all.

"Mrs. Van Der Maas..." she began.

"Yes, dear?"

"I should be getting back to Grand Rapids. Would you mind if I used your phone to call a cab?"

It was Klaus, rather than Dirk, who blurted, "Andi, you can't go anywhere now! What would Johanna think if she were to wake up in the morning and find you gone? Do you want to put us through this same thing all over again?"

"You can talk to Johanna," Andrea said. "You can make her understand."

Dirk's voice was very quiet. "I'll drive you back to Grand Rapids if you like," he told her. "We haven't the right to make you stay here against your will . . . no matter how much we may want you to stay." He paused. "Do you want to leave, Andrea?"

"Of course she doesn't want to leave, you idiot!" Klaus exploded. "You're the one who's forcing her away from here!"

"No," Andrea protested. "No, that's not true."

But was it true? Dirk was looking at her with that patient aloofness that could be so exasperating, and she was too weary to cope with it.

She sighed, and was relieved when Mrs. Van Der Maas said, "I don't think any of us can think too clearly just now. We've been through too much these past few hours." She smiled. "If you're half as tired as I am, Andrea," she added, "what you need is a hot bath and a good night's sleep. That's the prescription I'm going to follow as soon as I get you settled in, Klaus." She paused. "Thank God everything has worked out so beautifully. Johanna is safe and . . . I should tell you, Klaus, that I spoke to Julie Kuiper's mother this afternoon."

Klaus looked at his own mother as if she'd lost her senses. "What did you say?" he demanded.

"I phoned Mrs. Kuiper, dear. Julie's coming home from the hospital tomorrow. Her mother doesn't think she should have visitors immediately, but she's invited us to call on Thursday afternoon."

Klaus swallowed hard. "Are you saying that Mrs. Kuiper has invited me to come to her house?" he asked disbelievingly.

"Yes, she has, Klaus. And I have every reason to think that Julie will be in court the day you appear there. The other two young people who were in the car with you will be there, too. They want to tell their story to the judge, and they are prepared to swear that you hadn't had too much to drink. So you see, Klaus, some clouds do have silver linings."

Klaus couldn't speak. But after a moment he struggled to his feet and reached for his crutches. "If you'll excuse me..." he began.

"I'll go along with you," his mother said quickly. "Andrea, your room is just as you left it. Sleep late tomorrow. There's all the time in the world to catch up on things."

All the time in the world. Andrea thought wistfully of how wonderful it would be if that was true.

As it was, she felt as if the sands of time were running out for Dirk and herself, and he was not helping her to think otherwise. He'd taken the glasses they'd been using to the sink and was rinsing them out. He turned to say, "Mother's right. Tomorrow will be time enough to catch up on things."

He added, "I imagine Mark called back tonight. Probably my mother and Klaus forgot to relay the message to you. You'll want to talk with him in the morning, though. Meantime, sleep late, as my mother suggested."

He made no move to come toward her and she stared at him helplessly. He might as well have thrown up a force field between them. She couldn't possibly have made a move in his direction. She managed to mumble good-night to him, and the trip upstairs to the second floor was a long and lonely pilgrimage.

The pretty rose room looked so familiar, and someone had brought up her suitcase and her tote bag. Dirk, probably. Or Henry.

Andrea took a quick shower and then put on a sheer pale-green nightgown and slipped a matching robe over her shoulders. Tired though she was, she was also terribly restless and knew there'd be no chance of her getting to sleep.

She couldn't thrust Dirk out of her mind. He was giving her full credit for having found Johanna. There was no doubt of his gratitude in that particular area. But on a personal level. . . .

What was it he'd said when she'd asked if she could call a cab to take her back to Grand Rapids? Wearily, she decided the gist of what he'd told the others was that she had a right to leave if she wanted to...no matter how much they may have wanted her to stay.

She wondered if this was Dirk's oblique way of indicating that he wanted her to stay, and suddenly it became vital to find out whether or not it was.

She hadn't heard Dirk coming up the stairs, but he could have while she was in the shower, she reasoned. On the other hand, he might have decided to go across to his studio and spend the night there. In any case she had to find him.

She was nearly at the top of the stairs when she heard the music. Someone was playing the concert grand in the drawing room...playing it softly but beautifully.

She halted, recognizing first Debussy and then a movement from a Beethoven sonata. Then, slowly, she started down the stairs, trying not to make any sound at all as she crossed the entrance hall and went to stand in the drawing-room doorway.

Dirk's back was to her, and the light he'd switched on next to the piano was the only one to relieve the darkness in the room. It cast a pale glow across his hair, burnishing it to a rich bronze. Spellbound, Andrea started across the floor, watching his long fingers as they moved across the piano keys.

Then, swiftly, there was a transition. The music changed dramatically, merging into a lively tune reminiscent of a much earlier era.

Over his shoulder, Dirk said, "It's an old one."

So he knew she'd been standing there watching him, listening to him.

"The title," he said, "is 'Just One More Chance.'" He stopped playing and swung around to face her. "Do I have any hope at all of getting another chance from you?" he asked her, his voice tight.

He'd taken off his glasses, but he would have looked vulnerable anyway, Andrea knew, because he was gazing at her with his heart in her eyes. There was no stopping her response. Even as he stood, she was ready to go into his arms, and she clung to him as if she could never bear to let him go again. And she never could, she thought shakily.

Their kiss was more than a kiss could ever have been before. To Andrea it said more than all the words in the world's dictionaries. Then Dirk led her over to the brocade couch where, a thousand years ago—or so it seemed—Monica Van Der Maas had sat crocheting her afghan while Johanna practised scales on the same piano Dirk had just played so masterfully. He pulled her down by his side and she leaned her head against his shoulder, loving the feel of him, the scent of him.

He said, his voice still emotion filled, "I swore I was going to leave you alone tonight. I swore I was going to give you till tomorrow to recuperate from everything that's happened. Then I planned to do everything in my power to make you listen to me. But...I couldn't wait. I was praying you'd hear me playing for you and come downstairs."

He pulled her closer, nudging her hair with his chin. "Oh God, darling, what is it you do to me? Aside from driving me crazy. Do you know that you drive me crazy, Andrea Campbell? Clear out of my mind. I've never before in my life known a woman who could do what you do to me...and make me act the way you make me act. Like a damned idiot, most of the time," he concluded ruefully.

She started to pull away from him, but he tugged her back toward him. "Don't say anything," he implored. "Don't say anything until you've heard me out. Andrea...oh, darling, I love you so much!"

This time he couldn't hold her. She turned to face him, shocked by the expression in his eyes. He looked as if he was in agony.

"Dirk," she began, but he reached out a gentle finger to seal her lips.

"Please, dearest, listen to me," he begged her. "Right from the beginning, everything's gone so... so wrong. It started that very first time you were in my office. I wanted to take you to lunch, then Evelyn gave me the message that my mother had called. Klaus had been kicked out of school again. He'd just come home. He was packing up all his things, threatening to leave for good, and I had to go talk to him...."

"And then...well, it seems to me there's always been something to upset things between us. Often," he added slowly, "me."

"Dirk...."

"No," he said, shaking his head, "there's no point in your denying it. The problem is that I don't know how to explain everything I want to explain to you. For instance, I can imagine some of the things you've heard about Marietta. But how can I convince you that I got over my love for her a long, long time ago? And how can I make you believe that I never loved Marietta, I've never loved any woman the way I love you?"

A surge of happiness crested within Andrea, warming her so that her eyes glowed as she looked at him.

He smiled wryly. "I have to tell you that I was jealous as hell of you and Klaus today," he admitted. "For a terrible moment it seemed to me that history was repeating itself. Only it wouldn't have been history, Andrea. If Klaus had really been able to take you away from me, it would have been a thousand times worse than Marietta's marrying Gerrit."

"Dirk," she protested, "how could you possibly even imagine anything like that between Klaus and me? I felt very sorry for Klaus and, yes, I do feel a strong tug of affection toward him, but...."

"You don't have to explain that to me, dearest," Dirk said, and then added, "For that matter, I've been consistently jealous of Mark."

"But that's ridiculous," she cried. "I've told you from the very beginning that Mark is a friend and a business associate, nothing more."

"True. But I can't see how anyone could work with you without falling in love with you," Dirk insisted stubbornly. "There must be other men in your life. Or there must have been. You're too beautiful to have gotten to be twenty-eight years old without...."

Andrea said slowly, "There've been other men in my life, yes. But...both times it was all wrong, Dirk. Someday I'll tell you about them, if you want me to. But...."

"Yes?" he urged.

"It would be such a waste of time," she said, and knew this was true. "I never knew what love was till I met you."

"How can you say that after the way I've acted toward you?" he demanded. "Since I've known you, I've been a stranger even to myself. You see, Andrea, a long time ago I had to cope with so many different things, most of them at the same time. I admit it did something to me. I froze up inside. Nothing really seemed to reach me. That's why loving you has hurt so much. I guess you'd have to become an iceberg yourself to know the pain of slowly melting. And now...."

"Yes?"

"You have your career in Boston," he said. "I realize that. And I'm not such a chauvinist that I'd expect you to give it up for me."

She smiled. "I would think," she observed, "that the Van Der Maas enterprises might be needing a full-time director of public relations one day soon.''

Dirk shut his eyes and with them closed, asked, ''Is it a job you might apply for?''

''I think it might suit me very well.''

''What about the other vacancy?'' he went on, his voice very low. ''What about the job of being my wife?''

Andrea drew a long breath. Then she said softly, ''I thought perhaps they went together.''

She saw Dirk's face relax, as if a crisis had been met and passed. Then he opened his eyes and smiled at her in a way that led her to believe the very last of the iceberg had melted.

''I'm glad you've been reading the right want ads,'' he said unsteadily.

After a moment he asked slowly, ''Do you think you could be happy living in Holland? We wouldn't have to live in this house unless you want to. Remember that night you accused me of trespassing on someone else's property when we climbed up on the dunes overlooking Lake Michigan?''

She nodded.

''Well,'' Dirk told her, ''we were walking over my land. I bought that property while I was working in New York, and for years I've thought of building a place there, with a view of the whole surrounding area. I've even done a few sketches.''

''I know it would be beautiful,'' she said softly. ''But I don't care where I live, Dirk, as long as it's with you.''

He nuzzled her forehead with his lips. "How compliant that makes you sound, woman!" he teased, then he grinned.

"Do you know," he said, "I thought I was too damned tired to even make love to you. But you have an odd effect on me, Andrea. You revitalize me, you rejuvenate me. I have an idea you're going to lead me to the fountain of youth."

Andrea smiled impishly. "Just follow me," she challenged.

And until the darkness outside the window merged into a dawn streaked with the rosy promise of a beautiful day to come, Dirk Van Der Maas proceeded to do exactly that.

Author of GIFT OF A GOLDEN ISLE

**January's other absorbing
HARLEQUIN *SuperRomance* novel**

THE RIGHT WOMAN by Jenny Loring

Lia Andrews was a blackjack dealer. Flint Tancer
was a gambler. At least that's what it looked like to
the patrons of Lake Tahoe's Goldorado casino.

In fact Lia was a psychologist working on her
master's thesis. And Flint—all Lia knew for sure
was that the word *love* had had no meaning until
she met the charming high roller from San Francis-
co.

Lia had once been engaged to a gambler and vowed
never again. But how could she keep her resolve
when a moment shared with Flint Tancer sparked a
promise of paradise?

A contemporary love story for the woman of today

These two absorbing titles
will be published in February
by
HARLEQUIN
SuperRomance

THE HELLION by LaVyrle Spencer

Rachel Hollis had only just become a widow, and who should be pounding down her door but Tommy Lee Gentry.

Tommy Lee. Crazy boy. The hell raiser of Russellville, Alabama, had three marriages behind him and a string of fast women and cars. He'd never change, the townsfolk said.

Rachel knew differently. She had been in love with him at seventeen. Now, twenty-four years later, he could still excite her more than any other man. Then again, was it Tommy Lee she really longed for, or just a wistful memory from the past?

CRITIC'S CHOICE by Catherine Kay

Taking a potshot at a rival paper's snobbish dining columnist was all in a day's work for restaurant critic Sara Courtney. But she certainly hadn't intended to fire the first volley in a war of words that had all of Los Angeles talking!

Nor had she counted on falling in love with the object of her scorn, Paul Cabot Edgerton, but it happened. Protected by her pseudonym and her disguise as a nondescript matron while she worked, Sara had no trouble hiding most of her life from Paul.

Yet hiding her feelings was another matter entirely. . . .

These books are
already available
from
HARLEQUIN
SuperRomance

SANDCASTLE DREAMS Robyn Anzelon
AFTER THE LIGHTNING Georgia Bockoven
WAKE THE MOON Shannon Clare
EDGE OF ILLUSION Casey Douglas
REACH THE SPLENDOUR Judith Duncan
SHADOWS IN THE SUN Jocelyn Haley
DANGEROUS DELIGHT Christine Hella Cott
A QUESTING HEART Deborah Joyce
HEART'S PARADISE Lucy Lee
FORBIDDEN DESTINY Emily Mesta
SENTINEL AT DAWN Louella Nelson
TRUSTING Virginia Nielsen
AMETHYST FIRE Donna Saucier
A RED BIRD IN WINTER Lucy Snow

If you experience any difficulty in obtaining any of
these titles, write to:

Harlequin SuperRomance, P.O. Box 236,
Croydon, Surrey CR9 3RU

HARLEQUIN *Love Affair*

Look out this month for

FLIGHT OF FANCY   *Dorothea Hale*

Frank Andrews thought it was a whim. He loved his wife, Carol, he insisted, and wouldn't let her go. But Carol had never had any opportunity to be anything but Mrs. Frank Andrews—and she sought freedom. Now, despite the tiny flat and the routine job in the dress shop, Carol was uncovering hidden abilities, long buried talents, and something unexpected—a love for Frank that could not be denied!

TREASURES OF THE HEART   *Andrea Davidson*

Pine Lake Lodge, Colorado, was no ordinary resort. Luxurious and secluded, it was where the rich came to play, to think, to forget the world. Senator John Ryan had come for all three reasons. And Lana Munsinger was determined to discover why. Lana needed this story; her reputation and her job as a journalist were at stake. Yet from the first, Lana sensed a vulnerability, a weariness, in John Ryan that melted her determination and her heart. Lana's choice was impossible—between her love and her life . . .

TOUCH OF FIRE   *Cathy Gillen Thacker*

Kate Ryker considered her two-year-old marriage over. Her husband Alex had taken a job in Saudi Arabia and Kate refused to move with him. She had her own life to live—as editor of *Missouri Woman* magazine. Kate took control of her situation and filed for divorce, and when seven months passed without any word from Alex, she thought her actions were final. But obviously Alex did not . . .

HARLEQUIN *SuperRomance*

Your chance to write back!

We'll send you details of an exciting free offer from *Harlequin SuperRomance*, if you can help us by answering the few simple questions below.

Just fill in this questionnaire, tear it out and put it in an envelope and post today to: Harlequin Reader Survey, FREEPOST, P.O. Box 236, Croydon, Surrey CR9 9EL. You don't even need a stamp.

What is the title of the *Harlequin SuperRomance* you have just read?

_____

How much did you enjoy it?

Very much ☐   Quite a lot ☐   Not very much ☐

Would you buy another *Harlequin SuperRomance* book?

Yes ☐   Possibly ☐   No ☐

How did you discover *Harlequin SuperRomance* books?

Advertising ☐   A friend ☐   Seeing them on sale ☐

Elsewhere (please state) _____

How often do you read romantic fiction?

Frequently ☐   Occasionally ☐   Rarely ☐

Name (Mrs/Miss) _____

Address _____

_____

_____ **Postcode** _____

Age group: Under 24 ☐   25-34 ☐   35-44 ☐

45-55 ☐   Over 55 ☐

Harlequin SuperRomance, P.O. Box 236, Croydon, Surrey CR9 9EL.

SR